Praise from Australia
For *Suspect*

"Rowe's language seems, with each book, to become more terse and straightforward, not a word wasted. The pace in this one is unflagging."
    —*Australian Book Review*

"A classic mystery puzzler...A very entertaining read that is recommended for all aficionados of good crime novels."
    —*Canberra Times*

"Pleasant and engaging...Rowe is very good with the little details of human business—inappropriate dress, misconstrued meanings, and the messy conflict between work and personal life."
    —*Sunday Age* (Melbourne)

Please turn to the back of the book for an interview with Jennifer Rowe.

SUSPECT

Originally published in Australia as *Deadline*

Jennifer Rowe

BALLANTINE BOOKS • NEW YORK

For Hal McElroy

One

The man in the skeleton suit was sweating, skulking in the darkness. The darkness was thick with the smells of metal, people, paint, and dust, and the all-pervading tang of salt and dry seaweed that penetrated even here. The darkness was filled with sound. The dull rattling of the ghost train cars on the rails. Echoing wails and groans. The raucous screams and laughter of the customers.

A car rounded a corner and rattled towards him. It slowed, stopped. Inside it, a chubby girl, giggling, jiggling in a tight, low-cut pink knit top, clutched at a thin youth. The youth was leering, leaning back, his arms spread wide across each side of the seat back. Big man.

The skeleton-man waited. The darkness veiled him. Except for the glimmering white-painted bones, the hideous skull face gleaming.

"It's so dark! Oh, why have we stopped? Ooh, what if it's broken down?" tittered the girl, squeezing closer, scrabbling at the youth's shirt front. "Ooh, look at the skeleton!"

"It's just a dummy. What's wrong with ya?" the boy sniggered. He could feel one of her breasts pushing against his chest. Smell the perfume that rose from her warm, slightly damp skin in waves. He knew what she was after.

Still, still the skeleton stood. Like a dummy. Like a painted image.

The girl was closest to him. They always put the girls in the danger seat. He focused on the side of her plump, white neck, where the thin line of a gold chain clung. There. Just there.

With a jerk the car began moving again. Slowly, slowly. It was level with him now. It was almost past . . . Now!

He caught a glimpse of his own glowing bony arm, the nightmare clawing hand, as he stretched forward and brushed the girl's soft, folded flesh.

The girl screamed—a high-pitched shriek of pure terror. The thin youth swore violently. The car rattled on.

Sucked in, the skeleton-man thought. Cretins.

He drew back from the rails once more. Another car emerged from the darkness. Slowed. Stopped. It was empty. Stupidly gaping. But still it waited, for him to scare it. To lunge forward and touch, and wait for the scream.

An empty car. Customers must be thinning out, he thought. It must be nearly closing time. He had no watch. He had no sense of time in here. He could have been standing in this spot for minutes, hours, centuries, smelling the heat, hearing the sounds.

The empty car jerked and rattled past him. Because it was empty it rocked slightly on the rails. There was a wad of sickly-green bubble gum stuck to its torn seat. That was probably why no one had taken it. So maybe it wasn't near to closing time after all.

He felt overwhelmingly, absurdly disappointed. Thinking the shift was nearly over had made him suddenly frantic to be gone. He was conscious of a headache starting—a dull, bored heaviness pressing down, and spreading. There was no air in here. The Lycra suit clung to him like a clammy second skin. He was sweating like a pig.

He wished himself far away. Not just outside in the fun fair, all fake, all front, its screens of flimsy brightly painted wood masking the truth of it: grinding machinery, cynical men, and money tins. Not with the gabbling, hyperactive crowds, trailing home along the promenade after yet another failed night in search of something to make them feel they were really alive.

He wanted to be somewhere clean and open, with a breeze.

A beach, maybe. But not this sort of beach. Not a city beach, its flaccid waves and mean strip of sand hemmed in by a low concrete retaining wall, with flat, exhausted grass and roasting car parks beyond. Not a place with a bloody promenade lined with takeaways, cafes, supermarkets, and souvenir shops, litter bins and trees in little cages and crawling with kids and fat old guys in baggy swimsuits and snooty girls who acted like you were shit.

But a real beach. A beach that made you feel you were at the edge of forever. With waves swelling, breaking, froth hissing as it ran up thick, yellow sand.

If he had the money, he could get up the coast. Go on the dole. Drop out for a while.

Plenty of people did it. He could do it. He didn't even need much money. It was Monday night now. He'd get his pay on Thursday. There'd be a bit extra on top, this week. He could leave the next morning. He could hitch up the coast. Or maybe he'd go south. Might be cooler, down south. He could stop somewhere—anywhere he liked. Sleep on the beach. Just use the money for food . . . He could do that. There'd be others there . . .

Another car drew up in front of him. This time he'd hardly noticed it rounding the corner. Like the last car, it was empty. His heart lifted. He'd been right after all. Soon, then. Very soon . . .

His thoughts drifted back to his beach, his plans. He was just imagining the clean-skinned, long-haired girl, not too tall, who'd drop her towel next to his on the sand and tell him her name, when the cord slipped round his neck and jerked him backwards.

He gurgled once, fought briefly. Then there was only the sound of harsh breathing in his ear, and the terror, and the futile struggle for air, and life, and the blackness closing in.

As soon as the pager sounded, Tessa Vance knew. Knew what it meant. But still, as she crossed the room to turn it off, ring in, the glass of mineral water warming in her hand, Brett's eyes on her, she pleaded with fate.

Don't let it be that. Not now. Not tonight. Let it be something else. A reminder. A meeting for tomorrow. Something I forgot to do today. Steve Hayden, back at work tomorrow, wanting to introduce himself beforehand. Anything. Anything . . .

Her stomach knotted as she punched in the numbers.

But the voice at the other end of the line was the voice she had expected all along. In an odd sort of way, it was a relief. At least she didn't have to fear it any more.

Tessa listened to the voice, staring at the windows though there was nothing to see. The long curtains were drawn to shut out the city and the night. The curtains were a pale gold color. She'd wanted something lighter. Brett had wanted something brighter. Finally they'd settled on the gold. The curtains were a year and a half old now. She'd hoped they might fade a bit, but they hadn't.

The room smelled of roses, dinner cooked and waiting, the perfume Brett had given her. Glenn Miller was playing.

The voice stopped giving information, asked a question.

"Yes, I know it. I'll be there," she said quietly. "Soon as I can."

She hung up, put down her glass, and turned to face Brett, bracing herself. He'd put his glass down too. He was drinking the champagne he'd brought home. He'd presented it with a flourish. It was French. French champagne, for her birthday. French champagne, long-stemmed red roses, and perfume. The stuff of romance. He'd opened the champagne before she could stop him. He'd been so hurt, when she'd said she couldn't drink it.

He did it deliberately. He knows you can't drink when you're on call.

He'd just forgotten.

He hadn't.

He stood by the table, already set for dinner, where the roses lay dewy in their cellophane, waiting for water. He had his hands in his pockets. She knew that was so she couldn't see the clenched fists. He, too, had been waiting for this moment.

You could have had dinner last night. On Sunday night. You told him you were on call Monday. You said a day early wouldn't matter, but he said no, no, that's no fun. It has to be on your birthday . . .

She spread out her hands, tried to look casually, humorously resigned, as though she didn't know what this meant. "It's always the way," she heard herself say inanely.

He said nothing. Just looked. His eyes were angry, the hazel darkened almost to brown. When he was happy, or planning something, his eyes shone green. Whatever they'd been like at work, they hadn't shone green at home much lately. Not for a long time.

"I'm really sorry, Brett. I was so terrified this would happen."

She knew it wouldn't help. Apologizing never helped. In her head, the flat, ironic voice that so often provided a commentary on her life seemed to laugh. This is such a cliche, it was saying. Such a cliche. You, him, this situation . . .

"How long will you be?" he asked, though he knew the answer.

She shook her head, fighting down a wave of irritation. She reached for her phone, stuffed it in her handbag. Did she have time to change? She wasn't really dressed for the occasion. She was dressed for Brett. For the birthday dinner that was doomed the moment murder first entered the mind of someone yet unknown. "I don't know. Could be all night."

It was what she always said. But always he asked the question. She made an effort to change the pattern. "It's at Funworld. You know? The old amusement place on the promenade at Barrow Beach?" she said. "A young guy's been knifed. One of the staff. There were no witnesses—"

"I don't want to hear about it," he interrupted quickly. His face registered distaste. His hands bulged in his pockets as he clenched and unclenched his fists.

Tessa looked round for the car keys. The dialogue in her mind went on.

How did I get into this? How did it happen? It wasn't like this at first. He was proud of me, then. He liked it when people were interested in my job. Used to make jokes about me preferring corpses to him. All that.

He just got sick of it. He didn't think it would go on, and on, and on. A failure of imagination.

He's gone on with his job. He goes to conferences. He works long hours. Like tonight. He couldn't get home till nine-thirty. Dinner had to be late. I didn't mind. I never mind.

Get it through your head, you dope. He thinks it's different for him. He'll always think it. That's the way it is.

Tessa shook her head impatiently. She saw the car keys on the table where she'd left them, beside the roses.

"Brett, this isn't my fault. I can't help it!" Against all her resolutions, she was defending herself. It was instinctive, these days.

He shrugged. "You didn't have to ring in."

"Of course I did. I'm on call. I told you that, when you first said . . ."

"You could have changed with someone."

"I couldn't. God, I've only been in the place a few days. I couldn't start mucking them around. Brett, I told you . . ."

Same old thing. Same old pattern. Next he'll say . . .

"You'd better go then, hadn't you?"

Right on cue.

She'd thought moving to another division, closer to where she lived, would help. But nothing was going to help.

They stared at one another. The seconds ticked away. She knew she had to go. She should have gone by now. But the familiar feeling was rising. Anger mixed with guilt mixed with pain mixed with . . .

"Brett, it's not my fault! It's my job. It's what I do. I'm sorry if—"

"If you were sorry, you'd fix it."

Tessa dumped her handbag on the table and walked quickly from the room, down the short hallway into the bedroom. As she bent to the bottom drawer of her dressing table. she caught sight of herself in the mirror. Tizzed-up hair, perfect makeup, figure-hugging little black dress cut down to here at the front and finishing halfway up her thighs. Anything less like a homicide detective it was impossible to imagine.

She couldn't turn up like this. Not at a fun park right on the beach.

At Barrow Beach. Funworld. Remember . . . ?

Not on her first call with her new division. Not the first time she met Hayden.

But the dress fastened at the back, with a long row of tiny covered buttons. She couldn't get in or out of it alone. That was one of the reasons Brett liked it. But it would be grotesque to ask him to help her now.

Why did I put on the stupid thing?

Because it's the sexiest thing you've got. Because you wanted to please Brett. Show him you'd go to trouble for him. Make things right again. Great plan, Tessa. Worked a treat, didn't it?

She glanced at her watch and was shocked to see how much time had passed.

I'll be there. Soon as I can.

This was like one of those dreams she had sometimes. You're trying to get ready for something, and somehow you can't get it together.

But this wasn't a dream.

Her thoughts started to race, tumbling over one another:

You can't change the dress. Cover it up. Wear a coat. The gabardine thing.

It's too hot for a coat. I'll end up taking it off.

The shoes, then. At least change the shoes.

The high-heeled toe-peepers with ankle straps. "Follow me home and fuck me shoes" her friend Bridget called them—or used to, before she joined the rape squad and started to watch her language. Brett didn't like Bridget. Once he'd said she was a bad influence. Often he'd said she had no class. But she was probably Tessa's best friend, these days. They'd trained together.

Concentrate! Change the shoes!

The dress would look ridiculous with sensible shoes. Tessa decided it was better to try to carry the whole thing off. Being on call didn't mean you couldn't go out, dress up. She'd attended homicides in all sorts of gear. She'd seen colleagues do it, in her old division. She'd seen some of them turn up looking as if they'd had an invitation to a come-as-you-are party.

But this is the first time with this division. The first time I've met Hayden. What will he think?

You're wasting time.

Tessa ripped open the bottom drawer and pulled out her belt, holster, and gun. She strapped them around her waist. Looked in the mirror.

Absurd. No question.

She took off the holster again, grabbed her gabardine coat from the wardrobe, and almost ran back to the living room, pulling it round her shoulders.

Brett was still standing where she'd left him. He turned his head to look at her as she snatched up her car keys and stuffed the gun into her handbag.

"I'll see you later," she said. He didn't move. She went over to him, and kissed him lightly on the cheek. His skin was cool and damp.

He nodded, smiled slightly, but he didn't say anything, and he didn't touch her.

She was out the door and on the stairway down to the garage before she remembered that the roses were still lying on the table. She hoped Brett would think to put them in water. For a moment she thought of going back, but immediately realized she couldn't. She couldn't meet his eyes and tell him she'd only returned for the roses.

She put them out of her mind, and hurried on down the stairs.

"He was a lovely boy. One of the best. I'm telling you. No way anyone would've wanted to hurt Marty."

"Someone killed him."

Senior Detective Steve Hayden watched the old man reacting to this, mumbling his lips together over his almost toothless gums, his hands fiddling with the elaborate silver buckle on his belt. The beach murmured in the background like traffic noise.

"Plenty of weirdos hang round this place," the old man said finally. His face was as shriveled and intent as a monkey's. His hands, plucking at the silver buckle, were like leathery brown paws. He wore a baseball cap jammed tight over a hard, small head. His name was Ignatius Jackson. Predictably, everyone called him "Jacko." There was something utterly alien, yet incredibly familiar about him.

Steve knew what it was. There had been men like Ja
all the traveling circuses and carnivals that had ever tr
Steve's home town.

Those men hadn't worn baseball caps. And they hadn't always run ghost trains. Sometimes they ran rifle-shooting or
ball-throwing games, with a giant fluffy toy that no one ever
won stuck up at the back as first prize. Sometimes they sold hot
dogs, sometimes they sat at the doorway of the "half-man,
half-woman" exhibit, sometimes they seemed just to walk
around with their hands in their pockets. But every one of them
could have been this man's clone.

Jacko kept turning to look over his shoulder, past the scene
of crime tape to the silent ghost train, where a bizarre black and
white figure sprawled half-in, half-out of a car, skull head
lolling, a knife sticking out of its stomach, dead center between
painted ribs and hip bones.

The surrounding buildings were dark, except for a small,
brutal brick box tucked away to one side and screened by
shrubs. The office annex. Behind its dully glowing windows,
the ground staff who had been asked to stay huddled over weak
tea and coffee from the café bar, and ate the absent office staff's
undefended shortbreads.

But the ghost train blazed with light like a small, tacky is-
land in the middle of a black bay. The dead man was its center-
piece. But he was almost lost in the crowd. The forensic team
was crawling all over the place.

The tall, elegant figure of their superior, Lance Fisk, stood
surveying the scene. Beside Fisk stood Inspector Malcolm
Thorne. Very upright. Making his presence felt.

"Looking for fingerprints and that, are they?" the old man
mumbled. "Mine'll be all over everything. They would be,
wouldn't they? Like, it's my ride, isn't it?"

"Course," said Steve. "Relax." He knew what the man was
thinking. They're going to lumber someone with this, he
was thinking. That's how cops operate. And it could be me.
Never mind I was out the front pulling in the punters the whole
time. That won't worry them.

The old man glanced at him, wasn't reassured, and turned

back to the ghost train. His monkey-paw fingers went on fingering his belt buckle. "That your boss there in the front?" he muttered. "You tell him what I said. Poor young bloke getting topped's got nothin' to do with anyone here. Some weirdo done it. That's who."

"How long have you been doing this, Mr. Jackson?" asked Steve, to recall his attention.

The old man took a couple of seconds to react, as though he didn't realize Steve was speaking to him. He wasn't used to being called "Mr. Jackson." He'd been called Jacko for so long, and so universally, that he'd almost forgotten there was a longer version of the name.

"Worked the rides all me life," he muttered finally.

"Here? At Funworld?"

"Oh. Here? Nah." He thought for a moment, mumbling his lips. "Been here, on the ghost train, forty years, prob'ly. Give or take."

"Ever had any trouble before?"

"Nah. Never any trouble. Except for drunks. The odd stoush. Girls gettin' groped. Kids playing silly buggers and falling out. That sort of stuff. Bloke had a heart attack once. After he got off. Never nothing like this, but."

Steve made a note. Forty years. Forty years spruiking horrors, loudspeakers screaming in your ear, dealing with the drunks, the yobbos, the weirdos, the creeps, the lovers, the families, the mobs of kids. Packing them, singly or in pairs, into the battered little cars, wasting no time—time was money, and bums on seats was the name of the game. Seeing them laughing, chattering, squealing in anticipation as the ghost train swallowed them up through swinging doors. Hearing their amplified shrieks as the cars ran the dark maze inside. Watching them burst back into the open air through the exit doors, exposed in whatever state of hysteria, tears, laughter, or shock to which the tricks inside had reduced them. Then hauling them, limp, shaking, blasé or whatever, to their feet and out, and shoving more bodies into the empty cars while the seats were still warm.

Never any trouble. Till tonight, ten minutes before the park closed, when the exit doors flew open and a car sailed out carrying a man in a skeleton suit, stabbed through the stomach.

The old man fidgeted. But he wasn't going to ask when he could go. He wasn't going to ask what happened next. He was just waiting, not drawing attention to himself. He was one of those people who kept a naturally low profile where the cops were concerned. It was probably a lifelong habit, begun in the days when he was a skinny, sharp-eyed little boy dodging through the twilight world of the carnivals and fairs that had sustained him, and whoever cared for him. If it had been possible, Steve knew, he'd have melted away with the crowd who'd seen the dead man clatter out onto center stage, who'd screamed, stared, then scattered, long before the police arrived.

Steve became aware of a change of atmosphere, a stirring, among the throng of Fisk's gnomes even before he saw Thorne glance towards the fun park entrance.

Dr. Imogen Soames, pathologist, known to colleagues for reasons lost in her dim past as "Tootsie," was bearing down on the ghost train. Always a considerable presence—very tall, with a strangely sweet face, given her occupation, she was tonight looking even more impressive than usual in loose black trousers and a vividly striped tunic top that emphasized her height.

Fisk glanced at her warily. He'd had the field to himself up till now. But Tootsie wasn't the woman to wait patiently for his pleasure indefinitely. He drew himself up, preparing to defend his territory.

Steve caught the eye of a uniformed constable he'd found congenial on his arrival, and put Jacko into her care. He'd extracted about all he was going to get from the old man for now. And if Tootsie was about to charge Fisk's barricades, Steve was going to follow in her wake.

With or without Tessa Vance.

Tootsie was fronting Fisk now, hands on ample hips. The body of the skeleton-man, skull face turned upward to the glaring lights, lolled waiting for her.

As Steve ducked under the scene of crime tape and sauntered towards them, he noticed Thorne glance at his watch. The fearless leader wanted to leave. But he was waiting around for Vance. And Vance was taking her time.

You'd have thought she'd be fronting bright-eyed and bushy-tailed on her first call with the division. It looked like she'd decided to make an entrance instead. Well, that wouldn't impress anyone, least of all Thorne. Thorne's disapproval wasn't written all over his face—nothing was ever written all over Thorne's smooth, politician's face. But he'd remember this.

Steve hadn't yet met Tessa Vance. He'd been in court last week, when she started. He'd had today off. A day in lieu, they called it, though he thought they'd probably have to give him about a year off to make up for the actual hours of unpaid overtime he'd worked. But he'd started hearing bits and pieces about her as soon as she'd been named as his old partner's replacement.

From what he'd heard, Tessa Vance was a live wire, a handful, ambitious, unpredictable, a hotshot. He'd also heard she was neurotic, obsessive, aggressive, abrasive. And gorgeous-looking with it.

Steve liked women. He liked them a lot. He'd worked with women before, and enjoyed it. They'd been good mates, all of them—well, most of them. But Tessa Vance didn't sound to him as though she was going to fall into the "good mate" category.

She sounded more like a princess who was going to be a complete pain in the ass.

Two

Tessa pulled up on the promenade outside the Funworld gates, in defiance of a hulking uniformed officer who had started waving her away as soon as he sighted her car, and kept right on going as she tried to park, refusing to acknowledge her signs or calls. Finally, seething with frustration, she simply turned off the ignition, got out, and left the car standing where it was. He yelled.

"Hey, you! Back up! You can't stop here!"

Even in the darkness she could see that his face was dark and puffy with anger. He lumbered towards her, beckoning another, younger, officer who trotted to join him. Tessa fumbled for the identification wallet in her overcrowded handbag, finally found it, and flashed it at him as he towered above her.

He almost sneered, looking first at her identification and then at her, flicking his eyes up and down, taking in every detail of her hair, face, clothes, right down to her feet in their delicate high-heeled shoes.

You should have changed the shoes. He's looking at your shoes.

Let him!

Finally he stood back. "Through there," he said, jerking his head towards the gates as if she didn't know why she was here.

"Thank you," she snapped, and walked away from him.

She felt his eyes on her. She heard a snort of laughter as he muttered something to the younger man beside him.

A small crowd of onlookers stood on the sidelines. There were a few gangs of teenagers who'd been prowling the promenade. They nudged each other, slouching, grinning, catcalling, cigarettes hanging out of their mouths. There were a few shop-owners, too. And there were locals, some in dressing gowns and slippers, drawn out into the open by an entertainment that promised to be better than anything on TV at that time of night.

The media was there, too—cameras, lights, looking for action, but having to be content with filming and flashing cameras at parked police cars, the fun park's garish sign, the shop-lined promenade, the crowd. Tessa made a welcome diversion. She could hear their calls as she walked towards the scene of crime tape that had been strung across the park entrance. They were probably filming her. They wanted her to look around.

She forced herself to keep her eyes to the front, to walk at an even pace. She concentrated on ducking under the tape without tripping on her own high heels, or staggering because her dress was too tight. Thank heavens she'd had the sense to wear the gabardine coat.

Once inside the enclosure she felt safer, more in control. She pulled her coat around her, ignoring the heat, and moved forward with as confident an expression as she could muster, down the cracked concrete strip dotted with dark fairy floss stands and hot dog booths.

Her heels clicked on the paving. They, at least, sounded purposeful and authoritative. She ignored the dark, barricaded attractions lining each side of the paved area. Ahead of her, to the left, she could see her destination—a blaze of light surrounded with more scene-of-crime tape. Inside the tape people were milling, each seemingly without purpose, but actually following a predictable pattern.

It was a familiar scene, and it reassured her, despite her hurry, her nervousness. That taped-off area flooded with light was known territory to Tessa, however odd its surroundings. In the past two years she'd entered it from deserted carparks, from stinking rubbish dumps, from rivers, suburban houses, grimy shops, and a hundred other places. And now, wherever she was, once inside that tape she was at home.

As she neared the place, she realized that she would have found it easily, even without the light. She remembered the Funworld ghost train from her childhood. Remembered the smell of it, and the terror, even with her father beside her.

Thinking back, she realized that she'd only visited Fun-world once. It was strange that the memory was so vivid. Maybe it was because it was one of the very few times that her father had taken her anywhere on his own. It was usually her mother, on the weekends, on holidays, when Dad was working or sleeping the day away after nights without sleep. But her mother—always so loving and indulgent—had said no to Barrow Beach, and to Funworld. It was too far to go, she said. She couldn't cope with fun-park rides. She said they'd make her sick. And Tessa was too young yet to go on the rides alone.

But Tessa was wild to go. Barrow Beach wasn't near their landlocked suburb, but all her friends had been there, had swum, eaten fish and chips on the famous promenade, and been to Funworld. Most said it was fantastic, the best. Some had been so many times they were bored with it. All affected surprise that she alone hadn't even seen it.

She nagged and nagged at her mother. It became an obses-sion with her. When her father suddenly noticed, he said he'd take her.

There were a few false starts. She'd be dressed, ready, tin-gling with excitement, and then the dreaded telephone call would come and her father would have to leave. His work, a mystery to Tessa in those days, couldn't wait, it seemed. Barrow Beach could.

Tessa would cry and rage. Her mother would say brightly never mind, another day, and try to make up for it, with a visit to the local swimming pool, or the video shop. But Tessa re-membered the bitterness of the disappointment to this day. That, and the uncomfortable, guilty knowledge that her mother's sympathy for her was fueled by a hidden rage against her fa-ther, and the job.

But in the end they'd made it. She and her father had gone to Barrow Beach one Saturday afternoon. It wasn't a fine day. The tide was rising, but it was still very low. She hadn't done more than play around in the water for half an hour. The waves were flat and lifeless, just slapping at the sand. But at least she could say she'd done it. And when she'd dressed again, they went back to the promenade, and into Funworld.

It was strange, being with her father on his own. They didn't have much to say to one another. But they went on everything, tried everything—the ferris wheel, the dodgem cars, the pirate ship, the giant slides, and all the spinning, jerking rides with exciting names.

And the ghost train. It was strange, but it was the one thing that had stuck with her for years afterwards. Everything else was a wonderful blur. But the ghost train, with its gross images of evil and death, its shocks and deceits, its crafty manipulation of expectation, had shocked her. She'd sat rigidly as the little car rattled around the rails, beset by spooks and headless bodies appearing out of nowhere, assailed by horrible screams and groans. Her father had no idea how terrified she was, how confused by her own terror at things she knew were illusions, until she embarrassed him and herself by bursting into hysterical tears, right at the end.

"You're all right, love. You're all right," the man helping her out of the car had said as she shuddered with sobs, openmouthed, tears flooding, nose running, and the people watching laughed, or murmured "poor little thing."

But she wasn't all right.

She had nightmares, afterwards. Her mother coped with them, appearing at her bedside, stroking her forehead, turning her pillow over to make it cool, telling her everything was all right. Just a dream, Tess, just a dream.

That didn't help, really. In a way, it made it worse. Because there was nothing you could do to protect yourself against a dream. Dreams had their own agenda. You couldn't control them. It made you scared to go to sleep.

After a while, the nightmares stopped. Her unconscious, presumably, had sorted out that particular problem to its satisfaction, and gone on to other things.

But she never forgot.

Funworld. It was a weird feeling, being back in the place fifteen years on. Everything seemed so much smaller, so much less glamorous, so much more tawdry, than she remembered. Time had diminished it in more ways than one.

Tessa saw Inspector Thorne standing with Lance Fisk, the director of the forensic team. She'd met Fisk a few days ago. He'd been busy and distant at the time, though his first, sharp glance was appraising. She thought she knew why. His elegantly long hair was streaked with silver. Like Thorne, he was old enough to have known her father.

Doug Vance's daughter. Well, well.

Fisk was impeccably dressed in a cream-colored lightweight suit, plainly made to measure, with an open-necked forest-green shirt that Tessa could have sworn was silk. A flamboyant figure in these circumstances, and especially in contrast to Thorne, whose severely conservative dark gray suit would have been at home in the boardroom of a bank.

Thorne fixed her with a stony stare as she slipped under the tape and hurried towards him.

"You'll have to do better than this, Vance," he said, glancing—unnecessarily, Tessa was sure—at his watch.

"I will in the future. I'm sorry. I was held up," she said.

Don't say too much. Keep cool.

He nodded, coldly smiling, taking in her clothes, her hair, her shoes.

"At a party," he suggested.

"Sort of," she said.

You sound like a schoolgirl.

"You might care to be introduced to Senior Detective Hayden. He's up there, with Dr. Soames."

Tessa looked up to where a tall, dark man bent with Tootsie Soames over the ghost train car across which the body lay. Tootsie was pulling off the victim's black balaclava mask while a redheaded girl in police uniform took photographs with the vigor and enthusiasm of a paparazzo snapping stars at a society ball.

The dark man rubbed his chin, said a few words. So that's what Steve Hayden looked like. A stud, Bridget had called him. A heartbreaker.

Well, he was okay. Tessa had to admit that. But that wasn't

her concern just now. Was he going to work with her properly? That was the issue. From what Bridget had said, women hung round Steve Hayden like bees round a slice of bread and honey. How did he feel about having a new partner pushed onto him—someone with only two years' experience in Homicide? Would he expect her to hang around him too? Hoping for a sip of honey? And if she wouldn't play, would he get pissed off? Try to undermine her? Her stomach tensed at the thought.

Hayden seemed to get on with Tootsie Soames all right. That augured well. Tessa had only met Tootsie a few times, but she didn't seem to have been someone who'd put up with any nonsense. And the girl taking photographs didn't seem to be interested in anything but the corpse.

"Dr. Soames is examining the deceased," said Thorne.

"A member of the fun park staff," said Tessa, to show she'd listened to her brief. "Knifed. While on duty in the ghost train."

"I'd be most surprised," Lance Fisk murmured, staring straight ahead, "if he died of the knife wound."

It was the first time he'd spoken. Tessa saw Thorne glance at him.

But Fisk said nothing more. Despite the heat, he looked cool and controlled. It was hard to imagine him looking anything else. And it was impossible to estimate his age. Forties? Tessa conjectured. Fifties?

Thorne cast up his eyes briefly, jerked his head at Tessa to follow, and led the way to the ghost train.

Crouching over the body, Tootsie Soames was carefully examining the staring, discolored face that had been revealed by the removal of the skeleton-man's mask.

"Strangled," she pronounced. "Like I said." She pointed to the marks on the neck. "Cord, or rope, from behind. The knife in the abdomen was an extra. He was already dead when it went in. But not long dead."

"When?" Steve asked briefly.

Tootsie shrugged. "Ninety minutes?" she hazarded. "Less?"

"Thorne alert!" hissed Dee Suzeraine, the photographer.

"Thorne and a *very* snazzy babe. Hey—is that Vance? The new one?"

Tootsie glanced at the approaching pair, then at Steve. "You met her yet?" she inquired.

Steve shook his head.

"You'll like her," Tootsie assured him. "Don't be put off by the pedigree. She seemed all right to me."

"What pedigree?" Dee was alert.

"Her father was Senior Sergeant Doug Vance," Tootsie said loftily.

"Who?"

"Doug Vance. One of the good guys. Killed trying to talk a lunatic with a shotgun out of shooting himself. Bit of a legend in this division."

"I've never heard of him."

Tootsie sighed. "When you were still at school, Suzeraine. Ancient history."

"Is that why Thorne wanted her?" demanded Dee. "Because of her dad?"

Tootsie hooted with laughter, peering with a torch into the dead man's bulging eyes, checking for the red patches that would confirm her diagnosis. "Hardly. If anything, it's a downer as far as he's concerned. Thorne suspects legends."

"That's because he knows he'll never be one himself. You've got to have a personality to be a legend." Dee peered covertly at the approaching couple. "Hey, Steve, what do you think? Wow! Bit of a difference from old Barney, huh? Hey, have a look!"

But Steve just grinned good-naturedly, and ignored her. No way was he going to admit to curiosity about Tessa Vance, or make her feel more of a star than she obviously felt already.

He'd had no choice about taking her on as a partner. Barney Napps, his old partner, had left Homicide and gone back into uniform, finally bowing to the demands of his wife for a more settled life with sensible hours. Fair enough. These things happened. Steve knew he'd miss old Barney, but he wasn't going to pine away over it. He knew he'd get used to a new partner fairly quickly. He'd done it before. They'd shake down, and just get on with it.

But then he heard who Barney's replacement was to be. Senior Detective Tessa Vance, Doug Vance's daughter. Goddaughter, would you believe, of Superintendent Bob Murray. She'd wanted a move to their division, to be closer to home. She'd got it. Pays to have contacts.

Thorne had told him Vance was young, single, university-educated. Had pushed quickly through the obstacles along the usual path to Homicide—University, Academy, uniform, exam, CID. Had been with her previous Homicide division just on two years. She'd had some success there—though of course she was mainly dealing with suburban cases. She'd find their area a bit more complex than that. Seemed intelligent, if undisciplined. Needed watching—a duty, Thorne had said dryly, he was sure Steve would perform with his usual professionalism.

And then the talk had started. The scuttlebutt, the chiacking among the troops at the pub, in the lift, in the corridors and men's rooms. And Steve, shrugging laconically at each sly dig, had kept his thoughts to himself, and turned his mind firmly away from thoughts of what the future might hold.

But now it was crunch time. He could hear feet climbing the short, ridged ramp that led up to the ghost train platform, and Thorne's voice. Slowly he turned from the body of the skeleton-man to see a small, delicate-faced beauty with a mass of fair hair, dressed to kill under a sober gabardine coat. Smiling formally at him. Curved lips. Watchful, interested eyes. Suppressed energy radiating from her like heat. As they shook hands, her slim fingers firm under his, he was wryly aware that in other circumstances he'd have been strongly attracted. As it was, he was stiffening in all the wrong places—back, shoulders, arms, neck.

Tessa watched him nod, smile briefly in her general direction, then look over her head to say a few words to Thorne, and then to Tootsie Soames. The girl who'd been taking photographs had slid away from the group on Thorne's arrival, and disappeared.

Introduction over, apparently. Tessa felt a rush of heat flood her body, and hoped it wasn't showing in her face. She hadn't expected an effusive welcome. But she hadn't expected to be ignored, either.

Still talking to Thorne and Tootsie, Steve casually moved aside so that she could see the body of the dead man. He didn't glance back in her direction, but she knew he was aware of her. The way she was dressed, maybe he thought she'd scream, or shudder, or faint. She braced herself and looked down. The dead man's exposed face leered up at her. Strangled. Hideous.

Her stomach tightened. She'd never gotten used to the sight of violent death, of life wasted and abused. It no longer sickened her, but it still shocked her, filled her with fear, disgust, outrage, and pity. At first she'd fought the feeling, thinking it was unprofessional. But now she accepted it. In a sense she welcomed it. She wouldn't have wanted, really, to be able to remain unmoved. That would mean that the calluses had grown too thick—that she'd lost something, not gained it.

But that didn't mean she had to show what she felt, and she didn't show it now. She concentrated, as she'd learned to do, on seeing and memorizing every detail of the man. Almost certainly she'd only see him once more—on the autopsy table at the morgue. Then he'd be cold, stripped, washed down, laid out. This was her chance to see him as he'd lived. To know him.

He was young—mid-twenties, probably. His face was thin, a bit ferrety, with a slightly receding chin. He hadn't shaved for a couple of days. His neck was very white against the black of the skeleton suit, except for a single circlet of red where something had pulled tight, remorselessly choking out his life. He had two studs in one ear. One of the studs was surrounded by faintly pinkish, puffy flesh. A little infected. Maybe recently pierced. His short, gelled brown hair was half-flattened, half standing on end where the balaclava skull-mask had pulled it out of place.

From his stomach protruded the black handle of a knife. There was the slightest gleam of blood around the place where it had entered his body. An ordinary household knife, by the look of it. But it must have a sharp point. It had gone straight through the suit, and buried itself to the hilt. The suit was loose on him, but it was made of Lycra. Must have been hot . . .

Tessa became aware that Thorne was speaking to her, and looked up.

"You've got some catching up to do. Steve will brief you," Thorne was saying. "Dr. Fisk thinks he's clear where the attack took place. You can check that out, when Steve's ready. Then get on with taking the statements so we can let the staff go home. They've been waiting long enough. All right?"

Tessa nodded. Having delivered her into responsible hands, he was leaving. To deal with the press, and then to go home. Thorne, she had heard, didn't usually hang round crime scenes. He left that to lesser mortals. Why keep a dog and bark yourself? was his motto.

"I'll see you in the morning," Thorne added. "In reasonable time, please."

He turned on his heel, and left.

Tessa waited. She noticed the young photographer ease back to her place beside Tootsie. The girl saw her looking, and lifted her hand in greeting. "Dee," she said.

"Tessa. Hi."

"Okay. I'm finished here," Tootsie said. "Get the old guy up whenever you like, Steve."

"What old guy?" Tessa asked abruptly. She just had to get a handle on this. Had to make them include her.

They looked at her, as though she were a kid interrupting a grown-ups' conversation.

"The bloke who runs the ghost train. Name of Jackson," Steve Hayden said, after a moment. "He's going to do the formal identification. Deceased had no family. There's a girl-friend, but no one knows where she lives, and anyhow, she mightn't want to be dragged out of bed to look at that face, do you reckon?"

He spoke slowly, a country drawl very evident. Maybe emphasized for her benefit. There was something mildly aggressive about that last sentence.

Tessa said nothing. He smiled slightly and sauntered off,

down the ramp and across the paving into the dimness beyond the scene of crime tape.

The three women stood in silence. Then Tootsie fanned herself. "Hot under these lights," she said. She hauled the crocheted poncho over her head and slung it over one shoulder. "Mad," she said, presumably referring to herself.

"Should feel it inside," said Dee. "Like a sauna. Imagine standing in there in that costume day in, day out. Poor guy. What a job! Did you hear he even lived in a room out the back?"

"Saved him a bit of money, I guess," said Tootsie. "Steve reckons he acted as a sort of night-caretaker for the place. A security firm comes round. But they like to have someone on the spot."

"Skeleton staff," said Dee, straight-faced.

Tessa was gripped with a bizarre sense of unreality. These strangers were making small talk for her benefit. Small talk around a strangled corpse in a skeleton suit. It was absurd, horrible.

Like this whole night. This whole absurd, horrible night. Brett—dinner—her clothes—so late getting here—the cop on the gate—Thorne cold—Steve Hayden flashing a superior smile, turning away—

Suddenly, there was a devastating ache in Tessa's stomach, and a burning behind her eyes. Taken completely by surprise, she desperately fought the feelings down, swallowing and blinking, her head turned to one side so they couldn't see her face. She couldn't cry. She just couldn't. That would be the end. The finish.

"Right—here we go," she heard Tootsie say. "Tessa?"

The voice had been slightly sharp with warning. Tessa lifted her head, turned around. Tootsie nodded at her, and winked. She knew.

Steve Hayden was escorting a thin old man towards the train. The old man's shoulders were self-consciously hunched, and he stared at the ground.

Tessa felt a chill.

It's the same man. The same man I saw with Dad.

It can't be. That was fifteen years ago.
It's him. He looks exactly the same.

She remembered the old man's grin, the hard feel of his hands as he helped her into the ghost train car. He'd seemed taller, then. But it was the same man. No doubt.

The slight shock settled her. The ache in her stomach subsided.

The two men reached the ramp, and climbed up together. Jackson's face was expressionless. His monkey-paw hands gripped the ramp's chipped side rails, white-knuckled.

"Now, you know he doesn't look too good, Jacko," Steve was saying. "Well, you can imagine that, right? Poor young bloke's been strangled. But you'll be able to recognize him all right. Just take a quiet look. That's all you need to do. Then you can get on home."

The voice was quiet, reassuring. Not too gentle, not too formal. Just right. Tessa was for the first time impressed.

Steve glanced at her. His eyes moved a little, indicating that she should step aside to give Jackson a clear view.

She did so. The old man stared at the terrible upturned dead face, and swore under his breath. His mouth fell open, his hand crept up to it, and he started plucking at his bottom lip with brown, nicotine-stained fingers.

"Jacko," said Steve, touching his arm. "Can you . . . ?"

The old man stared, mumbled unintelligibly. They leaned closer.

"Jacko—" Steve said again.

Jackson looked up. His eyes were shocked and wet.

"It's not him," he whispered. "It's not Marty. Gawdalmighty, mate, it's fucking not him."

Three

"That's Pete Grogan," Jacko kept saying. "Bloody Pete Grogan." He was still repeating the name, over and over again, as if he couldn't believe it, long after they'd led him away from the body, and the ghost train. The shock had made him garrulous. All his previous reticence had disappeared. Now it was hard to shut him up.

They steered him towards the office annex. There they could get him something hot to drink, talk to him in private, sitting down.

"It was bloody Pete Grogan in the skeleton rig," the old man mumbled. "You can't credit it. He was supposed to have gone bloody home before I come on. I never thought it was him. Called him Marty. He never said."

"You spoke to him?" Steve asked casually. "When was that?"

"At the beginning of me shift. I bloody called out to him." Jacko was feeling for his packet of tobacco, stumbling a little on the tiny step that led up to the annex door. "Told you before, when you asked when I saw him last. I told you."

"Just tell me again, Jacko."

"I seen him out the back there—going in the back way, like always. He's in the rig. So I yell out. 'G'day Marty,' I say. 'Hot enough for ya, Marty?' I say. And he never says a thing. Never says, it's not Marty, it's me, ya silly old git. Never says nothin'. Just waves, like. Y'know?" He frowned resentfully. "He was having a lend of me. Bloody young smartass."

In another instant he'd remembered that the man he was abusing was dead. He stopped just inside the door, and looked confused, while his fingers worked on rolling a cigarette, in defiance of the clear "no smoking" notice displayed on the wall of the small, cheerless reception area. The area featured pale green paint, brown-flecked carpet, a single orange-upholstered chair, and a door marked STAFF ONLY. A hatch, presently sealed by a gray roller-shutter, had been let into one wall. Above the hatch was a flecked and faded sign: CUSTOMER ENQUIRIES—code for "Complaints Plus Minor Injuries and Illnesses," Tessa imagined.

"Did you go into the ghost train the back way, too?" Tessa asked impulsively. She felt, rather than saw, Steve glance at her. Jacko was his witness. He and the old man were getting on. She should leave it to him. Well, okay. But she had to know.

"Why'd I do that?" Jacko demanded, turning suspicious black eyes in her direction, and sticking a ragged cigarette into his mouth. "I work at the front, so I go in the front, don't I?" He lit the cigarette. The paper at the end of the thin tube flared up, the loose ends of tobacco frizzled and fell down the front of his shirt.

For a moment she was nine years old again, shuffling up that ramp with her father, piling into the ghost train car under Jacko's monkey-paw hands, glancing up at those little black eyes. *In you go, love.*

She lifted her chin, forced a slight smile. "I was just wondering why you were round the back in the first place," she said clearly.

He stared at her, expressionless. "Never you mind about that," he said finally. "That's my business."

Tessa's spine prickled. But she kept her smile in place. "It's our business too, unfortunately," she said.

He mumbled something.

"I'm sorry, I didn't hear you. Could you—?"

"I was in the bloody dunny, wasn't I?" he broke in loudly. "Gawdalmighty, can't a man go to the dunny without the bloody coppers poking their noses in?"

"There's a staff toilet out the back, is there, Jacko?" asked Steve easily, with a hard, warning glance at Tessa.

"Yeah," the old man muttered. "Behind Marty's room." He

sucked greedily at his cigarette, flicked ash in the general direction of the doorway.

"And you were coming out of that toilet when you saw a guy you took to be Marty Mayhew dressed in his skeleton costume." Steve went on. "It was about six o'clock, the beginning of the new shift. He was going into the ghost train by the back entrance. And you yelled out to him, calling him by name, and he waved, but didn't answer. So you went back out to the front of the ride, still thinking he was Marty." He paused. "That right?"

"Yeah. That's it," growled Jacko. "Like I said. Well, I never thought anything about it. Like, wearing the rig, you couldn't tell who it was. But I reckoned I knew who it was, didn't I? Marty's on nights this month. Pete Grogan's on afternoons."

He was still sulky. There was silence till he'd finished the cigarette and thrown it away. Then Steve ushered him through the door marked STAFF ONLY, leaving Tessa to follow.

The door led immediately into a bland, open-plan office area. There were two glazed cubicles at the far end, screened with venetian blinds. A clutter of desks, ruthlessly clear except for computers and phones, and looking strangely naked because their chairs had been removed, took up most of the rest of the space.

In a small open area just near the door, looking bizarrely out of place in this environment, the raffish crew of Funworld staff who were still waiting to give statements had set up camp around the cafe bar. Most of their colleagues had had their names and addresses taken, and had been allowed to go by now. The ones that remained—two women, three men—were those who worked closest to the ghost train, or knew Marty Mayhew best. All looked uneasy, unhappy, perched on or draped over the wheeled office chairs, huddled together, very aware of the young police officer leaning awkwardly against the wall, watching them. One of the women, the older one, with a mop of bleached blond curls, had been crying.

They glanced covertly at Tessa, Steve, and Jacko as they entered. And Jacko, seeing the familiar faces, suddenly came to life again.

"It wasn't him," he babbled to them. "Hear me? I saw. Not him. You coulda knocked me over with a feather. It's Pete Grogan. Not Marty at all. Not Marty."

They stared, baffled.

"Get him a cup of tea, will you?" Steve muttered in Tessa's direction. "We'll be in the office at the end. The one on the right. Other one's occupied."

"Strong, black, three sugars," bawled Jacko, as he was firmly propelled away.

Tessa was left standing with the young constable. He looked barely old enough to shave. The people around the cafe bar were still staring.

Steve and Jacko disappeared into the right-hand office and the door slammed shut behind them. At the same moment, like a scene in a French farce, the door of the left-hand office flew open to reveal a glaring, heavily-set middle-aged man with a high flush.

"That's the boss," murmured the constable. "Or the assistant boss, or something. A real pain in the ass."

He looked at Tessa properly for the first time. His eyes flickered as her appearance registered, and his pale skin began slowly to stain red. Tessa resisted the urge to wrap her coat around her, cover herself up.

"Name?" she asked crisply.

He straightened, looked fearful. "Constable Christopher Leon," he murmured. "Sir."

"*His* name," snapped Tessa. Would the idiocy of this night never cease?

"Papas. George." Constable Leon was scarlet to the hair-line now. "The Inspector talked to him earlier, but he's wanting more info. I couldn't help him, could I? I've been in here all the time since I got here."

"I'll see him," said Tessa crisply. "You get the tea for Mr. Jackson, will you? Take it in to him. He wants it strong. Three sugars, don't forget. Use two tea bags."

Domestic details dealt with, she left him, and went to tackle George Papas in his stronghold, glad to have something positive to do. Making tea for Jacko hardly qualified. Asking Jacko impertinent questions about his lavatory habits hardly qualified either.

But as it turned out, George Papas, grandly titled "Financial Controller," and very full of his own importance, was next to useless. He was a rigid, truculent man, who knew little about the entertainment staff, seemed obscurely to blame the police for failing to prevent what he called "the tragedy," and was far more interested in what was going to happen in the morning than in what was happening tonight. Could the whole thing be hushed up? he wanted to know. Would Funworld have to be closed? For how long? Could the ghost train be closed, and the rest of the park reopened?

He was the fun park's second-in-command. The manager wasn't available. He was uncontactable, away in the wilds on a school camp with his son. George Papas was on duty that night, a fact he obviously resented. It wasn't usual practice, but the night manager rostered on for the evening had just been diagnosed with glandular fever, and was at home in bed. Where George Papas would have preferred to be. None of the other night managers had been available to fill in. Or so they said. Typical. No one wanted to work these days.

Tessa found it impossible to turn his mind towards the idea that the murder of Peter Grogan was anything more than a potential financial disaster, or that it anything to do with him. He seemed to regard the Funworld amusements, and the people who ran them, as inconvenient appendages to his accounts department. He didn't even seem quite to accept that it was a man called Peter Grogan, not Martin Mayhew, the rightful worker on that ghost train shift, who had been killed. Marty Mayhew was on the shift roster. Marty Mayhew had not phoned in sick. So Marty Mayhew the dead man must be. There was a strict rule against switching shifts, he said. You couldn't let the staff start organizing themselves. They were too unreliable.

She couldn't decide if he was one of the most unpleasant men she'd ever met, or just plain stupid. The only useful piece of information she managed to get out of him was that Marty Mayhew had worked at Funworld for five years, and Peter Grogan for eighteen months. In the end she gave up, excused herself, and left, leaving him sitting behind his desk looking sulkily outraged.

She knocked at the door of the neighboring cubicle, and went in.

The manager's office was slightly bigger than the one she'd just left, and it had a small window paned with frosted glass. But otherwise it was identical. Just as stuffy, just as characterless. Unrelievedly dull. Like the rest of the annex, it was painted pale green.

Steve Hayden was slouched casually behind a grimly tidy desk. On the other side of the desk Jacko hunched on an orange visitor's chair, smoking his second economically skinny cigarette, which he was ashing when required into a polystyrene cup that contained the dregs of his tea. There was an orange filing cabinet beside the desk, and above it on the wall was a framed map of the park. A dusty-looking, shriveled cactus prickled in a plastic pot on the windowsill. Otherwise the office contained not a single ornament, personal object, or sign of life.

Tessa found herself thinking how strange it was that the manager of a fun park should work amid such joyless surroundings. But come to think about it, she'd once heard that there's no one so hard-bitten and cynical as a toy manufacturer. Maybe having to make money out of other people's pleasure soured you.

Or maybe this particular manager was just a very boring man.

Steve looked neither pleased nor sorry to see her. He had a good poker face, she decided. But he instantly made his wishes known all the same. He wanted her out.

"We'll be another five minutes," he said, as soon as she appeared. "Why don't you have a chat with the staff down the end? They've been waiting awhile."

"Be bloody glad they did bloody wait, now," Jacko piped up unexpectedly. "Better'n goin' home thinkin' Marty was the one who copped it, eh?"

"Peter Grogan wasn't very popular, apparently," said Steve, for Tessa's benefit.

"Nothin' wrong with 'im," Jacko muttered. "He was all right. But you know how it is. He was just—nothin' special."

He seemed to think about that for a moment. "Like most blokes," he added.

"But Marty . . . ?" Steve prompted.

The old man grinned—a wide, gummy grimace. "Marty's different," he explained. "Everyone likes Marty. 'Specially the girls." He leered excruciatingly, and winked. Then he added, surprisingly: "Marty's got charisma. That's what he's got."

"Is that right?" Steve grinned back at him. "Sounds like an interesting bloke. Where do you think he's got to?"

It was time to leave, let him get on with it. He'd get far more out of the old man on his own. Tessa withdrew quietly. Steve's eyes never wavered from Jacko's face as she silently closed the door.

"They were all working at the time Grogan was killed. All with witnesses to prove it. None of them knows where Mayhew is. Unless he's with his girlfriend. Her name's Val," Tessa said, as she and Steve moved out of the annex a little later, leaving Jacko, who wanted another cup of tea, to the ministrations of Constable Leon and the now-chattering group around the cafe bar.

Steve didn't answer. Just waited for her to go on.

"They all thought he was working tonight," she said. "They all thought he was dead till they heard from Jacko that he wasn't. They were very relieved. Still shocked, but obviously relieved."

She would have added, "Makes you feel a bit sorry for poor old Peter Grogan," had she known Steve better and been sure of his response. But under the circumstances, she kept her mouth shut.

He spoke at last. "Seems a bit funny. Mayhew and Grogan swap shifts, and don't tell anyone? Even Mayhew's mates? Even Jacko?"

"They wouldn't, the others said. Just in case word leaked. There's a rule against shift-swapping in this place. People have been sacked for it. The manager's got a bee in his bonnet on the subject. They say that if Marty Mayhew did it, he must have really needed to. He was taking a risk."

"Turns out it was Grogan taking the risk." Steve was pacing along, staring straight ahead. He'd loosened his tie, and rolled up his shirtsleeves. It had been hot and stuffy in the annex. Outside in the sea-scented air it was hot and sticky.

Tessa's skin was prickling with sweat under her coat as she tripped determinedly along on her high heels, just managing to keep up with Steve's long strides. She was certain that he was deliberately slowing his natural pace to accommodate her. Unfairly, this irritated her more than if he'd left her tottering in his wake.

They reached the ghost train. It was still brightly lit but, except for the uniformed female constable who'd acted as Jacko's minder and was now standing looking bored by the scene-of-crime tape, it seemed deserted. Peter Grogan's body had been taken away.

"They all inside, Maree?" Steve called to the woman on duty. She nodded and came towards him, her hand stealing to the back of her hair, patting it into place.

"They said it was okay for you to go round the back when you wanted," she said. "I asked them."

"Thanks." Steve grinned at her and she tilted her head and smiled back coquettishly.

"Anytime," she said.

Just whistle, thought Tessa, looking down at her shoes and wishing them to hell.

Sourpuss.

It's sickening. She's falling all over him.

What's it to you?

It's just irritating.

Sourpuss. Your shoes are too tight.

They're not. Feet swell in the heat, that's all.

"Want to come and have a look?" She realized Steve was speaking to her, and looked up.

He was standing watching her with his hands in his pockets. The flirtatious constable had gone back to her post.

"Got gloves on you?" he added.

She nodded sharply. She started for the ghost train ramp, but he called to her.

"Not that way. Easier to go round the back."

He began walking casually away, still with his hands in his pockets. She could only trot after him. She had no idea where he was going. Of course, he'd been here much earlier than she had. He'd found out the layout of the place.

"There's a path that runs behind all the stands. You can get to it round here," he said. They were passing the Laughing Clowns stand now. ("Try Your Luck! Test Your Skill! Every Player Wins a Prize!")

Suddenly Tessa had another flash of vivid memory. Fifteen years ago, she'd stood at this stand with her father, playing the game. She'd been determined to win a big prize. They had fluffy toys, dolls on sticks, vases, sets of hairbrushes, even radios lined up on shelves at the back of the stand.

After some elaborate calculations, and with enormous concentration, she'd pushed her six red balls one by one down the throat of her chosen clown as its head wagged silently from side to side. She'd watched each ball fall out at the bottom of the apparatus and roll perversely into one of the low-scoring slots. At the end she'd received a key ring attached to a little bright green fuzzball with eyes.

She didn't have a key to put on the ring in those days, but back home she put it into the flowered chocolate box in her top dressing-table drawer, where she kept her treasures. Years later, cleaning up, she'd found it and thrown it away. She'd had a proper key-ring by then. And the eyes had fallen off, anyway.

"You coming?" It was Steve Hayden's voice. He was peering at her from around the corner of the stand. Having attracted her attention, he disappeared.

Tessa shook her head in irritation, forcing her mind away from the past and focusing on the present. She felt she'd never been so mentally disorganized in her life. And it was showing. What this man thought of her she could just imagine.

But it's not my fault!

That's what you said to Brett.

Brett . . . what was he doing now? Pacing and fuming? Eating the dried-up dinner? Putting the roses in water? Watching TV? Maybe. Or maybe . . .

Steve had moved into a narrow space between the Laughing Clowns and a small ride called Go-Go Jalopies upon which brightly colored, toddler-sized cars hung. Tessa didn't remember that. When she joined him he was pulling on latex gloves he'd taken from his pocket, still in their plastic bag. She followed, pulling on her own gloves. She always carried some in her handbag.

Got gloves on you?

Just exactly how daffy did he think she was?

Four

In moments they'd made another left-hand turn and were walking back towards the Ghost Train along a dank, dark little path that ran behind the buildings, behind the rides, hard up against the Funworld boundary—a high, green, steel-paneled fence topped by barbed wire. The path was clean now, after its forensic sweep, but no doubt had been previously littered with cigarette butts, paper bags, and other detritus left by those who used the passage to eat, drink, smoke, shoot up, or have hurried sex out of the public view.

After a short distance, the path abruptly bulged and became a small, roughly square slab of concrete. Here a few scruffy bushes huddled against the boundary fence, beside a brick out-house bearing the inevitable STAFF ONLY label. The lavatory Jacko had talked about. Beside it was a wooden structure that must be Marty Mayhew's room. The door, once painted red but now bearing only the traces of it, opened onto a covered veranda-walkway which led to what was obviously the back entrance to the ghost train.

Marty Mayhew's door stood open, though the room was dark. The ghost train door was open too, and inside the cluttered space, light blazed and shadows flickered. As they watched, Lance Fisk emerged, his pale linen suit still fault-lessly clean.

"Anything?" asked Steve.

Fisk spread fastidious hands. His silvered hair gleamed in the artificial light. "Nothing particularly helpful, except that which you know already. A length of new nylon cord lying be-side the place where the skeleton suit man stood in the normal

course of his appalling employment," he said. "It was the weapon, we assume. This will be confirmed in due course." He
sighed. "Fingerprints everywhere. Thousands of them. No
blood. We have vacuumed the floor and walls. As to that, I'll let
you know."

"Can we go in?"

"Why not? It's a dog's breakfast already. Nothing you can
do will make it any worse, Detective Hayden. For once."

He stood aside so that Steve and Tessa could look into the
space beyond the doorway. Amid artificial horrors, forensic
staff were working in concentrated silence. Like finicky house-
keepers, they crouched, crawled, and stretched, collecting and
storing away minute traces that might one day be a court exhibit, or might be simply useless rubbish.

"Fortunately the lighting is excellent," Fisk said. "For maintenance, I understand."

Its tricks and illusions mercilessly exposed and made
commonplace by the light, the ghost train was revealed for
what it was—a cleverly-constructed, very compact maze. A
single gleaming set of tracks wound tortuously through the
small area, negotiating black partitions painted with scenes of
horror, running into mirrors, snaking through forests of plastic
spiders. Animated snakes, skulls, dummies of headless corpses
and ax-murderers swung from the ceiling rafters, presumably
timed to drop into view as each car approached. It was hard to
imagine such childish games could scare anyone.

"It would be better if we could see it in its normal lighting,
and running," said Tessa. "Is that possible?"

Fisk looked at her under his eyebrows. "Have we met?" he
inquired.

"Tessa Vance, Dr. Fisk. I saw you earlier, with Inspector
Thorne. But we did meet—at the morgue. With Tootsie
Soames. Last Thursday."

"So we did, Tessa. I didn't recognize you." He smiled. "Out
of uniform," he added.

Confused, Tessa took a second to realize that he meant out
of the well-cut jackets, skirts and shirts she usually wore to
work, out of her professional tidy hair and subdued makeup.

For a moment she'd forgotten she was tizzied up like a wanna-be photographic model.

"It's my birthday," she blurted out, floundering for something to say.

"Many happy returns," Fisk said dryly. He glanced back into the ghost train. "It seems someone has decided to give you a gift to remember."

Tessa, acutely aware of Steve Hayden's no doubt amused interest, furious with herself, could only smile weakly in response.

"Despite your enthusiasm for realism, or theatre in the round, whichever it is, I can't advise it," Fisk went on. "It's pitch black inside without the lights. You won't see anything."

"It doesn't matter—" Tessa began.

But to her surprise Steve Hayden cut in. "We'll try it, Lance," he said firmly. "She's right. It's worth doing. Can you give your guys in there five minutes' break?"

Fisk shrugged with exaggerated patience. "It's possible. But I repeat—you will not be able to see—"

Steve cut in again. "We'll be able to see what the killer saw," he said. "What the victim saw. And that's what we want. We don't need detail. We aren't looking for threads and bits of fluff, are we? That's your department."

Exactly, Tessa thought. She felt absurdly grateful that he'd understood.

Why shouldn't he understand? You think he's dumb, or something? So far he's acted a lot smarter than you have.

Give me time.

"As you like," sighed Lance Fisk. He seemed just a beat short of casting up his eyes. He walked without further comment into the ghost train

Steve turned to Tessa. "If we're lucky, Jacko will still be in the annex, nattering on. I'll go back to the office and get him. He can set this thing up for us. That'd be easier than fiddling with it ourselves."

"I'll have a look at Marty's room in the meantime," she said. "They seem to have finished with it."

"Help yourself. It looked pretty uninteresting when I saw it. But I only gave it a quick once-over from the door."

He was being non-committal, casually friendly, distant. For a moment Tessa was seized with longing for Tom, her old partner, who'd driven her crazy, but was at least comfortable, and for her old division, where she knew everyone, and everyone knew her.

You wanted this. You asked for this.

That only makes things worse.

She watched Steve walk back around the side of the brick toilet block, glancing into Marty Mayhew's room on the way. Only when he had disappeared from view did she follow. She pushed the door of the room open and stepped inside, pulling off the gabardine coat with relief.

The room was spartan. It was unlined, roughly painted white. A single lightbulb hung from the bare rafters, swinging on its flex in the draft created by the movement of the door. There was a small window that seemed permanently jammed open at the top by a framed fly-screen. A square of dull red vinyl sheeting in a tile pattern had been laid directly over the floorboards.

But the room wasn't grim, as it might have been. It was tidy, and had been carefully arranged. On one side there was an old free-standing wardrobe and a double bed covered by a South American–patterned cotton spread that fell almost to the floor. On the other side there was a clean sink, a white-painted cabinet that doubled as a bench, a clunking old refrigerator. In between, directly opposite the door, and below the window, there was a table pushed hard up against the wall, and one chair. A towel hung on a nail from the inside of the door, under a small rectangular mirror.

Tessa paced around the vinyl square, clutching her coat, taking everything in. Possibly this place had at one time been intended as a change and rest room for the ghost train staff. Or even as a storage room for spare equipment, and for maintenance.

Now a man lived here. Illegally, no doubt, as far as the local council was concerned. But the local council would no doubt be told, should it ever inspect or inquire, that the room was simply a staff rest and recreation facility.

Tessa noted an electric jug, a toaster, a small microwave, a mug and a plate washed up on the sink. In the cupboard under the sink were all the usual domestic items. In the cabinet were a few plates, mugs, and bowls, and some cutlery. As Steve had said, there wasn't much to see.

The arrangements were impressive in their simplicity. Marty Mayhew might be hard up, but he hadn't given up. Not by any means. He'd simply used the resources available to him to create the most comfort and convenience he could.

There were few personal items in the room. The cupboard contained a few clothes, all on metal hangers—even the T-shirts, jeans, and track pants that appeared to be Marty Mayhew's normal wear. Tessa saw no sign that he owned a pair of leather shoes, a conventional shirt, or a jacket other than a heavy, padded parka.

But she found it hard to believe that a man so apparently organized owned none of these items at all. There were some empty coathangers in the cupboard. Possibly, wherever Marty was, he was dressed in his best.

Hanging right in front of the other clothes were two skeleton costumes, apparent duplicates of the one Pete Grogan had been wearing when he died. Of course, she realized, there'd have to be more than one, because of cleaning and repairs, and because the people working shifts back to back had to be dressed before they did the switch.

There was a suitcase under the bed. It contained a blanket, a tartan rug, two sweaters, a woolly cap, and several pairs of clean dark blue socks. Also under the bed was a plastic sponge-bag, inside of which was toothpaste, a toothbrush, soap, shaving cream, a half-full bag of disposable razors, and a comb.

Tessa moved to the table, which did triple service as a bed-side table, a dining table, and a desk. Lined up at the back, against the wall, were a few well-worn paperback books, of the spy and high adventure variety. There was a page-a-day desk calendar, displaying the correct date. There were a couple of pens. On the side nearest the bed there was a desk lamp, and a phone. And beside the phone, standing up on display, was a cheap birthday card.

Tessa picked up the card. It looked new and bright. The front bore a vivid illustration of a bunch of balloons, and the words "Have a Happy, Happy Birthday!" Inside, there was no personal message, just the usual printed verse.

She put the card back carefully. The coincidence of finding it here on her own birthday spooked her more than she felt was sensible. Why should it spook her at all? Either Marty had bought the card to give someone else, or someone had given it to him. And possibly its existence explained the man's absence, and the absence of any "best" clothes in his closet.

Today could be his birthday, as well as hers. He and his girlfriend had wanted to go out, to celebrate. He'd arranged for Peter Grogan to substitute for him on the ghost train. End of story.

But something was niggling at her. What? Sure, it was odd the card wasn't signed. But . . .

Tessa paced the tiny room, thinking.

But surely the people she'd spoken to back at the office annex would have known if it was Marty's birthday. They were his friends. They'd all seemed very fond of him. They'd all said he was a lovely guy. Yet they'd said they had no idea why he'd have taken a Monday night off, running the risk he'd get found out and sacked.

Jacko had been astounded, too, to find that Marty was missing. He would surely have known if it was the man's birthday. He'd known him for five years.

It was strange. And another thing. If the birthday card had been given to Marty today, or he'd received it in the post, where was the envelope? She rechecked the red plastic wastepaper bin near the sink. A takeaway coffee cup. An empty packet that had contained cheese. Nothing else.

She heard voices outside. Steve Hayden and Jacko? It sounded like it. She walked quickly to the door and looked out.

They'd just walked around the corner of the lavatory block into the little courtyard. Jacko was gesticulating, shaking his head.

"They all say the same as me," he was saying. "No one'd want to kill Marty, like, personally. And no one knew it was Pete Grogan in the skeleton rig. So it stands to reason, don't it?

It was some looney did it. Some looney who reckons they was diddled by the park, say. Or just reckons the place stinks. An' where does that leave the rest of us? How do we know the bloke won't come back? What if he—?"

He broke off as Tessa joined them. He stared. Steve's face remained impassive. Tessa realized that she'd taken her coat off in Marty Mayhew's room, and hadn't put it on again. She lifted her chin. So what? It didn't matter what she looked like. There were more important things to think about.

"Was it Marty Mayhew's birthday today?" she asked Jacko abruptly.

He gaped at her for a few seconds, glanced at Steve, then shook his head.

"Are you sure?" Tessa persisted.

"Course I'm sure," he said indignantly. "I know when his bloody birthday is. He had his bloody birthday a couple of months ago. In September. He was twenty-seven. Getting old, I told 'im. Liz off the Laughing Clowns brought in a cake. Candles an' all."

"Is it anyone else's birthday today? Or anytime this week?"

"How would I know, love?" He was being patient with her.

"There's a birthday card in his room," she said to Steve. "Unsigned."

"Yeah. Saw that," he said easily. "Okay—we'll have a look at the ghost train now. If you're ready."

It was dark, very dark, in the place where the skeleton-man had died. The dark smothered angles and corners, hid the walls, the roof. In other parts of the ride, lights flashed on, illuminating terrors, then were cut off, leaving the eyes dazzled, and blinder than before. But here it was inky black. There was nothing to see. There was only sound—groans, cries, and screams booming from hidden speakers everywhere.

"It wouldn't have been hard for someone to sneak up behind Grogan, if they were careful," Tessa commented. "He wouldn't hear anything."

She waited for a response. None came. Her spine prickled. She looked around quickly, suddenly overcome by the creepy feeling that she'd been left alone without knowing it. But Steve was there. She could see the faintest glimmer of his face. He just hadn't bothered to answer her.

An empty car appeared around an unseen corner, and headed for them. It slowed, then stopped.

"That's so the customers can get a good look at the skeleton." Steve's voice. "They think it's a dummy. Like the hanged-man dummy we saw on the way in."

The hanged-man dummy that bounced down in front of you on the way in, he means. The dummy that scared you half to death. You screamed. Hayden must be so impressed with you.

I don't care what he thinks.

The car started moving again, slowly. Now it was passing them. Steve kept up his commentary.

"So then the skeleton leans out, touches the nearest person, and scares the pants off them. It's the fright finale. They've been doing it ever since the ride started. Works like a charm, Jacko reckons."

Tessa briefly closed her eyes. She remembered, from long ago. Only too well.

You're all right, love.

She cleared her throat. "Do we assume the killer came in the back way? Or actually rode the ghost train in, and got off at some point?"

"The idea seems to be that he came in the back. The same way he must have gone out. The crowds were thinning out by then. It was nearly closing time. Jacko can't remember putting any singles into cars for quite a while before that. Only couples."

"Would he notice?"

"He reckons he would. At that time of night, most people are in pairs, and any single men would be a bit sus. It's part of his job to watch it."

"We don't know the killer was a man. It could have been a woman, couldn't it?"

She almost felt him wince in irritation. But his voice didn't change tone.

"Sure. But a single woman would have been even more no-ticeable. Anyhow, I think it's most likely the killer came in the back. It wouldn't be hard to do. That path we came down runs right along the boundary behind the rides, from one end of the park to the other. There are quite a few places where you can get onto it."

Tessa nodded. She could see that he was probably right.

"Killer gets onto the path, and down as far as the ghost train without anyone challenging him," Steve said. "He gets inside the ghost train from the back—door's never locked while the ride's running. He makes his way to this spot. He kills Grogan, then he gets out fast the same way he came, while all hell breaks loose out the front."

"That means he knew what he was doing. He planned it," murmured Tessa.

Another car appeared around the corner. It came towards them, slowed, stopped.

"Why didn't he just leave the body on the floor?" Tessa wondered aloud. "That would have given him a lot more time to get away safely."

She didn't really expect her companion to comment. He seemed averse to responding to anything but direct questions. But on this occasion he varied his rule.

"I'd say it was an accident. He probably didn't mean the body to fall across the car. It just did. Look at this."

She felt him move past her. He stood in front of her, near to the rails. The empty car began moving again, slowly passing. He lowered himself into it sideways, leaving his feet on the ground. The car stopped. He lifted up his feet. The car started moving again. He did the experiment a couple more times, then clambered out.

"They're set up like that to stop accidents," he said, watching as the car rattled away. "Jacko told me. So. You can see what probably happened."

Tessa nodded in the darkness. She could see.

The killer hooked the loop of cord around Peter Grogan's neck, jerked backwards, and pulled tight. Taken completely by surprise, pulled off balance, Grogan struggled. Staggered, maybe, towards the rails, turning a bit, pulling his killer with him.

But the struggle wouldn't have lasted long. Soon Grogan

would have been a dead weight. Unable to hold him upright any longer, the killer let him fall. As it happened, the body fell not on the ground, as planned, but onto an empty car passing slowly by. It fell awkwardly: head and one arm hanging over the other side of the car, body on the seat, feet trailing on the ground. The car was halted by the drag of his feet on the ground. The killer plunged a knife into Grogan's stomach . . .

Why? He was already dead.

One thing at a time.

The car wouldn't move. None of the cars would move. The killer had to make a very quick decision. He had three choices.

He could leave the car and the body as they were, and run. But any second, Jacko would be coming inside to see what was wrong, what the blockage was. Jacko might turn on the lights. The train was full of people. The killer might be seen before he could escape through the back door.

He could fiddle around trying to get the wedged body out, but that would take precious time—time he didn't have if he wanted Jacko to stay where he was.

Or he could get the car going again, so the panic and alarm, if panic and alarm there must be, would be going on at the front of the ride, while he escaped out the back.

The last, obviously, was the safest choice. So he heaved the legs off the ground and into the car. The car started moving again. He took off.

A quick thinker, then. A pragmatist. The killing had been cleverly planned. Because even if there had been witnesses, who would take any notice of a strangling scene in a ghost train? Or of a dead body? But when there was a hitch, the killer didn't panic, just went into damage control.

"I don't think we're looking at some stray weirdo killing here," she said aloud.

She didn't really expect an answer. And she didn't get one.

Suddenly there was a shout from outside, at the front of the ghost train. The shout penetrated the inside din—the groans and cries and the rattling of the cars on the rails—with the ease of long practice.

"Hey!"

It was Jacko's voice.

"Hey! Steve! He's here. Marty's back! Wanna see him? Hey, Steve! Come out here and get the cops off the kid's back, will ya?"

Five

Marty Mayhew was incredibly good-looking. Slim, strong body, beautiful, finely boned face, thick, silky, honey-blonde hair, sultry dark blue eyes, wide, curving mouth. Combined with the indefinable, slightly dangerous, knowing air of someone brought up rough, the effect was devastating.

He looked younger than twenty-seven. He had a bluebird and rose tattoo on his left forearm and small studs in both ears. He wore a small string of Mexican beads around his neck. His clothes were cheap, and a bit flashy. But it wouldn't have mattered what he wore. He was a knockout.

Presumably this was what Jacko had meant by "charisma." It was genuine, animal magnetism. Tessa felt it instantly, and was almost as instantly shocked and embarrassed.

You're drooling. Pull yourself together, before they notice. What's wrong with you?

This must be how men feel when they . . .

When they're about to do something that'll get them accused of sexual harassment. Women are above all that.

Are they?

The problem disappeared, fortunately or unfortunately— Tessa couldn't decide which—as soon as Marty opened his mouth. His appearance of brooding, streetwise sophistication was so powerful that it was disconcerting to find him apparently ingenuous and uncomplicated, a simple person bewildered and shocked by what had happened. His voice was low and gentle. He kept saying he couldn't take it in.

Jacko, till they got rid of him, kept telling him that everyone was tickled pink he was okay, and asking where he'd been.

Marty just kept saying: "Pete, dead? I can't believe it. How could that happen? Pete. Dead. Killed. I can't believe it." He was almost in tears.

He was keen, even anxious, to cooperate. Except for one thing. He told them he'd spent the evening with Val, his fiancee. And he certainly looked as though he'd been out on the town. As Tessa had suspected, he was wearing his best. But he refused absolutely to tell them Val's last name, or where she lived. He said she had nothing to do with this, and he wouldn't have her dragged into it. He went with them to Homicide for further questioning without a murmur.

In the bare little interview room he told Steve and Tessa he'd been with Val because it was her birthday. They'd been going to have a late lunch, and the afternoon together. Val was working mornings only—waitressing. He was working mornings and evenings this month. Ten till two, six till ten. Pete Grogan was working the afternoons, from two till six. Marty and Val were to meet at this place they liked in the city—Sadie's Kitchen—at two. He didn't have to get back to Funworld till, say, a quarter to six. It was all organized.

But then Val was suddenly told she had to work through lunch and through the afternoon as well, because someone had called in sick. Val had only just gotten the job—she was scared she'd lose it if she refused to fill in. Her boss was a real old bitch.

She rang Marty up to tell him just after he'd finished his morning shift, while he was getting dressed to meet her. She was really disappointed. She'd been looking forward to her afternoon out. He told her not to worry. They'd have dinner together instead. He'd fix it so he didn't have to do the evening shift. That made her feel better.

There was really only one way he could fix it, of course, at short notice. He couldn't take a sickie—not living on the premises. Those bastards in the office would be sure to check up on him.

So after he and Val hung up, he nicked back into the ghost train and had a word with Pete.

Pete was a good mate. He agreed to do the double shift, to

help Marty out. Marty was going to give Pete the pay for the night, of course, plus ten bucks extra. It was worth it. Val was worth anything. Marty would rather have swapped shifts, of course, but that was too risky. People had seen Pete arrive for work. If they saw him leave again, they'd know what was going on. And Pete couldn't stay locked up in Marty's room all day. That would have been worse than working.

No one else knew about the switch, he assured them. How could they know? He didn't tell anyone. He went back to his room, after he'd fixed it up with Pete. Read a bit, tidied up. No one came near him. At 3:30 he nicked out, then went to Val's café—you had to get two buses—and waited there till Val got off. Then they went back to her place while she changed. Then they went out. No one saw them. And Pete couldn't have told anyone either. He was stuck in the ghost train all afternoon, all night. He was going to have to sneak out to the dunny to have a leak sometime, of course, but he'd be away five minutes. And if anyone saw him out the back, well, he'd be in the skeleton rig, wouldn't he, and how was anyone going to know he wasn't Marty anyhow?

He was right, of course. Jacko had seen Grogan "out the back," and even he hadn't had any idea.

"You went to quite a bit of trouble, just for a dinner out," Steve said casually.

Marty shrugged. "It was Val's birthday," he said simply. "I couldn't leave her on her own on her birthday, could I? Just because of my job. I had to work something out. If you love someone, you do, don't you?"

"Where's this boy been all my life?" muttered Dee Suzeraine, videoing the interview unseen from the narrow room behind the interview room wall.

And Tessa, sitting with Steve behind the one table in the interview room, the table with its recording machine, its notebook and pen, looking at Marty's earnest face, thought, "He's right. If you love someone, you work something out."

Steve started asking Marty again about whether he'd had a run-in with a customer recently. Whether there was anyone with a grudge against him. Anyone with a reason to hurt him.

They'd been through this before—twice at least. Bewildered, at a loss, Marty was still saying no, no, no. There was no one.

The interview was running out of steam. In Tessa's view it was time to let Marty Mayhew off the hook. After one last question, that is. A question Steve Hayden seemed determined not to ask.

Tessa glanced at her watch. It was 1 A.M. Brett would be asleep by now. When they first started living together, she'd come home to him at all hours, and he wouldn't mind. He'd stir as she slipped into bed, no matter how careful she was.

If he was sleepy, he'd turn over, cuddle up to her, murmuring, and slip back into sleep with his arm around her. And she'd lie there, hyper, her mind racing, till very slowly the warmth of the bed, his still, embracing body, would calm her and ease her into peace. If he'd slept enough to be more wakeful, he'd stroke her breasts, her thighs, press himself against her, whisper that he adored her, that she was beautiful. She always responded, though sometimes she was acting, because it was just too soon to relax, to forget. She didn't want to make him feel rejected. And she was so grateful for the acceptance, the love . . .

She forced her mind back to the interview.

"What about Pete Grogan, Marty?" Steve was saying now. "How did you two get on?"

"He was a mate. We got on really well." Marty's lips tightened, and his brow creased, whether from sadness, tiredness, or irritation it was impossible to say. "I told you."

"You've said you left Funworld mid-afternoon and didn't go back till you turned up after closing and found the police there. Are you quite sure you didn't go back earlier? To see how Pete was going?"

"I didn't go back. I was with Val all the time." Then, suddenly, there was a change. The dark blue eyes widened. The soft voice sharpened with panicky disbelief. Marty had finally caught on. "Hey, what are you on about?" he almost squeaked. "You don't think *I* killed Pete, do you? Why'd I do that?"

"I don't know, Marty. You tell me."

"Why would I kill Pete? I wouldn't do that! Are you serious?"

"We have to look at all the alternatives. Right? You've said you've got no enemies. No one who'd want to kill you. So maybe Pete wasn't killed by mistake. Maybe he was the target all along. But you've said yourself that no one knew it was him in the skeleton costume tonight. No one knew it but you."

Marty half stood, gripping the edge of the table, shaking his head compulsively from side to side. He was pale and hunted-looking. He licked his lips.

"I never saw Pete after one o'clock," he shouted. "I never saw him, I never touched him. Val and me went to dinner at Sadie's Kitchen like I told you, and then to a couple of night-clubs. Then I took her home. Her old lady was still up, so we just had a coffee and then I left and went back to Funworld. That's it, man. That's it! You can't . . ."

"You won't tell us where Val is, Marty. You won't tell us her name. You won't let us talk to her, check your story out. How do we know you're telling the truth? How do we know you aren't—"

"*All right!*" It was a cry of exhaustion, defeat. "I'll tell you. Her name's Val Nimrod. Valerie Louise Nimrod. She lives at 13 Poole Road, Knott's Park. With her parents. Her phone number's . . ."

Bastard, thought Tessa, as Marty babbled, and Steve wrote. You weren't going to let him go home without giving you that name and number, were you? You scared him into giving it to you. And for what? You know he's telling the truth. It's written all over his face. You know she'll confirm his story. Why scare him like that? We could have waited till tomorrow. He would have given us her number in the end. He was just trying to protect her. But you couldn't let him do that, could you? Not even for one night.

She was angry. Seething.

He's just doing his job. Making sure he ties up loose ends efficiently. Playing it by the book.

There are different ways of being efficient. Keeping this man's trust is more important than getting that phone number to check his alibi. There's something here we don't understand, and he's the key to it.

"Okay, good. Settle down, mate. Settle down, and sit down, will you?" Steve hadn't moved. Hadn't flickered.

Marty Mayhew hesitated, then finally slumped back into his chair, head bowed.

"We have to check it out, Marty," Steve said quietly. "You know we do."

Marty said nothing. Just nodded. He was totally demoralized.

Steve turned to Tessa. "I think we can finish here," he said politely. "Unless there's anything . . . ?"

"There's one thing." Tessa smiled at Marty, reassuringly, she hoped. "Did you give Val a birthday present tonight?"

He gaped at her, darted a look at Steve, looking for a trap, but answered. "Yeah," he said. "Some earrings. She'd looked at them in a shop window up on the promenade a few weeks ago. She really liked them. So I got them for her." Despite his fear, a slight smile trembled on his lips. "She was really pleased," he added.

"What about a birthday card?" Tessa persisted. "Did you buy a birthday card as well?"

"No," Marty mumbled. "I didn't have to. The shop wrapped the earrings. They were in a little box, really nice. They gift wrapped the box, free, with ribbon and that, and stuck a card on. I used that card. It was only little, but it had flowers on it."

He looked at her sideways—almost guiltily, in case it had been bad form to use the shop's free card.

"That sounds nice," said Tessa reassuringly. "I only asked, because there's a birthday card in your room. A card with balloons on the front. It's standing on the table. I thought maybe you'd bought it for Val, then forgotten to take it with you, or something."

He shook his head, looking puzzled. "It's not mine," he said. "It wasn't there when I left. Where did you say it was?"

"On the table. Who else knew it was Val's birthday today, Marty?" Tessa asked.

"No one," he said. "No one at Funworld, anyhow. I never said. I mean, there was no point. They don't know Val. She's never been there. Never seen where I work. I like to—you know—keep her out of it."

"Why's that?"

He hesitated. He seemed to be struggling for words. "She knows what I do, an' that. But seeing it's a bit different, isn't it?" he said at last. "Plus—they're good mates, but . . . they're a bit rough for a girl like her. You know. I like to keep her out of it."

He looked up at her. His eyes were thoughtful, guarded. Looking into those eyes, Tessa caught a glimpse of a life in which, perhaps, there had been little privacy. In which treasured personal things were kept safe, not talked about, not shared or exposed to public view and comment. She nodded, to show she'd understood.

"You told Peter Grogan about the birthday, presumably."

"Oh, yeah. I told him. Well, I had to, didn't I?"

"Maybe he put the card in your room—for Val."

Marty looked doubtful. "Can't see him doing that," he said. "And where'd he get a card from anyway? He was only in the ghost train."

"So where do you think the card came from?"

"I dunno." Marty wasn't interested in the birthday card.

Steve wasn't either. He terminated the interview for the benefit of the recorder, and stood up.

Marty leaned towards Tessa and lowered his voice. "Look— are you really going to ring Val?" he said. "In the middle of the night?"

"Yes. We'll have to, I'm afraid. And we'll have to see her— to take a statement."

He shook his head. "I really didn't want her mixed up in this. And she lives with her parents, you know. They'll get woken up as well."

"Don't worry too much. Look, I can understand how you feel. But don't forget—Val would want to do what she could to help you. In fact, she'll probably be mad because you didn't call her earlier." Tessa smiled into his worried eyes. "Women like protecting people they love too, you know," she added lightly.

His face suddenly broke into a beautiful answering smile. "Yeah," he said. Unconsciously, he straightened his shoulders. He glanced at Steve again, then turned back to her. "Could you be the one who talks to her?" he asked, loudly enough so that Steve could hear. "It'd be better. For her parents, too. Okay?"

"Okay." Tessa also glanced at Steve, whose face was expressionless. "Can I come with you, when you go to see her?" Marty asked it wistfully. He knew what the answer would be. But of course he still had to ask.

Val Nimrod's father had answered the phone when Tessa called. He'd said little—just mumbled for Tessa to hold on, dropped the receiver, and bawled for his daughter to come. When Tessa arrived at the cramped little semidetached house thirty minutes later, he was nowhere to be seen. Neither was Val's mother. Presumably they'd both gone back into bed, leaving Val to get on with it. One of the two bedroom doors off the narrow hallway was firmly shut.

Val herself turned out to be a small, sharp-faced girl with short, wispy bleached blond hair and a surprisingly loud, nasal voice. In preparation for Tessa's visit, she'd wrapped herself in a mauve kimono and stuck her feet into matching mauve slippers which clashed with her bright red-painted toenails. A ring of smudged mascara under her eyes gave her a raccoon-like look. She kept yawning. She was nothing special to look at. Nothing special as far as personality was concerned, either.

What did you expect? Helen of Troy?

The way Marty talked about her ... something a bit better than this. And he's so incredibly good-looking himself. And very engaging.

She's not good enough for him. Is that what you're saying? Come off it! He might be a babe, but let's face it, he's not a mental giant, is he? The fact is, he thinks she's Christmas. He thinks he's lucky to have her. So he is. Right?

Right.

But laboring on with the statement in the stuffy sitting room, watching Val yawn and pick at her nail polish (scarlet, to match the toes), Tessa decided she'd be very surprised if this girl's feelings for Marty Mayhew were as deep as his were for her. She'd marry him, though, unless someone with better prospects came along. She wanted to leave home, have a place of her own. Marriage was the appropriate way to achieve that. And Marty, devoted, would work himself into the ground trying to give her everything she wanted.

Val didn't seem to be able to focus on the fact that her boy-friend had only narrowly escaped death. She seemed to assume that fate had intended Peter Grogan to die, and not Marty, and that was that. Her main concern was that Marty was going to lose his job because of taking the night off.

But however disappointing she proved to be in other ways, she did confirm every detail of Marty's story. Letting Tessa out into the dark, deserted street, its tightly packed, tightly locked houses blind and deaf in the grip of sleep and the night, she agreed to come to Homicide after work, to sign the statement, as long as the police provided transport—or at least paid her fares.

It was 4 A.M. by the time Tessa, numb with tiredness and dispirited by the events of the night, turned the key in her apart-ment door and let herself into the dim, silent living room. She shut the door behind her, tested it as she always did to ensure it was deadlocked. It was. But there was no key in the lock on the inside.

She switched on the light, and blinked, looking around. Pale gold curtains screening out black sky. Answering machine, blinking red. The stumps of burned-down candles on the still-set table. Open champagne bottle, half full. Red roses limp and dying in their cellophane . . .

Tessa stuck her own key into the lock. It was habit. Whoever came in first. She and Brett had agreed. Whoever came in first left their key in the deadlock. In case of fire. In case of accident. They both had a horror of being trapped.

Seal intruders out, but don't seal yourself in . . . we're on the third floor here. No way you could jump . . .

But there'd been no key in the lock.

Tessa kicked off her shoes. At last. She dumped her heavy

handbag on the table, next to the roses, stripped off her gabardine coat. The light on the answering machine was blinking slowly. She noticed almost absent-mindedly that there were books missing from the bookshelves. A gap where the CD player used to be . . .

She crossed the room to press the button on the answering machine. One silence and hang-up, at midnight. Another at 1 A.M. Nothing more.

Slowly she walked to the bedroom. Tidy, as she'd left it. Empty. Bed pristine. The wardrobe doors stood half open. Her clothes hung bunched up on one side. She'd bunched them getting out the gabardine coat in a hurry. The other side of the wardrobe was empty, except for a row of coat-hangers and a tie lying like a discarded snake-skin, tangled on the floor. She bent and picked it up, smoothing it between her fingers. Dark blue silk with yellow stripes. Her mother had given that to Brett. He'd quite liked it. She'd have to make sure to send it on. Once she found out where he was.

She felt nothing. Nothing at all.

In a shadowy room, words slowly collect on a computer screen, as they do every night. Words, sentences, paragraphs . . .

". . . but I am really looking forward to when we do get together. I can understand that you feel nervous about it. I feel nervous too. I am scared you will be disappointed in me. But we will see each other soon, won't we? You promised."

The hands on the computer keys still. It's late, and there's nothing else to say. Not just now. The fingers begin to move again.

"I had better go now."

Lips smile. Three more words.

"Love from Baby."

Six

Tessa gave herself four hours of sleep. She hadn't bothered to set the alarm, just left the bedroom curtains open to let in the morning light. She knew she'd stir after four hours. It seemed to happen naturally. Like babies waking in the night to be fed, she often thought. She'd stir, and she'd wake. When there was something on her mind there was no temptation to roll over and sleep again.

The apartment seemed strange. So quiet and empty. She wondered about that as she stepped from the shower, her hair flat and dripping on her shoulders. It wasn't just Brett's absence. Brett had often already left for work when she woke after a late night. He often went away on business trips. But this was different.

The difference was in her. In what she knew about the silence, the emptiness. Brett wouldn't be returning. For the first time in eighteen months, she was living alone.

She rubbed herself down, dried her hair, brushing it smooth. She went back to the bedroom and dressed quickly and carefully, rejecting colors for a cream shirt, dark suit. After last night, she felt the need to look extremely businesslike.

She walked to the kitchen through the still-darkened living room, ignoring the mess on the table, and drank orange and mango juice standing up at the kitchen window. No one to tell her to eat something. No need to try to straighten things up. No need to think about dinner. Tonight it wouldn't matter if she came in late. And she could clean up anytime.

Twenty-five minutes after she opened her eyes in the bedroom, she was walking down the stairs to her car. She glanced at her watch as she slid into the driver's seat, and was surprised to find how little time had passed.

No distractions, she thought.

No distractions.

When Tessa arrived at Homicide, Steve Hayden was already there, talking on the phone. He looked fresh and relaxed. His computer was on—he'd been typing a report. A folded newspaper and an empty take-away coffee cup sat on his desk. How long had he been in? He nodded and raised a hand in greeting as Tessa slid behind her desk. She felt obscurely at a disadvantage.

Last week he'd been in court. She'd had the office space to herself. Now the office was full of his presence.

There's a little irony for you. Home's empty. Work's full.

She wished she'd thought of buying take-away coffee. Now she'd have to make some. She'd done it every other day on her arrival, but then she was alone. It made her uncomfortable to think that he would see it as her first act. As though she had nothing more important to do. Or maybe that it was her role to make the office coffee.

You're paranoid.

There was a message on her desk. "Ring Bridget" in firm, sloping, unfamiliar handwriting. His, presumably. At the top of the note he'd scribbled "Tues. 9 A.M." So he'd been here in the office, answering her phone calls, while she was walking downstairs to her car, congratulating herself on her efficiency. Great.

She switched on her computer, and pulled her notebook out of the top drawer of her desk. She'd type up Val Nimrod's statement. Get that done, at least.

Ignoring her caffeine addict's pangs, she started work. She heard Steve finish his phone call. He'd been talking to Tootsie Soames. The skeleton man's autopsy, presumably, had been scheduled. Tessa kept her head down, typing automatically, waiting for him to speak to her, but he didn't say a word. She heard the scrape of his chair, the rustling of paper, the clattering of a file, and then his footsteps quietly leaving the room.

Surely he wasn't going to the autopsy without her? However aggro he was, he wouldn't do that. Would he?

Why didn't you say something?

It was up to him.

What's the matter with you?

Her fingers stilled on the computer keys. "I don't know what's the matter with me," she said aloud.

Now you're starting to talk to yourself.

Angrily, she snatched up the phone. A friendly voice. Some normal conversation. That's what she needed. She punched in Bridget's number, praying she'd get an answer.

"Murphy." Bridget's voice, warm and husky. Normality. Relief.

"Bridget, it's Tessa. You left a message—"

"Tessa? You okay?"

"Of course I'm okay. I'm fine. Why shouldn't I be okay?"

"You just sounded funny, that's all. Listen, Tess—oh, happy birthday for yesterday, by the way. Sorry—I meant to ring on the right day for once—had it down in my diary, but then I got busy and I forgot about it till last night. And then I thought I wouldn't interrupt the famous dinner. How did it go?"

"It didn't. Remember I was on call? I had to go out."

"You're joking."

"Wish I was."

"God. How did Brett take it?"

Tell her. Get it over.

"Not well, you might say. He moved out."

"He actually—Oh, Tessa . . . oh, I'm really sorry . . ."

Tessa closed her eyes. There was a roaring in her ears. The sympathy in Bridget's voice was almost more than she could bear.

Why? You called her for sympathy, didn't you?

I suppose I did. But . . .

But sympathy was inappropriate. Tessa realized that as soon as she uttered the words "He moved out." Suddenly she knew that there was part of her that didn't deserve pity. Because there was part of her that was glad Brett had gone. Glad the tension was finally over. Glad she was her own woman again, having to answer to no one for her job, her eccentricities, her untidiness, her insomnia, her intensity—her everything.

And if that was true, what had she been doing living with Brett at all? Pretending everything was fine? Sleeping with him? Doing all those things . . .

"Tessa?"

She cleared her throat. "It's okay, Bridget. It's fine. I'm okay." She heard a faint noise from one side of the office and saw that Steve Hayden had returned. He was pouring water into the coffeemaker. He'd just gone out to wash the jug. To get water. He was making the coffee.

She hadn't noticed him come back into the office. Had he overheard what she'd said? How much had he heard? She felt herself blushing.

Bridget was saying something, but she hadn't been listening. She forced herself to pay attention.

". . . want to give you your present. Can you meet me for coffee later? Or lunch?"

"No. I can't. I'll be working through. Listen Bridget, I'd better go. It's a bit busy—"

"You've got company," said Bridget with quick understanding.

"Right."

"How're you getting on with him?"

"Oh—you know, okay."

"He's got a sexy voice."

"You never change. Okay, then—"

"Why change when you're perfect? Tess, look, before you go—" Bridget's voice, always expressive, had suddenly taken on a rather strained, hesitant note. "There was something else. Ah—it's probably nothing. It's in the paper—maybe you know already, but—just in case—"

"What?" Intensely aware of Steve Hayden, Tessa was now impatient to end the conversation. The coffee was dripping into the jug, smelling marvelous. Steve was moving back to his desk. Taking up a file and flicking through it. Working. While she chattered on . . .

Bridget's voice penetrated her confused thoughts. Bridget's voice saying a name.

". . . Brady Mumm. He's out. Got out the day before yesterday. Paroled. So . . ."

Brady Mumm. Pale eyes, staring. Brady Mumm. Out.

". . . I thought I should warn you. Just in case—"

Just in case . . .

"Have you heard from him or anything? . . . Tessa?"

Tessa licked her lips, found her voice. "No. I haven't heard from him. Bridget, I really have to go."

"Sure. Right. Well, I just wanted to let you know." Bridget sounded just a trifle put out. She was trying to be a good mate. She didn't like being held at arm's length.

Tessa tried to rise to the occasion. "Thanks," she heard herself saying. "I really appreciate—everything."

The voice at the other end of the phone warmed immediately. Bridget was infinitely forgiving. "That's okay. Look, keep your chin up. I'm really sorry about Brett. I mean, I know things have been a bit off for a while, but you must feel awful. Call me tonight if you want to talk. Doesn't matter how late it is. Okay?"

"Okay. Bye, Bridget."

Tessa hung up. She felt numb. It was the shock. She hadn't been prepared for this. Had the years gone so fast? She tried to work it out, counting back on her fingers. It had been five years ago. Five years . . .

Steve had gotten up again, and was pouring himself some coffee.

"Want some of this?" he said, without looking up.

"Yeah. Thanks." She got up stiffly, picked up her mug, and went to join him. He poured the coffee out for her, as if she were a guest.

"Sugar?"

"No thanks."

"PM on Peter Grogan in half an hour," he said, adding three teaspoons of sugar to his own cup.

"I'd like to go," Tessa said quickly.

"Good," he said. "That lets me off the hook."

He wandered back to his desk, sipping as he went.

Now he thinks you're a frigid ghoul.

I don't care what he thinks.

Brady Mumm's out.

Brady Mumm . . . in the paper. Bridget said . . .

"Anything in the paper about last night?" she asked aloud, keeping her voice as calm and cool as possible.

"Page three." Steve pulled the paper out of his bin, flicked a finger at it, indicating that she was welcome to take a look.

She picked it up from his desk and went to her own, clutching her coffee. She put down the mug carefully and leafed through the paper, steeling herself.

Page three. A shortish story on the Funworld murder. She flicked through it, barely understanding what she read, only gathering that it was big on picture, little on real information. The victim's name, the story said, had not yet been released. His family still hadn't been contacted.

Tessa turned the page casually, folded it over. And there he was. Staring at her. In a story about early releases. People complaining about early releases. Brady Mumm. As if she needed to be reminded what he looked like. She still saw his face in her dreams, sometimes. The almost albino look of him. His strange, no-color eyes. His shock of very fair, nearly white hair. They'd used an old photograph. Part of one she remembered seeing before. He'd look different now, probably. But not so much. Five years wasn't a long time.

"Catching up on your reading, Tessa?"

Thorne. Without thinking, Tessa crumpled the paper in her lap like a kid caught reading in class. She cursed herself as soon as she did it, but it was too late to change anything.

He stood smiling sarcastically just inside the door.

She hadn't heard him come in. People round here moved like sneak thieves. Or was she so rattled she was deaf to anything but her own thoughts?

"We've got a bit to do," he said, still smiling.

Tessa folded the paper and stuffed it into her desk drawer. The drawer was already overcrowded. The paper stuck. She shoved it in, hard.

Anything else you can think of to make yourself look bad?

Then Steve Hayden was standing up, coffee mug in hand. He was walking towards Thorne, lazily saying something about statements and reports. He was showing Thorne a file, telling him Tessa was going to the autopsy soon, leading him out the door.

He thinks he's protecting me.

He is protecting you.

I don't need protecting.

You do. You're making a real mess of this.

Too much is happening. New job, new partner, Brett gone, Brady Mumm . . . I can't . . .

You can. You have to.

The morgue: cold, smelling of disinfectant and death. Tootsie Soames, tall and strangely wholesome in brown-stained white coat. Coffee stains, or blood? It was hard to say.

The body that had been a living, breathing creature was lying washed, naked, and cold on the stainless-steel slab. Tessa looked at the choked, swollen face, red-patched eyes. There was a deep scarlet wound right through the umbilicus, as if the man was a giant-sized baby from which the cord of life had been ripped.

Peter Grogan, whom nobody had claimed. Over whom no one had wept. The man who was—just ordinary.

He had a brother, presently traveling overseas. Still not contacted. Did he love Pete? Would he miss him? Would anyone really miss him?

The hairs on your head are numbered.

Tootsie was examining the body minutely, speaking into a cassette recorder as she worked. Perhaps Peter Grogan had never been looked at so carefully, so tenderly, since he was a baby, and his mother had care of him, and loved him.

If his mother loved him.

The diagnosis of death by strangulation was confirmed. The knife wound had definitely been made after death.

"Why?" asked Tessa, remembering her question of last night. "I mean, why strangle someone, then knife them?"

Tootsie shrugged. "Just to make sure, maybe. Have you seen the knife since it was removed?"

Tessa shook her head. "I thought it looked very ordinary, though. Like a steak knife."

"A steak knife it was," Tootsie said. "Sold in sets of six or eight in every supermarket in the land. But that's the short answer. Our Dr. Fisk is no doubt compiling a twenty-page treatise on its weight, length, make, sex, and date of birth as we speak. No doubt he'll give you the benefit of his inquiries in due course."

There had been no cutting yet. Just external examination. The body was turned over. Tootsie bent, scanned, then leaned closer.

"See that?"

She'd brushed aside the straggling hair at the back of Grogan's neck. The pallid skin was marked by a savage, deep-red line—the mark of the ligature that had choked off the man's life. But above the line, there was something else. Another mark. A small tattoo.

Tessa bent to look. How strange. A blue-gray outline of a koala clutching the branch of a tree. It seemed oddly familiar. Then, suddenly, she realized why.

"It's not a tattoo," she exclaimed. "Hey—isn't it—?"

"A rubber stamp impression," said Tootsie. "Yes."

"Like you used to get on your hand at school, if you were good." Tessa was fascinated.

"Not at my school. At my school if you were good you got a religious picture and a day off a thrashing."

Tessa glanced at the pathologist, But Tootsie was absolutely straight-faced, and seemingly totally absorbed in examining the koala stamp. It was impossible to tell if she was joking or not.

Of course she's joking.

What if I laugh, and she isn't?

"Now why would he have a koala stamp on the back of his neck?" murmured Tootsie.

"A joke, maybe," said Tessa doubtfully. "Someone messing round. I'll check up with the people at Funworld. Maybe the office staff . . . How long do you reckon it's been there?"

"Not long at all. It's quite fresh-looking. Depends when he had his last shower, doesn't it? He's scruffy, but he wasn't dirty. His neck's not dirty. He washed fairly regularly, in other words."

"Ordinary washing wouldn't have taken it off," said Tessa, remembering angel and koala stamps on the back of her own five-year-old hand, and notably the time she'd stamped "Not Negotiable" all over her forearm on a visit to the bank with her mother. "You have to scrub."

"True. But ordinary washing would have at least blurred the lines a bit. As would a shirt collar, for example. There's no sign of blurring. No—I'd say he got the stamp yesterday sometime."

"He was inside the ghost train all afternoon and all night. No one came near him."

"Except his murderer."

Except his murderer.

The rest of the day went in a blur of interviews, the taking of statements. Tessa worked doggedly, concentrating on the case, screening out everything else, or trying to, but every now and then the screen would fracture, and she'd become freshly aware of the lowering cloud that hung over her, threatening to press down, smothering and disorienting.

Three times she took phone calls to hear only silence, and then a click as the caller hung up. The last time it happened she slammed down the receiver angrily, and turned to see Steve Hayden watching her.

"Problems?" he asked casually.

She shrugged, shook her head, bent over her work, shutting him out.

Why don't you tell him? Tell him you think it's Brady Mumm.

He'll think I'm unprofessional. Nervy. Paranoid.

You are. Why should it be Mumm? It's irrational. Why would he even remember you?

But she knew he did. She'd felt him, on the other end of the phone line.

* * *

She was still in uniform when she'd testified against Brady Mumm. Her evidence wasn't particularly important. Her part in the trial had been very minor, really. But Mumm had noticed her. He stood in the dock and didn't take those no-color eyes off her. He stared at her while she testified, and he went on staring afterwards, all the time till he was led away. She'd read the hate, and the promise, in that look.

Mumm was a rapist, a cold killer. She knew it. But he presented well in the witness box in his dark blue suit—well-schooled by his lawyer, or just a natural deceiver. He seemed earnest, unbelieving, deeply troubled—a decent young man trapped in a situation that had gotten out of control.

He said he'd met Melanie Bernstein in a bar, that she seemed quiet, and shy. That she'd said she had a car, suggested they go somewhere quieter. He said she took him to a park, one thing led to another—she initially consented to sex, seemed very keen, in fact, then had changed completely and pulled a knife on him. He'd struggled with her, of course he had. As far as he knew he was fighting for his life. The girl ended up dead. And he ran away. He was sorry about that now. But he'd panicked. Wouldn't anyone?

Liar, Tessa remembered thinking. Liar. As she sat stiffly in the courtroom, carefully not looking at Melanie Bernstein's parents, Libby and Brian, holding hands, stupefied, in misery.

But the jury believed Brady Mumm. And the judge was sympathetic. If Mumm hadn't run, he might have gotten off the charge completely. As it was he was convicted of manslaughter and given a minimum sentence.

Now he was back on the street. Far earlier than she'd thought he would be. And the first thing he'd done with his freedom was to track her down.

You don't know that.

I do.

That night, when Tessa left to go home, every fair-haired man she saw on the street looked like Brady Mumm. She checked the back of her car before she drove away, hurried out of the carpark when she reached home, glanced over her shoulder as she emptied her letterbox. She sorted through her mail nervously, hurrying up the stairs. Bills. A padded envelope addressed in her mother's writing. A couple of letters for Brett. Nothing unusual. Nothing to fear.

Inside her apartment, deadlock in place, she should have felt safe. But the curtains were drawn, and the rooms were full of shadows. The answering machine blinked furiously, an angry red eye in the dimness. She ignored it, went to the bedroom, and pulled off her clothes, carefully hanging the creased suit, putting the shoes away, throwing the shirt, underwear, and tights into the laundry basket.

You don't usually do this.

Tonight I feel like being tidy.

It's a substitute for thought. You know it is.

She went and stood under the shower for five minutes. There was only one of her now. She could afford the hot water. She dried herself carefully, put on moisturizer and a long, loose caftan her mother had made her, and padded barefoot back to the living room, turning on lights as she went.

The table was still set from last night's dinner. The roses lay limp in their cellophane, bud-heads drooping. They'd never open now. She turned her back on them and went to the answering machine.

"Tessa? Are you there? I thought you'd be home by now. Tessa?"

Her mother—loving, plaintive, with that note of faint reproach that always tinged her conversation these days.

" . . . Anyway, if you're still out . . . I just wanted to hear how your birthday dinner went, and if you got our present. Let me know if it hasn't come. It should have by now. It's just a little thought. Guy sends his love. Love to Brett. Bye."

Short and sweet. Ringing long distance, her mother never talked long to the answering machine.

Ring her back. Thank her for the scarf. Tell her about Brett.

I can't face it. She'll be upset. She'll say it was the job.

It was the job.

No. It was me.

"Tessa. Leonie. Look—um—Brett's told me about—everything, and—um—"

Brett's twin sister. A computer analyst who played the recorder and collected blond jokes. She and Tessa had always got on. Tessa would miss seeing her.

" . . . just wanted you to know I'm really sorry and—um—maybe we could have lunch or something—sometime? I mean, just because you and Brett aren't—um—it doesn't mean we can't, does it? Well, I hope not. If that makes sense. Anyway, that was all, really. It's weird. His voice is still on the machine. Feels like he's there. He's an idiot, I think. I told him. Bye."

Double beep. End of messages.

Tessa turned on the radio in the kitchen for company, and started clearing the table. The French champagne still had enough life left in it to froth as she poured it down the sink. The roses wouldn't fit into the kitchen tidy. She had to bend them. It seemed like sacrilege.

The phone rang. Brett's recorded voice answered. Loud. Confident. "We can't come to the phone right now . . ."

His voice is still on the machine. Feels like he's there.

Whoever was on the other end hung up.

Who was that? Who . . . ?

Tessa found the booklet for the answering machine and spent the next fifteen minutes remembering how to record. Then she deleted Brett, and put her own message onto the machine. "We can't come to the phone right now . . ." Exactly the same words as his, she realized when she'd finished. But she couldn't be bothered recording the message again, and she couldn't think of anything much else to say, anyway.

She ate an avocado and the grapes she'd bought for last night's dinner. She paced. She thought of doing some ironing. She knew she'd never sleep.

It was almost a relief when she was called out again. There'd been another murder.

Seven

Tracey Fernandez. Ballet dancer. Twenty-four. Strangled. No sign of break and enter. No sign of robbery. Husband, Guido Fernandez, helping police with their inquiries.

The tiny terrace house blazed with yellow light. The narrow street on which it crouched arm in arm with identical others was crowded with parked cars, some of them pulled onto the footpath. Neighbors stood around, gaping. A thin, frizzy-haired woman in a T-shirt and bright green shorts, her arms tightly folded against her chest, was haranguing a uniformed police-man near the front door. A witness. A neighbor, probably. Tessa drove past, around the corner, found a place to park in the tiny lane that ran behind the houses, and walked back.

She'd nearly reached the house when a car drew up outside and Inspector Thorne got out. The car drove on. The onlookers watched respectfully as Thorne walked briskly to the house gate, authority and rank displayed as clearly in the lines of his well-cut suit as in those on his confident face. Tessa's footsteps quickened. Thorne glanced around, and saw her, then turned away, smiling pleasantly as the frizzy-haired woman fastened onto him with avid determination.

By the time Tessa joined them, Thorne had it all worked out. "Thank you, Mrs. Andicus. Very useful. Detective Vance will take your statement down," he said smoothly. "Just tell her everything you've told me." He nodded to Tessa, and disap-peared through the front door, shutting it firmly behind him.

Mrs. Andicus, Mrs. Lynette Andicus, lived next door. She had a lot to say about Tracey and Guido Fernandez. She'd talked about them unceasingly to her friends ever since they moved in next door to her a year ago. Now she wasn't just a gossip, but a witness. She found this most satisfying. She'd told her story to the uniformed copper. She'd told it to Inspector Thorne. Now she was telling Tessa. Tessa wasn't as impressive as Thorne. But at least she took notes.

"Fought like cat and dog," she said, her lips thin, her arms strapped tightly across her chest. "Never stopped. It was him. Jealous? You've never heard anything like it. He'd scream and yell. Especially when he was drunk. Accusing her of going with other men. Threatening he'd kill her. Or himself. You could hear it through the wall. Not that I'm saying he didn't have a reason. The way she dressed. You could see by the undies on the line how she went on."

Tessa glanced up from her notebook. Mrs. Andicus was a sandy woman with small, bitter eyes. Her face, haloed by the dried frizz of her hair, was crazed with fine lines. Sun damage plus permanent discontent. She was probably younger than she looked. Maybe no more than forty. It was a chilling thought.

Mrs. Andicus saw Tracey Fernandez come home with some shopping bags at six o'clock. She knows it was six, because the six o'clock news had just started on the television, and she had tea for the kids on the table. She was looking out the front for her eldest, Troy, who was late, and she saw Tracey going in the gate.

At 7:30, about, she heard the next-door gate squeak again, and slam shut. She looked out her front window, and saw Guido Fernandez coming home. He looked drunk to her. Been at the pub with his mates as usual. She said to Troy, we're in for another brawl. You wait. The television was on, so they didn't hear anything for a while. But next thing, the police were arriving. Guido was raving and yelling about Tracey being dead. She said to Troy, told you. He's done it this time. This time he's really done it.

It didn't really take long to pick the few useful grains of fact from the mass of supposition and prejudice Mrs. Andicus had to offer. It just seemed long. After ten minutes Tessa was able to thank her and let her go. She watched as the woman marched away into the crowd of watching neighbors, arms still folded, mouth shut like a trap, chin high. Now she could tell her story all over again, repeat her forebodings, say she'd always known something like this would happen. She'd be the star turn.

Impatiently, Tessa turned to the house. She hadn't seen Steve Hayden go in. But he could have arrived before either her or Thorne. He could have gone in the back way. She found the thought that he could have been on the scene all this time, while she was stuck outside, supremely irritating.

This isn't a competition, you know.

It feels like it.

The front door opened into a narrow hallway lit by a swinging bulb covered by a round white paper shade. Ahead, a stairway led up to the bedroom floor, and a passage ran back to the kitchen. But voices were coming from a doorway to the right of the front door. Tessa stood at the doorway and looked in. Living room. White walls, another light in a paper shade, a young woman lying sprawled on her back on the fussily patterned red carpet.

Lance Fisk and his forensic troops were in control here. Dee Suzeraine was videoing the scene. Thorne wasn't there. Fisk glanced at Tessa warningly, but she knew better than to enter the room, and even Fisk couldn't stop her looking.

The room looked like a stage set. The lurid carpet. The light. And the dead woman—slim, simply but dramatically dressed in tight black leggings and leotard topped by a loose green jacket made of some silky fabric. The bright pink rayon scarf that still clung, twisted, around her neck was out of place. Almost certainly she hadn't been wearing it. It had simply been used to kill her.

Tracey Fernandez had been unusual-looking. Beautiful. Her very long, straight red hair was caught back in a ponytail. The hair was pulled tightly away from her face—she'd had no need to hide or disguise those high cheekbones, fine arched eyebrows, enormous, slightly tilted eyes, or that flawless milk-coffee skin. Her front teeth protruded very slightly—a tiny, attractive imperfection that would have made her face very memorable in life.

Dee Suzeraine drifted towards Tessa, face glued to the eyepiece of the camera. Her face was intent. She was chewing gum. "The fearless leader's in the kitchen," she muttered. "With the husband."

"Steve?"

"Not here yet."

"Excuse me." Tootsie Soames had arrived. She edged around Tessa and went to the body. Steve Hayden had come in behind her. He took the scene in at a glance, then left the room again, and headed for the kitchen. Where the action is, Tessa thought.

Lance Fisk also removed himself. He acknowledged Tessa as he passed her. "We seem to be determined to keep you busy," he said. He smiled pleasantly, and went upstairs. Where the action wasn't. But where fingerprints and fibers, papers, signs and marks in the dust lay quietly waiting to offer up their mute testimony to the experts.

Tessa didn't move. She watched as Tootsie bent, then crouched. Then she forced her eyes away and looked around, fixing the picture of the room in her mind. The body was lying beside a small table on which was a phone, an address book, a pen, and a memo pad. The phone was cream, and smeared with blood.

Blood?

Tessa glanced quickly back at the body, and as Tootsie moved to one side her heart thudded as she saw a dull gleam on the blackness of the leggings, near the waistband. How could she have missed it before? She'd been diverted by the scarf, the ruined face, the dramatic clothes. Tracey Fernandez had been injured—shot or stabbed—as well as strangled.

"Stabbed," said Tootsie, as if reading her mind.

She bent again over the body. Tessa bit her lip, not wanting to spoil the pathologist's concentration by asking the questions that were stacking up in her mind.

What sort of knife? Have we found it? Where exactly was she stabbed?

Don't rush it. Finish looking around while you can.

The walls and ceiling were white, recently painted. There were posters on the walls. Reproductions of old movie posters. A newish TV set, video. A CD player. A gas heater featuring fake coals had been brutally crammed into the space where the fireplace used to be. The furniture was old and knocked around. A three-piece lounge suite covered in mustard-colored vinyl with blond wooden arms, an ugly seventies sideboard with sliding glass doors, the phone table, a bookshelf. It didn't look as though it could have been chosen by the woman on the floor. The terrace, perhaps, had been rented furnished.

Near the body were two white plastic carry bags, about a meter apart. They'd both slipped sideways, and packets, tins and vegetables had spilled out onto the hectic carpet. Tracey had been shopping. She'd come home, carrying a bag in each hand, and met death.

A look back at the body. Yes. Another detail previously unnoticed. The thin black leather strap of a shoulder bag pulled tight over the black leotard, half-hidden by the green jacket. The bag itself, presumably, was trapped under the body.

A wailing voice rose from the back of the house. A slurring voice crying and groaning. The husband, presumably. Guido Fernandez. Tessa looked down the hallway, towards the sound. Steve was walking towards her, tall and dark, expressionless. If anything, he looked bored. He said nothing as he joined Tessa at the living room doorway and peered.

"Not long ago," said Tootsie, without turning round or looking up. Did the woman have eyes in the back of her head? "Rigor hasn't started yet. Maybe an hour or two."

"Husband says he came home at about 7:30, found her lying on the floor. Tried to revive her. Couldn't. Rang emergency. Emergency call registered 7:37," drawled Steve.

Tootsie pushed aside her glove to look at her watch. "It's 8:40 now," she commented.

"We're going to take him in for questioning," Steve said. "We've got a car coming round the back. Tessa, you right?"

It was a courtesy. A throwaway line. Why shouldn't Tessa be

right? She hadn't been necessary in the first place. The gang had it all sewn up.

"Why are you so sure the husband did it?" Tessa asked politely.

Steve shrugged. "He's covered in blood. He's drunk as a skunk. Neighbor's heard him threatening his wife before. He met the cops at the door with the knife in his hand."

"What does he say about that? About having the knife?"

Steve's smile was grim. "Says he thought she'd fallen on it, and he pulled it out. Didn't realize she was dead."

"That could be true."

"Sure."

He was humoring her. He thought she was overcomplicating things.

Any minute he'll start quoting statistics. About how often it's the spouse.

I know the statistics.

"She was strangled from behind. If it was the husband, that's unusual," she said.

"Unusual but not unknown," he answered formally. "Look—"

"There's something else," Tessa went on doggedly. "The husband came home ninety minutes after she did, according to the neighbor. But I think she was killed as soon as she came into the house. She's still wearing her shoulder bag. Her shopping's still on the floor where she dropped it. I think someone was waiting for her in the living room. He could have come in the back way without the neighbor seeing."

"There's no sign of break and enter."

"Is there a deadlock, or a bolt?"

"No."

"Then he could have used a credit card to force the latch. He could have even had a key to the back door."

"The husband has a key to the back door."

"Why would he bother to ambush his wife in their own house?"

"You tell me."

They were fencing, getting nowhere. Tessa was aware of

Tootsie and Dee glancing at one another. So, obviously, was Steve. He hitched at his belt impatiently. Thorne was waiting. And maybe, after all, game-playing wasn't his scene.

"Nearly ready to move her, Tootsie?" he asked.

"Any minute. You want to get the husband out first?"

Slowly Tessa withdrew from the doorway, leaving the field to him. She had something she needed to do. She considered the kitchen, then decided to try the easier option first, and walked upstairs.

Lance Fisk was in the larger of the two bedrooms. He looked at her sharply as she hesitated at the door. He hadn't expected interference up here. What was there to see?

The bedroom was untidy. Clothes everywhere. But it looked like the usual domestic chaos. Like a room where two people had dressed hurriedly, after a late bedtime the night before.

White paint. French doors to the balcony beyond. Green carpet square over painted bare boards. Double bed, lots of pillows, sheet thrown back. Bedside tables. Large wardrobe. A dressing table covered with jars and bottles. Some dead flowers in a vase. A fireplace with a pretty wooden mantelpiece.

And on the mantelpiece, a birthday card.

Tessa pointed to it. "Is that signed?" she heard herself saying.

Lance Fisk glanced at the card. His eyebrows rose. He picked the card up with gloved fingers, and opened it. He shook his head. No signature.

"I gather you'd like it tagged and taken?" he inquired.

"Yes—please."

Tessa withdrew from the bedroom and ran downstairs again. Her heart was beating fast.

Could be a coincidence.

No.

Don't get carried away . . .

Steve was still in the living room. He was standing in front of the two bags of groceries, considering them as if perhaps measuring the distance between them. As Tessa came in, he looked up.

"Looks like she was carrying one in each hand," he said. "As you said—came in, put them down."

"Yes. And why didn't she go straight to the kitchen? Why come in here? Unless she heard something."

"There's no sign of theft. No disturbance." But he was getting interested. She could see it. She took the plunge.

"She was strangled from behind. She was stabbed after she was dead. Have you seen the knife? What sort was it?" she asked abruptly. She held her breath.

"Ordinary household steak knife." he said. Then suddenly he looked watchful. He'd realized where she was heading. "Are you saying you think this is connected to the ghost train thing?"

"It could be. There's a birthday card in the bedroom upstairs. It's unsigned. Like the one in Peter Grogan's room."

He regarded her thoughtfully. Then, without saying anything, he turned and went back to the back of the house. Tessa watched him go, then looked back at the body of Tracey Fernandez. Tootsie was crouched again over the body, peering at the neck. Dee was watching, camera poised.

"Tootsie—" Tessa began.

"I'm looking," the pathologist said, without glancing up.

Steve returned from the kitchen, covering the short hallway in a few long strides. "It's not his birthday, and it wasn't hers," he said briefly. "He says his wife could have bought the card for one of her friends. But he doesn't remember seeing a card in the bedroom last night or this morning."

"Is the knife the same? The same sort as the one used on Peter Grogan?"

"I don't know if it's the same. Similar, sure. A steak knife." He said this slowly, unwillingly. She knew what he was thinking. That doesn't prove anything. Those knives all look alike. Black handles, brass studs, sharp, serrated blades. And even if it is the same exactly, those sets are cheap as chips, and cutting up steak in thousands of houses all over the city right now. But she didn't care about that. She pushed.

"Do they have any other knives like that in the kitchen?"

"Don't seem to. But the cutlery's all just bits and pieces. It's not compulsory to have matching sets of everything."

And that includes murders, I guess.

"Do you want to have a look at this?" Tootsie's voice was low.

Tessa and Steve looked around. She glanced up at them, her face serious.

She was holding the dead woman's hand. She'd pushed up the sleeve of the loose green jacket to the elbow. She twisted the hand slightly, so that the pale skin just above the wrist was exposed.

Both of them saw the mark at once. But they had to go closer to see it clearly.

It was a rubber-stamp mark, dull blue against the creamy skin. The outline of a koala in a gum tree.

Weeping, Guido Fernandez was escorted to a car brought around to the back lane, and discreetly driven off, watched only by two cats and a small boy in pajamas sitting on a tool-shed fence. But the neighbors still gathered at the front of the house got their vicarious thrills anyway, when minutes later the shrouded body of Tracey Fernandez was carried from the front door and loaded into the mortuary van. Strangely, once she had gone, and only an outline on the red carpet remained to show where she had lain, the house seemed desolate.

In the stuffy, stale food and grease-smelling kitchen, break-fast dishes still piled in the sink, Inspector Thorne, apprised of the new developments, made a few things clear—among them, that if Tessa had thought for a minute that she'd gained his good opinion over the last fifteen minutes, she was dead wrong.

"It's all very nice and exciting to be the one to discover that there's an apparent link between yesterday's crime and today's, Tessa," he said, with a thin smile that was a mere curving of the lips. "But I want to remind you that the rubber stamp mark would have been discovered at the autopsy in due course in any case. This would have led us back to the house, and the birthday card. And while you've been playing at being pathologist and forensic expert combined, the door-to-door that should already be underway hasn't even started."

"I'll be starting on that now, sir." What else was there to say?

"Yes, you will. And you will say nothing to anyone about either the card or the rubber stamp mark. Understood?" His cold eyes briefly met hers. She nodded, stifling a quick rush of resentment. What did he think she was going to do? Rush out and describe the crime scene to all the neighbors? Babble to the press? Just how unprofessional did he think she was?

But Thorne was continuing, speaking now directly to Steve Hayden. "So from now on we do things in order, and by the book. We don't jump to conclusions. We don't let the similarities between the cases throw us. We check out the husband's story. Check the wife's movements. Check the neighbors. We don't neglect one single, solitary piece of routine. Whatever theories anyone might have about mysterious strangers, we don't forget Fernandez."

Anyone? He doesn't mean anyone. He means me. He thinks I'm a dingaling.

Calm down, will you? He'll be gone soon.

"We bear in mind that Fernandez could have killed them both," said Thorne. "He's unstable. The woman next door says he was jealous as hell."

"She—Tracey—a chick like that—she wouldn't have been involved with that guy in the ghost train!" exclaimed Dee Suzeraine. "He wasn't in her league."

"You've seen her husband. Her taste in men wasn't too good," Steve said briefly. Tessa saw him jerk his head slightly at Dee, warning her to shut up. But Dee seemed careless of Thorne's stony disapproval of her interference.

"It's not on," she argued. "Look, believe me. I know these things. Grogan was . . ."

"We're not necessarily talking about Peter Grogan, are we?" Steve interrupted easily.

Dee fell silent. Then she shrugged. "Yeah—well—I'd forgotten about that. Marty Mayhew's a different story. She could have fallen for him. That's possible. If they met somewhere—"

"Marty Mayhew's in love with someone else," Tessa couldn't help putting in.

Dee laughed. "What's love got to do with it? He's a guy. Don't tell me he wouldn't have a flutter if he got the come-on."

Thorne's urbane expression didn't flicker. "Steve?" he said, as if there had been no interruption. "What does Mayhew know about the way Grogan was left?"

"Jacko would have told him about the knife. He knows about the birthday card. But he doesn't know about the koala stamp."

"Unless he and his girlfriend diddled us and he killed Grogan himself. I want you to contact him. Find out where he is now, where he was an hour ago, where he was at six."

"As far as I know he was working. Ghost train was reopening tonight. I'll check."

"Thought he was going to get the sack. For switching shifts," Dee put in.

"Didn't happen," said Steve. "Jacko stuck up for him. Told management that with Peter Grogan gone, he needed him. Couldn't get on without him. So he got off with a warning."

"Right. You check him out. Get him in again if necessary. If he was away from plain sight of a dozen witnesses for five minutes any time between six and seven-thirty I want to know about it. Get back to the office when you can. I'd like to interview Fernandez ASAP, and I want you in on that, but he can simmer for a while. He'll need to sober up a bit before the interview anyhow, and he might insist on a lawyer. That'll hold things up. I'll let you know."

He walked to the door. As an apparent afterthought, he turned and addressed Tessa. "You can get on with things here, Vance. Talk to that harridan next door again. Then start the door-to-door. Don't skimp it and don't rush it. We don't want to have to come back, do we?" He didn't wait for her murmured agreement before turning on his heel and leaving, straightening his tie as he went.

"That's right. He's a real sweetie," said Dee, grinning at Tessa. She wandered off, presumably in search of Fisk.

Tessa quickly readjusted her expression, which had obviously been far too revealing. But not before she'd caught Steve's eye.

"He's not dismissing the idea that there was someone else, Tessa," he said quietly. "He's just checking Fernandez and Mayhew thoroughly. He's just saying 'first things first.'"

"Favorite cliche number sixty-seven," she said hastily. She saw him turn away. He didn't actually shake his head, but she suspected he wanted to.

Eight

Checked again, Mrs. Andicus confirmed that she'd seen no one but Tracey and Guido Fernandez enter the Fernandez house. She seemed to resent the suggestion that there had been anyone else, to resent the fact that they were persisting in asking her.

Her little eyes narrowed suspiciously. She knew what police were. She knew what was going on here. They were going to let Guido Fernandez get away with murder. He'd paid them off, or was going to. In her head she was already rehearsing what she'd say to the neighbors tomorrow. Maybe, even though it was getting late, tonight. She could ring. Shocking, she'd say. Shocking. And one of the detectives was only a girl. . . .

Grudgingly, however, she admitted that she wouldn't have noticed anyone entering the Fernandez house from the back. Conveniently forgetting her previous references to Tracey's underwear, she said she had better things to do than peer over her neighbors' fence. Besides, she added, overdoing it and ruining everything, she knew they weren't home. They always came in the front.

The four Andicus kids—all boys, all sandy-haired, all sharp-faced, all monosyllabic—hadn't seen anyone either, between getting home from school and when their mum called them in for tea. Troy had gone off on his bike, down to the park. The younger ones had played with some others in the back lane after school. They'd had a game of cricket, as usual at this time of year, with a tennis ball and a box for stumps.

Mr. Andicus was a long-distance truck driver. He was halfway between somewhere and somewhere else right now.

He'd be home Friday. Or Saturday. His wife seemed to care little one way or the other. Mr. Andicus was plainly unimportant in the scheme of things, except as an irritant requiring extra cooking at mealtimes and quiet while he slept, and as a source of income.

The neighbor on the other side of the Fernandez house was an ancient man who was deaf and partially blind. His back door was permanently bolted shut. Spiders, lizards, cats, and morning glories reigned in his backyard. His windows were so filmed by years of grease and smoke that they seemed paned with frosted glass. He left the house only on Sundays, when his son-in-law came to pick him up. Every Sunday, he mumbled, he went to his daughter's place for lunch. Roast lamb, baked vegetables, a sweet. Very nice. Other days, regular as clockwork, Meals on Wheels brought his dinners. They were very nice, too. For breakfast he had Cornflakes and a banana.

His world had shrunk to a few dust-filled rooms. His needs had shrunk to food and warmth. His thoughts were vague and drifting. He didn't know who lived next door to him. He'd stopped caring about such things years ago. But he patted Tessa's hand as she left, and said she was a good girl.

Methodically Tessa checked every house in the street, interrupting people at their late dinners, in the middle of television programs, hacking out overdue essays, painting their fingernails, having a last cup of tea before bed. No one had any extra information to offer. Everyone had been at work all day, or watching TV, or doing housework, or out shopping, or in bed with the flu, or just in bed. If a stranger had entered the Fernandez house, from the back or the front, during the hours before Tracey Fernandez arrived home, no one had noticed it.

Steve rejoined her after about an hour. He'd seen Marty Mayhew, who was in the ghost train, where he'd apparently been since the ride had reopened at six o'clock.

"He could have sneaked out," Steve said. "But with Grogan dead, he'd have had a tough time finding someone to stand in for him. And he couldn't just leave and trust to luck. I stood out the front with Jacko for a while after I talked to him. You get a glimpse of the skeleton as the exit doors open to let the cars out. I reckon Jacko would have noticed if Marty was missing for longer than a few minutes."

"What did he say about Tracey?"

"He doesn't know anyone by that name. Doesn't recognize the description. So he says."

They continued the house-to-house together. Up one side, down the other, around to the few houses that backed the small back lane. No result. They'd finished by the time Steve heard that Guido Fernandez had at last been pronounced fit to be interviewed, and he was wanted. He suggested Tessa go home, get some sleep, but she wanted to watch the interview, and in the end they went back to Homicide headquarters together.

He thought she was being obsessive—she could see that. And maybe she was being obsessive. But that's how I work, she told herself. That's how I've always worked. I can't help it.

That's a rationalization. This is different. You're drugging yourself. So you won't have to think about—

I'm not drugging myself.

You are.

Guido Fernandez didn't do it.

If he didn't, they'll find out without you watching. Don't you trust them?

No.

Fair enough. They don't trust you either.

There was little new gained from the formal interview, at least as far as Tessa was concerned. She stood with a yawning Dee in the small video area that adjoined the interview room and watched the process unseen as it cranked itself along a track that led nowhere.

As Mrs. Andicus had theorized, Guido had had what he called a few drinks with some mates after work. This was his usual practice. He drove taxis. He hated it. Loathed the people. If they weren't pigs, they were idiots. The ones who tried to talk to him were the worst.

He was a poet, really. He'd had stuff published, too. But you couldn't make a living doing that, and no one was going to give him a grant. You had to be one of the in-crowd to get a grant. And Tracey earned peanuts.

He was in the pub by 4:30. The local pub. He didn't leave till about 7:15. He walked home. He and Tracey had a car, but it had packed up. Needed a new motor. He cursed about this. It was just one more piece of proof that fate had turned against him. Then he cried, because the car was a wreck, his life was a shambles, and Tracey was dead.

Asked about last night, Monday night, he at first weakly protested, asking what it had to do with tonight. With Tracey. But emotional exhaustion had sapped his will, and dulled his curiosity, and when they told him it was just routine, he accepted it and told them.

Monday night he'd been at the launch of a friend's book, at a local bookshop. It was an embarrassing book, which hadn't deserved to be published, and the launch was a piss-weak, embarrassing little affair. Everyone thought so. He'd rather not be published at all than be published like that. But he'd had to go. You had to go to these things.

After, a few of them went on to the pub. He stayed till the pub closed, at midnight, then three of them shared a taxi home. He gave names and addresses of people who would confirm the story. He was apathetic, uncaring. Either he was the world's best actor, or he was telling the truth.

"So it wasn't him who killed Peter Grogan," yawned Dee, checking the tape.

"Of course it wasn't." Tessa was weary, her mind churning.

"He still could have killed his wife."

"What about the koala stamp? The birthday card?"

"Coincidence?"

"Pretty bizarre coincidence."

Dee shrugged. "It happens."

"Not this time."

I can feel it. I can feel him out there.

Setting yourself up as a psychic now, are you?

Dee fiddled with the equipment, turned away from the monitor, from the black and white images of Thorne, Steve, and Guido Fernandez, slumped forward on his side of the table, his head in his hands. "A serial killer. That's what you're saying, isn't it? You're saying there'll be more."

"I guess so." Tessa suddenly shuddered all over. Dee glanced at her.

"You cold?"

"No." Tessa tried to smile. "Goose walking over my grave."

"You should go home. Get some sleep."

That's what he said. Your nerves are showing. Pull yourself together.

It was well after midnight by the time Tessa got home.

Wednesday morning, and all's well.

The garage was full of parked cars, and deserted. The building was hushed. There was no sound but the hum of the air-conditioning, the buzzing and pinging of a flickering fluorescent light, and the swishing of her own feet on the carpeted stairs. She hurried, gripping her keys.

If anyone's waiting for me . . .

Her apartment door opened on thick darkness, pierced only by the tiny, rapidly blinking red light of the answering machine.

Should have left a light on. Next time I'll leave a light on. The lamp, on the round table . . .

Baby.

She lifted her chin and deliberately closed the door, cutting off the light from the stairs. She turned the key in the lock, tested it, then walked straight through her living room, down the hall and into her bedroom in the dark.

What are you trying to prove? What about the answering machine? Don't you want to know who called?

It's too late. I'm tired.

But who called? It was flashing fast. Several calls. Who?

Tessa tore off her clothes and fell onto the bed.

The window.

She got up again, opened the window, lay down again, pulling up the sheet, burrowing down. She closed her eyes.

Who called? Could be urgent. How would you feel if . . . Mum—heart attack. Brett—car accident. Bridget—waiting up.

She lay rigidly for five minutes, then threw aside the sheet, crawled out of bed, and padded to the living room, turning the lights on as she went.

Bridget, brisk and breezy, hoping she was okay, tactfully making no mention of the new message on the machine. Someone wanting her to buy tickets in an art union, hopefully leaving a return number. A hang-up. An old school friend trying to organize a reunion dinner. Another hang-up, this time preceded by ten seconds of the dull sound of traffic, the distant wail of a siren. Someone ringing from a public phone box. Someone who didn't talk, just hung on the line, then put down the phone.

Tessa knew who it was. She could see him in her mind, standing in a booth on a corner, turned away from the traffic, shoulders hunched, white hair gleaming in the light. He'd be smiling. Wondering if she was there, holed up in her flat, not picking up the phone, listening to his breathing and the traffic, and understanding his unspoken message.

I know where you live.

Two long beeps. End of messages. Tessa's finger stabbed down onto the delete button. Too late she realized that she'd cleared her school friend's careful repetition of her phone number, along with everything else.

She switched off the lights and went to the bathroom to clean her teeth, wash her face. She went back to bed. Then she lay still, eyes shut, trying to think of nothing, till finally she drifted into a state that wasn't sleep and wasn't waking, jerking into startled consciousness with every sound.

The computer screen glows with light. The words gather slowly. The writing has been hard work, tonight. But the screen is nearly full, and when it is full, that will be enough.

" . . . it seems funny, but I feel lonely. I didn't before. I hope I will be seeing you or hearing from you very soon. I think about you all the time."

One line left to write. The fingers move fast for the last three words. They've been typed so often before.

"Love from Baby."

Nine

Wednesday morning. Armed with a publicity photograph of Tracey Fernandez, Tessa doggedly plowed through the routine allotted to her—the gradual collection of threads that, woven together, would eventually form a picture of the dead woman's last day. The dance class she attended on Tuesday morning. The hair appointment immediately after that. The rehearsal she attended on Tuesday afternoon. Her colleagues in the Corps de Ballet fluttering and grieved in tights and leg warmers, flexing their feet as they gave their statements. The health-food supermarket where she'd done her shopping the day she'd died.

The supermarket was in the cluster of shops ten minutes' walk from the Fernandez home. Tracey often went there. Annabel Wise at the checkout remembered serving her just before closing. They closed at six.

Annabel had checked Tracey's purchases through, then Tracey had seen some honey and macadamia nut bars on the counter, and had picked one up, asking for it to be added to the total. She'd said she was starving: hadn't had lunch. She'd paid for everything, and gone off carrying her two bags in one hand and the nut bar in the other, eating as she walked. Several of the shopkeepers had seen her pass. They all knew her, and she was a memorable figure that day, graceful and striking in her green and black, with the long red ponytail.

She'd finished the snack by the time she was halfway home. Mrs. Delimar at the laundrette, gazing in frozen boredom through the plate glass windows of her chlorine-smelling prison, saw her eat the last bite, stop, screw up the empty, sticky cellophane wrap, and stuff it into one of her shopping bags. Mrs. Delimar remembered thinking that was nice. A lot of people would have just thrown the sticky cellophane onto the footpath, for someone to tread in. There were no litter bins in this part of the street. Mrs. Delimar often had to sweep the footpath herself.

Tessa rang in after that. At last she had something useful to tell. Tracey had eaten something just after six. This would help pinpoint time of death.

But when she finally made contact with Thorne, she found that the investigation had moved on without her, and that the information she had to tell was of little interest, except as confirmation. Tootsie Soames, working over the slim body in the chill of the morgue, opening the stomach disfigured by a knife thrust directly through the umbilicus, had already discovered the honey and nut bar. The pieces were still in the stomach, intact. Digestion had barely begun. Tootsie would be very surprised if even half an hour had passed between that final bite and death. Fisk had found the empty cellophane pack and the receipt for the bar in one of the plastic shopping bags.

It had therefore already been established that Guido Fernandez, whose pub mates had confirmed his story, who had entered the house ninety minutes after his wife, could not have killed her. He was definitely out of it. But Steve's investigations of the morning, plus information from forensic, had confirmed that the two murders had been committed by the same person. A person unknown. Tessa should come in for a briefing.

Tessa hung up wondering if Thorne would have bothered to call her if she hadn't called him. Wondering, too, if his failure to indicate that he remembered that it was she who had first suggested a link between the murders was simply professional offhandedness, or a deliberate snub.

"The steak knife used on Tracey Fernandez is identical to the one used on Peter Grogan. Both knives, in Fisk's opinion, were new or at least unused previous to the murders. No fingerprints on either of them."

Thorne's voice droned on, summing up Steve's discoveries of the morning and early afternoon.

The steak knives were freely available. Sold in sets of six. The manufacturer had directed them to the fact that there had been a recent bulk sale to a supermarket chain which had been advertising and selling the sets at a reduced price for a couple of weeks. Thousands of sets had been sold nationwide.

Self-inking koala stamps whose imprint matched the stamps on both victims had been available at the same chain of stores for years. Birthday cards identical to the ones found in both Marty Mayhew's room and Tracey's bedroom were also stock items. Both cards came from the same range, which had been introduced to the chain exclusively a year ago, was comparatively inexpensive, and sold well.

Checks were being done, but it was extremely unlikely that anyone would remember checking through such popular items, even as a group, unless the purchaser was acting extremely oddly. If they were bought with cash, as was likely, they had to accept that there was practically no chance. And of course it was by no means certain that all the items listed had been bought at any one store.

As for the forensic report: Fisk had reported that Tracey's card bore no fingerprints, or traces of fingerprints, which was odd, because it would have been handled several times by supermarket staff at least before being sold. Presumably it had been carefully wiped over, and thereafter handled with gloved hands.

The first card had now been retrieved from Marty Mayhew's room. It bore Marty Mayhew's prints, which wasn't surprising, because he'd picked it up and looked at it on being allowed back into his room on Tuesday afternoon. There were no other prints on the card whatever.

Fingerprints in Marty Mayhew's room and the ghost train had been compared with those found in the Fernandez house. No match. The killer, presumably, had worn gloves. Analysis of hair and fiber found at both scenes was still underway. It had, however, been confirmed that dark blue fibers, consistent with fibers present in track-suit fabric, were present at both scenes, as were beige-toned Berber carpet fibers. Neither Tracey nor Guido Fernandez owned a dark blue track suit.

Marty Mayhew had a couple of pairs of black track pants, but no blue ones. Peter Grogan, the only other person to regularly use Marty's room, had no track suit pants at all. He wore jeans or nothing, apparently.

"Fisk isn't committing himself to anything, naturally," Thorne finished dryly. "But he's suggesting we consider the strong possibility the same person was present at both scenes."

"So we start looking for a link between the victims," drawled Steve. "Tessa, have you started on the address book yet?"

The Fernandez address book, crowded with names.

Tessa shook her head. Not yet. She caught Thorne's eye. "I've talked to the people she worked with," she heard herself saying, in a voice that sounded strangely thin and immature. "She seems to have been popular. Not a great star, so no real professional jealousy. No enemies that anyone knows about. No one likes the husband much, but most of them barely knew him." She made an effort. "I was thinking, though—both the victims were performers. Could that be a link?"

Stupid.

"Think we'll have to do better than that," said Thorne, smiling slightly. "I wouldn't have thought dressing up in a skeleton suit and jumping out at screaming teenagers was exactly equivalent to dancing classical ballet."

"I don't know." Steve looked at Tessa thoughtfully. "There could be something in it. Hard to see how else Tracey Fernandez and Marty Mayhew make a pair. They were about the same age, but it's not likely they had friends in common." He grinned. He had, Tessa noticed again, a very nice smile. "They moved, as my Auntie Rose would say, in different circles. You can't imagine Tracey and Guido taking herbal tea with Jacko and Marty on the ghost train steps, can you?"

Jacko. Jacko's voice, echoing in the bricked courtyard behind the ghost train. "It was some looney. Someone who reckons they was diddled by Funworld, say. An' where does that leave the rest of us?"

Galvanized, Tessa leaned forward. "What about Funworld?

That could be the link. Tracey didn't make a lot. She could have taken a casual extra job or something at Funworld—"

Steve shook his head. "Checked that this morning. What's-his-name, Papas, the Financial Controller, swears blind no one called Tracey Fernandez has worked at Funworld over the past seven years, even for a day. He's punctilious about keeping the records, he says. For tax reasons."

"She could have stood in for someone without Papas knowing. A private arrangement. Papas didn't know about Peter Grogan substituting for Marty Mayhew, did he?" Tessa's voice was rising. She could feel the adrenaline surging through her body, tingling at her finger-tips.

Don't come on too strong—they're staring at you.

She moderated her voice, forced herself to sit back in her chair. "Look, don't you think we should—"

"Check it out?" Thorne put in, smoothly regaining control. "Yes. You do that, Tessa. Whenever you're ready."

It was a polite dismissal. Tessa nodded briefly, got up, gathered her things, and left. She had the distinct impression that the two men were going to start talking about her as soon as she was gone.

No one at Funworld recognized the photograph of Tracey Fernandez—no one admitted it, anyway. The quest took hours, and was fruitless. Tessa went back to the office to type up her report. Steve wasn't there. Neither, it seemed, was Thorne.

Much later, she left the office, picked up Thai takeaway for one, and creeped (she felt she was creeping) back to her increasingly unwelcoming flat.

It was hot. There was no light showing on the answering machine. She'd forgotten to turn it on.

You didn't forget. You did it deliberately.

She ate the food mechanically, watching a television program she later couldn't remember. After that, she rang her mother, and thanked her for the birthday gift.

"Are you all right, darling? You sound so tired." The soft, concerned voice was full of warmth. It seemed to caress Tessa through the phone line. She suddenly had a childish urge to throw herself into that warmth. She wanted her mother with her. She wanted to snuggle up, hide her head, pour out everything that was worrying her, have her mother say, "Never mind, darling, you're safe now, everything's all right, it was only a dream . . ."

But of course she couldn't do that. She couldn't have that. For lots of reasons.

"I'm fine, Mum," she said into the phone. "I am a bit tired, though. I've got a case, not going so well. That's why I couldn't ring last night."

"Oh, right. I see." The voice had changed a fraction now. It was just a little more distant, a tiny bit strained, and trying hard not to show it. "Are you still enjoying—the new place?"

"Oh, sure. It's fine."

"Must be nice to be closer to home."

"It's marvelous. You can imagine."

"Yes."

The phone line hummed between them—the strained, helpless silence thick with unspoken words.

Talk to me, Tessa.

I want to, but I can't. I can't talk to you about what's most on my mind. This job—

That bloody job. How could you, Tess! How could you! With all your talent, all you could have done . . .

It's what I wanted.

How could you do it to me? After your father . . .

Mum, please!

Tessa made an effort. "How's Guy?"

Guy, nice Guy, neat and dapper, clipped mustache, shorts with long socks. As different from Dad as . . .

"Oh, he's fine. Sends his love. We've been playing tennis today. Told you we joined the club, didn't I?"

"Yes, I think you did."

Another pause.

"Well, darling, you'd better go. We haven't got any news. This is costing you and Brett a fortune."

"It's okay, Mum. It's cheaper at night. But anyway, yes, I'll go. Try to have an early night."

"That's a good idea. Talk to you soon. Glad you liked the scarf. Love to Brett."

Brett's gone.

"Thanks, Mum. Okay, talk to you soon. Bye."

Tessa hung up, and wandered to the window. She stood looking out, wondering if her mother felt as flat, as despairing, almost, as she always felt after some of their phone conversations.

She probably did. But she probably hid it from Guy, as Tessa had always hidden it from Brett. Because—how could you explain it? Without sounding damaged and neurotic.

Brett knew her mother disapproved of her job. He agreed with her, heartily. It was one of the main things they had in common. But he didn't know how deep the rift was.

It wasn't just the job. It had started long before that. When Dad was killed, thought Tessa, staring out at the night.

She left the window, and wandered to the bathroom. She'd have a shower. Cool off. Change into something loose.

She pulled off her clothes, and dropped them on the floor. She stepped into the shower and turned it on, wetting her hair, turning her face up deliberately to catch the shock of the cold water, only gradually turning the hot tap till the stream was lukewarm.

Senior Detective Tessa Vance, Homicide. She couldn't blame her mother for seeing her job as some sort of betrayal. In a way it was. She couldn't blame her mother for failing to understand how she could have even thought of it, except as a form of revenge.

They'd both adored Doug Vance. When he was at home, the house seemed to be filled with his vast, warm, and dependable presence. The trouble was, he was more often absent than present. At every family gathering the phone was the enemy.

As she got older, Tessa resented it as much as her mother did. She resented the way the job took him away from them, from school concerts and prize-givings, from promised trips and outings, the way it consumed his energy and his time. She sided with her mother, often, against him. They talked about it, on evenings alone together. There had never been any other children. Tessa's mother said that raising one child alone was trouble enough.

Her father had tried to talk to her about it once. She was fourteen. There'd been an argument. Mum was in their bedroom, crying. Her father, red-faced, stubborn, defensive, came out onto the veranda where Tessa was sitting on the step. He said she was old enough to understand. She should try to understand. He said he was what he was. He said he loved her, and her mother, but what he did was important, and meant a lot to him too. He said he was sorry.

He was asking for acceptance, but she turned her face away from him and wouldn't speak.

A few months later, he was dead. Tessa was paralyzed with grief and guilt. She'd never made peace with him. Her mother, distraught, mourning, then embittered, said she'd always expected that her marriage would end like this.

And somehow the death pushed a wedge between them, instead of drawing them closer together. They never spoke about it, never breathed a word, but they both knew they'd ganged up on the man they loved. Each had fed the other's anger. Like conspirators, they blamed each other in their hearts.

Compensation and a pension saw Tessa finish school, go to university, move away from home into a shared house. After university she went overseas, and stayed away a year. She came back to face the realities of the family home sold, her mother remarried and living in another state.

So it goes.

She barely remembered the next few months: they were just a blur of sporadic casual work, sporadic attempts to find a "proper" job, sporadic contact with old friends. Nothing seemed to matter. Then, one day, waitressing in a suburban cafe, she met an old friend of her father's—Bob Murray. He'd been a homicide sergeant in her father's day. Now he was Detective Chief Superintendent. He was her godfather, though she hadn't seen him since her father had died.

They talked. He told her the service needed people like her. He told her that people like her, like her father, needed to serve.

Corny.

It was corny, but the meeting changed her life. Suddenly, everything fell into place. She knew what she wanted to do. And over her mother's dead body (almost literally) and her old university friends' astounded disapproval, she did it, joining the police service and starting to work towards the place where she wanted to be.

And now she was there. In the place where she wanted to be. *Are you? Is this what you want? This?*

Tessa turned off the taps abruptly. She stepped from the shower and pulled on a kimono. She was still wet, but it didn't matter. She padded out into the living room and rang Bridget.

"Tessa! You all right?"

"Why does everyone keep asking me if I'm all right? Of course I'm all right."

"Has anything happened? I mean, has Mumm . . ."

"I've had a few funny phone calls. Could have been him." *You know it was him.*

"Might have been Brett."

"No, I don't think so."

"Tess, you'd better tell someone. Just in case." *Just in case.*

"What am I supposed to say? I want protection because I've had a few funny phone calls? Because I've just got this feeling this guy I saw for a few days five years ago is out to get me? These people think I'm neurotic enough as it is."

"Tessa—"

"Look, I should be able to cope with this. It's my job. The fact is, Mumm probably doesn't even remember my name. I'm just a bit overtired. Jumpy. You know? It's hot. I'm not sleeping too well. We've got a big case—"

"Yeah, I heard—you join the division and they have two murders in two days. Good work. You going to go for the trifecta?"

"Don't say that."

"Tessa, you don't sound too good."

"Thanks. Bridget, I've got to go. Just rang so you wouldn't worry. All right? See you soon."

"Okay. Take care."

Take care.

Tessa put down the phone and wandered around the living room, touching things, absently noting dust, the dining table, still partly set for the birthday dinner that never was.

Clean up. It'll make you feel better.

"Two murders in two days. You going for the trifecta?"

Clean up.

Monday, Tuesday . . .

Nothing happened today.

How do we know? A body could be being discovered right now. Knife through the belly button. Koala stamp. Birthday card. The pager could go any minute . . .

Clean up, then sleep. Do it!

Someone types, in a shadowy room. Only the computer screen lights the night. Lips move, murmuring the words.

" . . . but I can't help thinking something's wrong. Every day I think—maybe today. I know that you meant what you said. You couldn't have said those things if you didn't mean them.

"Love from Baby."

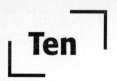

Ten

It was the next morning at six-thirty, the sky a glorious arc of shimmering blue, the sun already promising a day of relentless heat, when the call came.

"Would you say a butcher was in show business?" Thorne inquired pleasantly as Tessa came quietly through the butcher's shop to join him at the door of the freezer room.

Tootsie, crouched among the hanging rows of carcasses over the stiff, chilled body of Lloyd Greely, twenty-nine, turned her head to look at them. She didn't like jokes about the dead.

"It's another one," Tessa said. It wasn't a question, but a statement. She could see the black-handled knife protruding from the man's stomach. She could see the koala stamp on the back of his hand. But Lloyd Greely hadn't been strangled, and the stomach wound had been made before death. It had bled freely.

"Hit on the back of the head, with a heavy metal object, almost certainly the hammer you found," said Tootsie briefly. "Then dragged in here, stabbed in the stomach, through the umbilicus, and locked in. Sometime last night. Before midnight, I'd say. That's three in three days." Her breath made puffs of mist as she spoke.

Three in three days.

Tessa had seen the desk where Lloyd Greely had been sitting when he was struck down—a battered little desk in the back room of the shop. The scene was easy to read. He'd been doing his accounts. Lloyd always did his accounts on Wednesday nights, after closing, his apprentice Alistair Skinner had said, between chattering teeth.

Alistair had discovered the body. He was seventeen—tall and lanky, with bright blue eyes and traces of teenage acne still visible on his soft chin. He was still shaking all over when Tessa saw him, despite the blanket the paramedics had wrapped around him. He was blinking incessantly, talking to Steve. He'd come to work, seen blood smears on the floor, the bloodied hammer lying near the upturned chair. He'd gone looking for Lloyd—and in the freezer he'd found a nightmare that would haunt his dreams forever.

Steve was handling him well. Like an older brother. Calm, strong, reassuring. Tessa had left them alone. She had a feeling the boy would try to be macho in the presence of a woman. But she knew he shouldn't try.

She found her voice. "He froze to death?"

Tootsie's face was grim. "I can't tell you the exact cause of death at the moment. The cold would have contributed, of course. But there's a very severe concussion, and the knife wound. The knife went straight through the umbilicus, like the others. He lost a lot of blood. With attention he probably could have pulled through all right, but as it was . . ." She pressed her lips together.

She's angry.

"There's an alarm button here near the door," said a voice close to Tessa's ear. Tessa jumped violently, bumping Thorne with her elbow. She hadn't realized Fisk was there. Thorne glanced at her, raised his eyebrows slightly, and moved away.

"He wouldn't have been able to get to the alarm," snapped Tootsie. She bent again over the body.

Would he have regained consciousness? Known where he was? Known he was dying? Head swimming, bleeding, in pain? Trapped and freezing?

Don't think about that. Don't ask Tootsie about that. That's what's upsetting her. That thought. He could have lived. With attention. But someone left him here to die.

Tootsie stood up. "I can't do any more here," she said crisply. "You can take him." She pushed her way through the swinging carcasses to the freezer door. Tessa stood back for her as she brushed past, in a draft of chill air. Her arms and hair were spangled with flecks of frost.

Tessa watched as she walked straight through to the back of the shop. Steve Hayden was there, standing alone. Tessa saw him stop Tootsie and say a few words. The pathologist shook her head. He put his hand on her shoulder, briefly. She grimaced, smiled, shrugged, and walked on, through the back door and out into the sunshine. Steve looked after her, hands stuck in his pockets.

Tessa went to join him.

"They've taken the kid to hospital," he said. "He's a mess."

"Have they found a birthday card?" she asked abruptly.

"No. Could be that was a furphy."

"It can't be!"

"Where is it, then?" He moved uneasily, troubled by her vehemence. "You right?"

Yes, Tessa was right. Right to leave this place, anyway. She'd seen the desk, accounts neatly laid out, checkbook, pens, phone, the photograph of the young woman smiling, eyes squinted in the sun. She'd seen the bloodied hammer. She'd seen the smears of blood from the head wound on the vinyl-covered floor, and the marks of Lloyd Greely's dragging heels as he was hauled to the freezer room by his killer.

She'd seen the shopfront, stainless-steel shelves bare except for bright green plastic ferns neatly laid out to cover their gleaming nakedness, the plate glass window plastered with "Specials" signs, the "Closed" notice on the door, the still almost deserted early-morning street outside. She'd seen the untouched cash register, the posters of meat cuts on the walls, the recipe pamphlets and jars of marinade on the counter. She'd seen the coolroom. She'd seen the freezer, and the body.

Nothing more to see. Nothing more to do here.

"I'm going round to the Greely house," said Steve. "How about you stay here till the rest of the shops open up? Won't be long. Newsagent's open already. Someone could have seen something last night."

"Maybe the chicken shop next door. Everyone else would

have been closed. Anyway, yes, I'll do that. I'll show the picture of Tracey Fernandez around, too, in case she shopped here."

"I doubt she did. Doesn't look like her sort of place."

A moment's silence. Awkward. Tessa's gaze drifted around the small room. The battered filing cabinet. The electric jug on a tin tray. The cluttered desk. The photograph. The bloodstains on the floor. A man's life had ended here. Violently. Unexpectedly.

"He chooses his times, this merchant," Steve muttered. "He watches them. Finds out their habits. Finds out when they're alone. Plans it."

Tessa shivered.

He watches them. Plans it.

"The hammer came from the toolshed out the back. It was his. The kid recognized it."

"The picture on the desk. His wife? Girlfriend?" Tessa's stomach churned at the thought of telling the laughing woman what had happened to Lloyd Greely.

"Wife. Joy. She died a couple of months ago. We'll check it out, but according to the kid it was just an accident. Electrical accident. At home. Greely was devastated." Steve grimaced. "She was three months pregnant."

"Oh, *no* . . . Oh, how—"

How unfair. How cruel! What had he done to deserve—

Don't you dare cry. Remember who you are, where you are. What's wrong with you?

Tessa glanced quickly at Steve, but he was staring through the doorway, off into the distance, giving no sign that he'd noticed her distress. His face was very subdued. "The kid says Greely only came back to work three weeks ago," he muttered. "He was still very depressed. Knocked for six. If it hadn't been for the blood, the drag marks, the kid would have thought it was suicide."

He paused. "Greely wasn't a very big bloke. But he was young. Well-muscled. You'd think he'd have put up a fight."

"He didn't get the chance to fight," Tessa reminded him wearily. "The killer got in, crept up on him while he was working at the desk, with his back to the door, cracked him over the head."

"Yeah. Doesn't make sense to me. You plan to kill the guy. You plan it carefully. But then you just take a chance he'll be sitting at the desk when you come creeping in the door—instead of up stretching his legs or making coffee or whatever—and that you'll be able to get close enough to hit him without him hearing you and turning round. There was nothing wrong with Greely's hearing, the kid said. The killer took a bloody big risk. An even bigger risk than he took with Tracey Fernandez."

"He wouldn't have taken a risk," said Tessa positively. "He minimizes risk."

"You're saying he knew Greely? Maybe knew Tracey Fernandez, too? So they trusted him? Turned their backs on him?" Steve demanded. "A tradesman, maybe?"

Tessa shrugged, shook her head. She didn't mean that. It could be true, but she didn't think so. The crime scenes didn't tell that story. She couldn't explain it. All she knew was that this killer had it all worked out. This killer was obsessive, cold, intent. He might take a risk, if he had to, to cope with something unforeseen. But a foolish risk wouldn't be part of his plan. No way.

The shopping center was small—just two short lines of shops on either side of the road, catering almost exclusively, Tessa would have thought, to local residents. There would be little passing trade here, so far from the main highway. The newsagent and the cake shop were open. The others—fruit shop, supermarket, delicatessen, hardware, haberdashery and craft supplies, and all the rest—began unlocking their doors within half an hour.

One by one, Tessa checked them out. As she'd expected, none of the shop owners had seen anything, heard anything suspicious, noticed anyone loitering near the butcher's shop on Wednesday evening. Most of them closed at five or six, were gone by seven at the latest.

Try Milo Rossi at the char-grilled chicken shop, everyone

suggested. He stays open quite late. He's next door to Lloyd. He might have seen something. But the char-grilled chicken shop was still firmly closed.

Rossi would be turning up soon, the newsagent across the road said. But he doubted Tessa would get very much from him. Milo Rossi was a surly bastard who took no notice of his neighbors. He never so much as said g'day to anyone except his customers, and from what you heard, he barely spoke to them if he could help it. He'd only taken over the shop six months ago, and the newsagent confidently predicted he wouldn't last.

Everyone knew Lloyd worked on his books on Wednesday nights. Lloyd, it seemed, was a creature of surprisingly regular habits for a man so young. He had been well-liked. He'd taken the shop over from his uncle Stan, who'd retired and gone up the coast to fish and play golf for the rest of his life.

Lloyd was young to have had his own business. But his uncle had helped him out, set him up, according to the newsagent who, perhaps influenced by the atmosphere of headlines, news, information, gossip, and innuendo in which he spent his days, seemed to know every detail of all his neighbors' lives, and to enjoy discussing them.

Lloyd had done a good job with the shop, working hard at it, adding to its range some expensive cuts and ready-to-cook stir-fry and casserole mixtures his uncle had thought were risky, and introducing a new range of fancy sausages. Lloyd hadn't been the same since Joy died, the newsagent and all the other neighbors said. But life goes on. He would have gotten over it. Everyone thought so. Everyone wished he'd had the chance.

Steve rang her from the Greely house. He and Fisk had found a birthday card propped against an empty vase on the dressing table in the main bedroom. He thought she'd like to know.

Of course I would!

At least he's talking to you.

"Why did the killer go to the house? Anything stolen?"

"Hard to tell. Doesn't look like it."

"He left the card in Marty Mayhew's room as well. And the

card was in Tracey's bedroom, not the living room. What's the point?" Tessa hadn't really thought about this before. But, of course, it was strange. Why did the killer go to the extra trouble—take the extra risk, in fact—of going to a second location to place the birthday card?

"We've got a briefing at midday. Forensic psychologist. Ask him. You need to come in anyway. Thorne's put together a task force. We're not on our own any more. You nearly finished there?"

"Not quite. I'm waiting for the chicken shop guy. I've talked to everyone else."

"Got anything?"

"Not much."

Not much? Not a thing. No information, no observation that could help. No one had seen anything. Because Lloyd Greely had been alone in his shop, doing the books, and the shopping center was deserted, except possibly for the surly Milo at the chicken shop.

He chooses his times, this merchant. . . . He watches them. Plans it.

No one had recognized the photograph of Tracey Fernandez. Well, it had been unlikely that Tracey had ever come to shop in this ordinary little suburban center far from her home.

As Steve Hayden said.

It was worth a try.

Milo Rossi, when he did arrive for another sweltering day over the char-grill, turned out to be, as the newsagent had promised, a man of few words. He didn't even know Lloyd Greely's name. He didn't recognize the photograph of Tracey Fernandez. He hadn't noticed anything unusual on Wednesday night. He closed at eight, then typically spent another hour cleaning up, he said. He didn't look happy about it.

"You heard nothing?" Tessa asked, desperately trying to break through his taciturnity. "Nothing at all? Not a car? Not a cat? Not the squeak of a mouse?"

Milo Rossi glowered. "No mice," he growled. "You think I run a dirty shop here?"

She sighed, thanked him, put away her notebook and turned

to leave. The phone rang, and Rossi slouched over to the wall to answer it. The man next door might be dead, but it was business as usual at the char-grilled chicken shop.

What do you expect? Like they said, life goes on.

"Hey!" The door was closing behind her, but Rossi was calling. He was beckoning to her imperiously, his other hand clapped over the mouthpiece of the phone.

"The phone ring," he shouted to her.

"What?"

He jerked his head impatiently. "The phone. Next door. I hear it ring. Last night."

Tessa's heart thudded. "When?" she asked quickly.

He shrugged. " 'Bout 8:30, maybe."

"Did Mr. Greely answer it?"

"Someone answer it. Only ring a couple of times."

"Did you hear anything else?"

He scowled, perhaps already regretting communicating his sudden flash of memory. "I'm cleaning up," he said. "I hear nothing."

She waited till he'd finished his phone conversation, which seemed to concern a delivery of frozen chips, then she tried for further details. But he had nothing more to tell her. He only heard the phone next door because he happened to be in the back of the shop at the moment it rang. But he didn't hang around there. He wanted to finish the work and get home.

"What's it matter, anyhow?" he growled as she left. "Little phone call. Doesn't matter."

But Tessa thought it did.

"It was the phone," she was saying thirty minutes later to Steve Hayden at the office. "I'm positive. The killer rang Lloyd Greely on a mobile and kept him on the line till he got to him. So there was no risk. He knew exactly where Lloyd would be. Sitting or standing at that desk, on the phone. And I bet he did the same thing with Tracey Fernandez. The phone started ringing as she opened the front door. That's why she went straight into the living room with her shopping. The phone's in there. Right next to where she was lying."

Steve was impressed. She could see it. "He could have been actually hiding on the premises somewhere. In both cases. Then he could just move in on the victims while he was actually talking to them."

She nodded vehemently. "He didn't have to do it the first time. He knew exactly where the skeleton man stood, and it was dark and noisy in the ghost train. But the other two . . ."

"We'll get mobile billing records checked." Steve was galvanized by the prospect of some hard evidence. "Find out who rang the Fernandezes just after six on Tuesday, and the butcher's shop at around 8:30 on Wednesday."

Tessa didn't want to burst the bubble. Approval, at the moment, was very appealing to her. But she had to say it: "I think it's really unlikely the killer's using his own phone. He's too clever for that. He'd know we could use the billing records to track him."

But Steve's enthusiasm didn't falter. "He might think he's clever too," he said. "Might think we'll never catch on to the phone thing. There's a good chance." He went to the door. "Coffee's fresh," he said, as he left, no doubt to seek out Thorne.

Tessa, left alone, found herself pacing, fidgeting, unsatisfied. She'd been excited about the phone call idea. But now that she'd passed it on, there was a sense of anti-climax. If the killer had used his own phone, it was going to be the key to his unmasking. But the more she thought about it, the more she doubted that it was going to be so easy. And it would take time.

She poured herself some coffee and forced herself to sit down at her desk and turn on the computer. The briefing was in forty minutes. She had reports to write, statements to type. But she couldn't settle to the work. It seemed pointless. Steve was already working on the phone call idea. Everything else she'd found out was of little interest. Negative evidence at best.

Three killings in three days.

Why did this have to happen just now? When I've just started here? When I've got all this other—?

Forget the other. Concentrate on . . .

Three victims, apparently unknown to one another, apparently with nothing whatever in common. Lloyd Greely, a well–set up, hardworking young butcher in a suburban shopping center, a still-grieving widower. Tracey Fernandez, a bright, pretty young dancer, living in the inner city, not very well off, married. Peter Grogan . . .

No, not Peter Grogan. Not Peter Grogan.

Tessa looked across at the office whiteboard, now displaying the photographs of the victims. Three victims. Four photographs. Marty Mayhew's photograph was up there beside Peter Grogan's, because though Grogan had died in the ghost train, Marty Mayhew must have been the intended target.

Publicity about the killings would warm up after today. Links would be made. The police would have to confirm that they were seeking a serial killer. But for now the ghost train death was old news. The media was concentrating on the murder of the glamorous Tracey Fernandez. Soon, it would be Lloyd Greely, perfect headline fodder, his death in the freezer room of his shop so grotesque, the tragic loss of his wife and unborn child so recent.

Peter Grogan's name had never been published. It hadn't been released, because his brother still hadn't been contacted.

Almost certainly, then, the killer didn't know Marty Mayhew was still alive. He didn't know that with his first murder, he'd made a mistake.

How would he feel about that, if he did know? Would he care, this clever, clever killer?

Briefing soon. Save the questions for then. You know how Thorne is about paperwork. He told you. You'll be out on your ear if you don't . . .

Tessa gritted her teeth, faced her computer again, set her fingers firmly on the keys.

Three killings in three days. Why did this have to happen now?

That's not the question you should be asking. Three killings in three days. How many more? That's the question.

There are six steak knives in a set.

Eleven

Tessa arrived at the briefing room at five to twelve to find it already crowded with detectives and uniformed police, thick with heat, and vibrating with the sound of overwhelmingly male voices. Most of the seats were taken. The only ones that remained were scattered through the two front rows. Several people were standing against the back wall.

Inspector Thorne, presiding over the gathering, nodded to her as she entered. Heads turned to look. She felt like a kid starting at a new school. She glanced around, and saw that Tootsie Soames was among the standing group, and was looking her way, smiling. Gratefully, Tessa went to join her. Better that, far better, than to have to walk conspicuously to the front.

"I'm standing up because I'm only here for a while. Want to hear the star attraction. He's speaking first," Tootsie whispered. "Steve's down at the front. See? Second row. There's a seat beside him."

Tessa shrugged, murmured that she was fine, she'd rather stand. She didn't know Tootsie well enough to say that Steve Hayden might be her official partner, but this didn't mean they were joined at the hip. Or to comment that Steve obviously didn't think so, anyway, since he showed no sign of looking out for her.

Dead on midday, Thorne called for silence, asked for the doors to be closed, said a few words, then introduced the man Tootsie had called the star attraction.

Dr. Dolf Hermin, forensic psychologist, was a small person with beady eyes, an exquisitely crafted goatee beard, and an odd, crouching posture.

"Where'd they dig him up?" a sweating detective beside Tessa muttered, hitching at his belt. "The wrong side of the funny farm fence, if you ask me. Looks like he'd take an ax to you soon as look at you."

The man next to him snorted appreciatively.

"He's in fact most impressive, once he gets going," Tootsie murmured, leaning peacefully back against the wall. "I've heard him before. He knows his stuff."

Dr. Hermin began to speak. He had a high-pitched, rather sing-song voice. He swayed slightly from side to side as he talked. He told his audience to feel free to interrupt with questions that were relevant to any point he raised. Better that than save them all to the end—through questions, we gain knowledge. . . .

Already, Tessa was feeling slightly mesmerized. Overtiredness, the heat and stuffiness, and her jangled nerves were playing havoc with her powers of concentration.

After ten minutes, the figures in the room had taken on a dream-like quality. Dr. Hermin had the strange habit of pressing the backs of his wrists against his chest and wiggling his fingers at his audience for emphasis. The combined effect of this mannerism, the man's appearance, and his name made Tessa think of a hermit crab. Once she'd thought of it, she couldn't put it out of her mind. She felt a little hysterical. She was seized with fear that she'd start laughing.

Forget it. Concentrate on what he's saying. That'll sober you up.

The hermit crab was saying that this series of killings, which he was certain would extend beyond three in due course, was in some ways classic and in others, unusual.

The killer attacked from behind, and killed quickly. This implied that unlike many other serial killers he did not receive his gratification from seeing the victims' fear and pain. The three victims thus far were both male and female, and of different types and socio-economic backgrounds. Yet the killings were plainly not random, or impulsive. Careful planning was required for each murder. All three victims had been stalked for days or weeks beforehand, because all were killed in a place and at a time when they were guaranteed to be alone.

"It would be reasonable, therefore," the hermit crab went on, "to come to the conclusion that this serial killer has chosen his victims carefully."

A hand went up in the third row. The questioner was a woman, earnest and blushing, asking if Hermin was using the male pronoun deliberately, or for convenience.

The sweating detective beside Tessa groaned under his breath.

"I use it deliberately," said Dr. Hermin, smiling briefly in the questioner's direction. "Even if a woman had the physical capacity to commit the crimes—"

"No reason why not," Tootsie muttered.

"—female serial killers are rare. And history teaches us that they overwhelmingly restrict themselves to the disposal of children, the sick, and the aged. So I would regard a female as an unlikely perpetrator of the crimes we are dealing with here. It is not out of the question, you understand, but unlikely."

The earnest woman subsided into her chair and tried to return to invisibility.

Dr. Hermin resumed, waggling his fingers with relish. "As I was saying," he said, "our killer chooses his victims carefully. He has now killed three persons. I would suspect that he has already marked others for death. He has a reason for his choices. We do not yet know what that reason is, but we will know. He is carrying out some obsessive plan, perhaps treasured for months, perhaps for a lifetime. He is making a pattern for himself, and for us, and he is leaving us signs to tell us what the pattern means, and who he is.

"He is leaving birthday cards in each victim's home, a rubber stamp imprint on each body, a steak knife inserted in the navel. Also, he has so far killed on subsequent days. It remains to be seen whether this part of the pattern will continue."

Lloyd died yesterday. That means today—maybe right now . . .

Tootsie's elbow nudged her. "Steve's trying to get your attention, I think," she said in a low voice.

With difficulty, Tessa focused on the tall figure in the second row, turning in his seat, staring inquiringly over his shoulder at her, jerking his head slightly. Did he want her to come and sit with him? How could she do that, in the middle of everything? She smiled faintly, shook her head and looked away.

Out of the corner of her eye she saw his hand go up. She heard Dr. Hermin respond. Then Steve was speaking—asking if Dr. Hermin had a theory as to why the killer chose in each case to leave the birthday card somewhere other than the crime scene. In the place where the victim sleeps. Why did he take that extra risk?

Heat rushed to Tessa's cheeks. That was what Steve's inquiring look had meant. He'd been reminding her that she'd wanted to ask Hermin a question. Telling her that this was the appropriate moment to ask it. Prompting her. And she'd responded like a gauche teenager being asked to dance by a boy with sweaty hands and bad breath.

Fool. Fool!

"It is an interesting question," Dr. Hermin was saying approvingly. "The answer is also interesting. I would think it forms part of the ritual for him. He decides that it is safest for him to kill the first and the third victims at their work. The second, he kills in the living room of the family home. Because, I would surmise from information received just previous to this meeting, the telephone is there. Inspector Thorne, I understand, will be informing you of this development later on."

Tessa saw a few people glancing at one another with raised eyebrows, and felt a slight flutter of pleasure. Very slight, though. The embarrassment over her misunderstanding of Steve was still overwhelming.

Listen to Hermin!

". . . He kills where it is most convenient. But still he must enter his victims' most private places, display their vulnerability, you see. He has to show his power over them, his ability to penetrate their most secret lives. This is how, you see, he attains the gratification he seeks."

Tessa's stomach churned.

"The symbolism is fairly straightforward." Hermin smiled blandly.

"Sickos. I hate 'em," muttered the sweating man next to Tessa. He shoved up his hand, to the immediate discomfort of everyone standing near him. "Why leave the card?" he asked loudly.

Hermin hunched his shoulders, pressed the backs of his wrists against his chest, wiggled his fingers.

Hermit crab.

"It is not enough for him to know he has succeeded. Everyone else, you see, must know it too. We must know it. We must understand his power. He cannot trust us to find traces of his presence unaided, though doubtless—" he bowed courteously in the general direction of Lance Fisk sitting upright in the front row "—his distrust is ill-founded. So he leaves the card. Why a birthday card, we do not know. At this time."

He must penetrate their most secret lives. . . . We must understand his power.

The room seemed dimmer. The outlines of the figures in the chairs, the bizarre outline of the swaying hermit crab were ringed with light.

Hermin's singsong voice was moving on through the classic serial killer profile. Youngish, middle-class white male. Almost certainly looks and acts quite normally. Psychopathic. Low self-esteem combined with intense, self-protective vanity . . . possibly tortured animals as a child. Sees his victims as having no rights. Does not empathize. Feels no remorse. Compulsive. Once begun, will continue until . . .

There are six steak knives in a set.

. . . probably abused as a child. Probably impotent. A sexual basis to his behavior, though so far with this series, no sign of normal sexual contact with the victims . . .

. . . *must penetrate their most secret lives.*

"The knife in the umbilicus has fairly obvious sexual connotations," the hermit crab sang, hunching its shoulders, wiggling its fingers. "Similar to the invasion of the bedroom, you see. Never forget. Nothing in this sort of crime happens by chance."

His voice seemed very loud. Echoing. The thick air shimmered.

I feel sick.

Tessa felt strong fingers grip her wrist, an arm go round her shoulders.

"Out!" Tootsie's voice hissed in her ear. She felt herself pushed forward, hustled past the sweating detective. His pale blue eyes bulged, staring at her. His lower lip hung loose and moist.

Never forget . . .

The man at the front of the room was talking. "Everything is meant—consciously or unconsciously. Everything is a message for us."

Everything is meant. . . . everything is a message . . .

Through the door, cool air, into the ladies' room across the corridor. A chair, someone's hand—Tootsie's hand—pushing her head down. The world slowly steadying. Water running. Wetness on her forehead. Fingers on her pulse. The sickness gradually receding.

"Better? Keep your head down. I'll get you a glass of water in a sec."

"Thanks." It was hard to speak. The words came out in a mumble. "I've never fainted in my life. I can't understand why . . ."

"Couldn't be pregnant, could you?"

"Oh!" Woozy panic. Rapid, confused calculation. Relief. "No, no. I couldn't be pregnant."

"Well, it was just one of those things." The calm voice ran on. Soothing. Professional. "It was very hot in there. Ridiculous. They should have kept the doors open. Bet you didn't have any breakfast either."

"I don't think I did."

"You're a goat then, aren't you?"

Yes.

"Never mind. You'll be right. Lucky I noticed you going green before you keeled over."

They'll think I can't cope . . .

"Hardly anyone noticed. Too interested in Hermin. Fascinating bloke, isn't he? Get anything out of it?"

He's making a pattern . . . nothing in this case happens by chance. . . . Once begun, will continue until . . .

Tessa nodded dumbly. She started trying to get up, but her legs were wobbly, and firm hands pressed her down.

"You just stay there for a while."

"I'd better get back. I'm missing—"

"Just stay here. Five minutes. Doctor's orders. Hermin was nearly finished anyway. You'll only be missing Thorne, anyway, and you know what he's going to say. You've been in this from the start. You'll be back in time for Fisk. Then you go out and get yourself something to eat. All right?"

"All right." Tessa roused herself, looked up. "Thanks, Tootsie," she said. "Look, I'm keeping you. Don't wait. I'll be fine."

Tootsie smiled. "I'll stay for a few more minutes. No problem. I was only going back to the morgue. And my clients aren't going anywhere."

Lance Fisk was speaking when Tessa finally returned to the briefing toom. To her relief, the doors had been propped open in her absence, so she was able to slip into the room unobtrusively.

A lot of people had left. Like Tootsie, they had presumably only turned up to hear Dr. Hermin's part of the proceedings. The room was much clearer now. No one was standing up, and there were plenty of vacant seats.

Tessa sank gratefully into a chair at the back. Her neighbor barely glanced at her. She saw he was taking notes, and felt for her own notebook and pen.

Fisk had a dry, occasionally hesitating delivery. His every sentence was hedged around with disclaimers and warnings against precipitous conclusions. Although he must have been used to public speaking, one got the impression that he wasn't enjoying this situation at all.

Strange, thought Tessa. He always seems so confident. Arrogant, even. I would have thought he'd love holding forth.

She sat listening for a while, watching the elegant man's closed face, his stiff gestures, trying to reconcile them with what she knew of him. And slowly she realized her mistake. It wasn't the public speaking Fisk disliked. It was what he had to say.

She found herself smiling—her first natural smile for days. Fisk was literally in pain. He hated exposing his work half-finished. He liked to treasure up every little fact, until the day when he could present it to the world with all its brothers and sisters in the totally controlled form of a bulky report (with diagrams) and all the ifs and buts in place. Theories were his intellectual property, to be tested till they either failed or crystallized beautifully into known truth, not public property to be polluted, misunderstood, trampled on, pulled about, and otherwise mistreated by unscientific minds.

But events had overtaken him. Three homicides in three days. No time for the niceties. His meager findings so far had to be laid bare. Track suit fibers (dark blue, inexpensive, imported, origin to be ascertained) and beige Berber carpet fibers (origin as yet unknown) present on all victims' clothing, at all three crime scenes, and throughout the victims' homes (as far as had been checked at this stage). Fingerprint checks still underway, though the signs (enumerated) were that the killer had worn gloves (possibly disposable polyurethane) in each case. Weapon in each case (rope, scarf, hammer) belonged to the victim or the premises, and had been left on scene. The steak knives . . .

Tessa's mind began to drift. She knew all this. Fisk had nothing. He knew it. Everyone knew it.

The killer is making a pattern. Leaving signs to tell us what the pattern means . . .

Marty, Tracey, Lloyd—they didn't form any pattern. They had nothing in common at all, except that they all looked to be around the same age. They were all in their mid- to late-twenties.

She felt a tiny flicker of excitement, sat up a little straighter in her chair. Age—that fitted into the birthday card theme.

Nothing in this sort of crime is by chance. . . . Everything is meant—consciously or unconsciously. Everything is a message for us.

But the victims weren't the same age exactly. They didn't even share a birth date.

Fisk's voice droned on. Tessa no longer heard it.

What about star signs? No. Marty, in early September, was Virgo. Tracey, in March, was Pisces. Lloyd, in October, was Libra. All different.

Still—maybe it was the difference that was important. Was that it? Star signs? Hadn't there been a movie about that? A killer who chose his victims by working through the twelve star signs? This killer could have seen that movie. Liked the idea. Decided to . . .

There are six steak knives in a set. Six not twelve. Six not twelve.

She beat off the thought. The difference between the numbers couldn't be that important.

Everything is meant . . . There are six steak knives in a set.

Six steak knives notwithstanding, the birth-sign theory was still worth raising with Steve and Thorne, she told herself. But as she framed what she would say, how she would put the theory to them, the dwindling flame of her excitement went out with an ignominious puff of smoke.

She could just imagine it. Steve and Thorne's faces. Tessa, hot on the trail, announcing triumphantly that she'd discovered a pattern in the crimes. All the victims had different birthdays! Well, blow me down, they'd say. Different birthdays, eh? Extraordinary! Tessa, you've done it! Eureka!

The man next to her moved restlessly, returning her to consciousness of where she was. Fisk was still talking, winding up at last. And not before time, it seemed. The whole room was a mass of small fidgets. Scraping chairs, muffled coughs, easing of cramped legs, scratching of chins.

" . . . but it is very early days yet," said Fisk, folding his notes, his gaze sweeping his audience disapprovingly. "And as the individual responsible for these crimes persists, he'll eventually lose concentration, and give us something further to go on."

"So we just wait for the next one," the man next to Tessa muttered, apparently to himself. "That's bloody lovely, that is."

Tessa wholeheartedly agreed.

After the briefing, Tessa trailed out obediently to the sandwich shop and bought herself some lunch. She arrived back in

the office to find the photographer, Dee Suzeraine, standing beside her desk, replacing the phone on the hook while Steve
watched with interest.

"I answered for you, but they just hung up. Didn't want to
talk to me," Dee said. "What have you got that I haven't got?
Can't be brains. Can't be looks. Must be money."

Tessa forced a smile.

It's him. It must be. What am I going to do?

Don't think about it. You don't know who it is.

I do.

"I've given Steve copies of the pics from this morning,"
Dee chattered on, while her bright, sharp eyes darted over
Tessa's face.

"Right."

Tessa sat down at her desk, and started re-arranging the
papers there. The tidying was meaningless. Just a way of
avoiding those curious eyes.

She collected a handful of pens and pencils and pulled at
her top drawer so she could put them away. The drawer
opened a couple of centimeters, then jammed. She tugged at it
ineffectually.

"We're going to the pub tonight," said Dee casually. "You
want to come? Give you a chance to get to know a few people."

No.

You should. Get to know a few . . .

No.

*Do you really want to be alone at home? Scared to answer
the phone? Waiting for . . .*

Tessa looked up. Again she forced a smile. "Thanks. Yes. I'd
like to. Where is it? The pub?"

"Steve's coming. He'll show you."

Oh, no.

Too late to back out now.

"Hey Steve? You bring Tessa to the S & M tonight, will
you?" Dee called.

Steve, looking through the photographs, nodded. "Sure," he
said, without looking up.

Great.

"See you then." Dee was already at the door. "Unless the wacko with the steak knife set arranges for us to meet beforehand. Tootsie says the psychiatrist guy was on about a death a day." She grinned cheerfully, and left.

She's seen Tootsie. Tootsie's asked her to look after me.

So what?

I don't need looking after.

You don't?

Gritting her teeth, Tessa stuck her fingers into the partly-open drawer, far enough to feel that it was jamming on the folded newspaper she'd thrust inside it the day before. She scrabbled around, and finally managed to press the bulky newsprint down far enough to get the drawer open.

She tore the paper out, and threw it into her waste-paper bin. The she changed her mind, pulled the paper out again, and put it back into the drawer. She glanced across at Steve, but he wasn't looking at her. He was leafing through Dee's photographs, and apparently giving them his full attention.

He doesn't fool me. He thinks I'm a dingaling. He's wondering what he's been lumbered with.

You're paranoid. Eat your sandwich. Drink the juice. Then talk to him. Find out what else Hermin said. What's happened about the phone thing.

Brady Mumm . . .

Forget about Mumm. Forget about everything but the case. Three deaths in three days . . .

A death a day . . . why a death a day?

Nothing is by chance. Everything is meant. Consciously or unconsciously.

Everything is a message, for us.

Twelve

The Stars and Moon pub, popularly known as the S & M, was already crowded when Tessa and Steve arrived that evening. A sea of unfamiliar faces greeted Tessa as she edged through the throng at the door.

She had seen the Stars and Moon from the outside many times over the years, but she hadn't taken much notice of it, had never been inside it, and certainly hadn't realized till tonight that it was a popular meeting place for her new division. It seemed rather too elegant for that. The Stars and Moon probably had a checkered history, but its original art deco glamour had now been restored to appeal to a trendy city clientele.

Tessa felt a pang of homesickness. The Miller's Arms, where her old division congregated after work or for celebrations, was suburban, sprawling, and ordinary. Built in the fifties, it had never been beautiful, and renovations since, notably the application of Spanish-style swirled stucco to most of the internal walls, and the apparently random scattering of dark false beams and heavy iron-laced lanterns throughout, had made it worse.

How bizarre that she could ever miss that place. The Miller's Arms was dark and hot summer and winter, it smelled overwhelmingly of hot cooking oil and stale beer, and the endless pinging and beeping of the game machines drove you crazy. The food was terrible: sweet and sour pork in bright pink sauce, dubious chicken curry in which someone had once found what they swore was a beak, rock-hard Wiener schnitzel, and salad whose main features were radish roses and presliced cheese. But the place was known territory, and the faces at the tables and at the bar were, if not always friendly, at least familiar.

In six months this place, these people, will be just as familiar. If you last that long.

A couple of people in one particular group at the bar called Steve's name. He raised his hand in greeting and began ushering Tessa through the crowd towards them. She was relieved to realize that she vaguely recognized a few faces, and even more relieved to see Dee playing pool at a table nearby.

Her father must have often come to the Stars and Moon after work, but it was hard to imagine him here, big and shambling, tie pulled loose, shirtsleeves rolled up. At nine she'd suspected that he wasn't the world's sharpest dresser. At fourteen she'd been embarrassedly certain of it.

Still, the renovations looked relatively recent. The place had probably been shabbier in his day. And if it had been the division's favorite pub forever, as Steve had told her, then Doug Vance had been here. She remembered him often coming home smelling faintly of beer, talking about having had a game of pool with the blokes. They would have all been blokes then. All but the barmaids.

But there were several women in the group they were now approaching. Everyone knew Steve. The men greeted him casually, the women less casually. Tessa was introduced, welcomed, provided with a drink, engaged in polite conversation by a few, and treated to rather forced jollity by some. Then, social obligations having been satisfied, normal conversation gradually resumed around her, and she was left in peace with her warming glass of mineral water in her hand, to join in or not, as she liked.

But she was aware of sly glances in her direction. She knew she was being sized up. She was Steve's new partner. An unknown quantity, and a woman. Not only that, she was Doug Vance's daughter. Everyone must know that. She had too much respect for the police grapevine to think otherwise.

She'd been prepared for this. She must have been. When she asked for the transfer, when she got it, she knew what she was giving up. She knew, too, that she was taking something

of a risk, moving into her father's old division. But she hadn't
hesitated—hadn't even really thought about it. She hadn't ever
doubted her ability to cope with a new working environment.

Why should she? Lots of people changed jobs, moved
around. The important thing was to try to smooth things down
with Brett. Less traveling time meant more time at home. If she
had more time at home, Brett would have less to complain
about. Less reason to resent her job and its demands.

But things with Brett had moved on while the transfer was
applied for, granted, acted upon. She hadn't really understood
that. So busy, so absorbed, so tied up with cases and paperwork, so focused on the minutiae involved in disengaging herself from one place and starting at another, she hadn't seen it.

*That's because you weren't looking at Brett. Not as a lover.
Not as someone you depended on. He was just another piece of
the jigsaw. One that wouldn't fit. Just another problem to solve.*

That's not true!

But it was. She felt hot as she faced it, standing in this unfamiliar place, surrounded by strangers. How could she have
been so blind? Why hadn't she realized what was happening?
She hadn't been having a relationship. She'd been managing a
problem. Or, more accurately, not managing it. She'd been
evading it. Getting around it. Pouring oil on it. Sweet-talking it.
Doing everything but facing it.

You're no more alone now than you've been for months.

She sipped at her water. The thin slice of lemon floating at
the top of the glass tingled on her lips.

"Wakey, wakey!" She jumped as someone snapped their fingers in her face. Her mineral water slopped over, wetting her
hand. She focused on the grinning, fleshy face of the detective
they'd introduced as Simmo.

"Steve wants you to give him a game," Simmo said.

For a second she didn't know what he meant. She gaped at
him foolishly.

He jerked his head at the pool table. It was unoccupied. Dee
and the man she'd been playing were walking towards the bar.

"Steve likes a game," Simmo said. "Thought the new partner should give him one."

The double entendre was obvious. There were a few appreciative sniggers.

Kick him in the balls.

He's harmless.

"Drop off, Simmo," Steve said pleasantly.

"Don't you play?" persisted Simmo, leering.

"Forget it, Tessa. He's a clown." Steve was letting her off. Protecting her again.

I don't need protecting.

Tessa put her glass of water carefully on the bar and wiped her fingers on her skirt.

"Why not?" she said. She smiled briefly at Steve and walked to the pool table.

"She's taking you on, Hayden!" she heard Simmo call raucously. "Hey, watch it, mate. She's a little one, but by the look of her she's going to be rough."

They were all laughing, now. But Steve wasn't. His face was expressionless as he followed her to the pool table.

She expected him to tell her Simmo was okay, really. Heart of gold. Expected him to tell her, then, that he really didn't want to play. Try to let her down gently, so she could escape embarrassment, and he could get back to the bar, and out of the limelight he didn't enjoy.

She was ready for that. But it never happened. He calmly picked up a cue, and waited.

The group at the bar were all watching as they started to play. Tessa began nervously. She hadn't played pool for quite a while. There wasn't a pool table at The Miller's Arms. But grimly, she persisted.

Bloody Simmo, Steve thought, watching her set face. Against his better judgment, he'd found her small heroism at the bar endearing. She wasn't going to be bullied by anyone. She'd called Simmo's bluff. She was tougher than she looked.

He was starting to wonder about Tessa Vance. She wasn't as open and shut a case as he'd imagined. He'd expected supreme confidence, aggression. Well, she'd shown that—in patches. The business about the mobile phone, for example. The insistence that the first two crimes were linked. She'd stuck to her guns, and she'd been right.

But she obviously wasn't a team player. Maybe that went with the hot shot image. He'd kept a place for her at the briefing this morning, but she'd ignored that, coolly leaning against the back wall with Tootsie and the other blow-ins as though it wasn't particularly important for her to hear what was being said.

Then she hadn't wanted to ask her own question about the placement of the birthday cards. She'd given him a superior little smile and turned her head away, leaving it to him to put the question to Hermin himself. Maybe she'd worked the whole thing out to her own satisfaction already, and just hadn't bothered to tell him.

A lot of the time she didn't seem to have her mind on the job. She was incredibly nervy, too. She'd been jumping at shadows all week. She seemed stressed out. Trouble with the boyfriend, he gathered, from the fragments of conversation he'd over-heard when she was talking to her mate Bridget. He wished she'd keep her affairs to herself. Everyone had personal has-sles, but that shouldn't interfere with work. The last thing he needed was some self-absorbed, neurotic girl with love prob-lems messing him around. Especially with these steak-knife cases going.

He heard cat-calls from the bar, turned his mind back to the game, and discovered to his surprise that the scores were level. While he'd been wool-gathering Tessa had found her feet and, by the look of it, was preparing to thrash him.

He pulled himself together and fought back. Taking it easy to help the girl out was one thing. Losing to her was another. But he could see that he'd almost let things go too far already. She was an unconventional player. She took risks. Sometimes they didn't come off, but when they did, the results were devastating.

"Where'd you learn to play pool?" he asked her. He wanted her to talk.

"My father taught me," she said briefly. "We had a table at home."

End of discussion.

Their audience was losing interest in them now that it was clear that they were evenly matched, and that Simmo's little joke had backfired. People were turning back to the bar, ordering another round of drinks, starting new conversations. It would be gossip, jokes—Steve knew the rhythm. He wasn't missing much.

Some of them would be talking about the case. About the briefing this morning. Simmo would be trying to get a sweep going, wanting to bet on when the next body would turn up. He was glad Tessa wasn't there to witness that. He had a feeling she'd be disgusted, though she had no right to be. She should be used to the way things were by now. Cops couldn't afford to be sensitive little flowers. They handled their job the best way they could.

"Do you think the steak knife merchant'll have another go tonight?" he asked abruptly.

"Yes," Tessa said. She looked up at him, her eyes dark and serious. "I was just thinking about that. We're here playing a game, and someone's going to die."

"You've got to take a break. Helps you think."

That's what Dad used to say when Mum complained about him going to the pub on the way home. Gives you time to relax, to think, he'd say.

He also used to say—gives you time to talk. Swap ideas . . .

Steve watched her as she rested her cue on the edge of the table. "I've been thinking," she said. She wet her lips and went on carefully, as though she was feeling her way—either with what she was saying, or maybe just with him. "Hermin said that the killer was making a pattern, following through some obsession."

"They always say that. There's always a pattern," said Steve, lining up his next shot.

"But this is different. This guy doesn't always go after the same sorts of people. They aren't all old women, or street people, or young women, or gay guys or whatever. But there must be—there must be—something about them that made him choose them."

"You think he's playing a nursery rhyme with their postcodes, or spelling out his old fourth-class teacher's name with their middle initials," he drawled. "You've been watching too many movies."

He thought she'd be needled, but to his surprise, she laughed. The idea that she didn't take herself as seriously as he'd thought pleased him immensely. He felt himself relaxing with her for the first time since they'd met.

But suddenly she stopped laughing. Her face grew serious. She leaned on the pool table, and said: "Look, Steve. I have to tell you something . . ."

Uh-oh, he thought.

"I know I've been acting a bit strangely. It's—I've got a bit of a problem—"

He held up his hand quickly, his skin crawling at the thought that she was about to tell him some personal thing he'd really rather not know, and that she'd probably regret telling him anyway. "Look, it's fine," he said. "You're fine. You don't have to—"

Her phone rang. She froze. It rang again. Slowly, biting her lip, she pulled it out of her handbag, and answered.

Steve saw her face change. "Oh. Brett. Hi," she said, and turned away slightly as she listened. "Yes. No, it's okay, I understand. . . . No, I'm fine. I can manage the rent okay." She listened again, and her voice took on a defensive tone. " . . . Well, yes, I am in a pub, actually. We've been working . . ."

She glanced around at Steve, obviously wanting privacy. Steve withdrew to the bar.

"Who won?" said Simmo.

Steve shrugged. "We didn't finish."

"Poolus interruptus," giggled a woman called Christie, who prided herself on being one of the boys.

Simmo guffawed appreciatively.

Steve could see Tessa, shoulders hunched, phone pressed to her ear, one hand running through her hair. This Brett guy—the boyfriend who'd moved out—the one she'd been talking to Bridget Murphy about, presumably—was giving her a hard time.

She hung up finally and looked over to him, stuffing her

phone back into her handbag. He put down his drink and went to join her.

"Sorry about that," she said stiffly. "It was just—"

"No worries," he said, cutting her off. "Look, let's just call it a draw. I'm bushed, and this place is too noisy. Think I'll head home in a few minutes. And like you were saying, you're a bit hassled at the moment."

She lifted her chin. Suddenly it was as though shutters had come down over her eyes. "Oh. Sure. Okay, then."

"Would you like another drink?"

She shook her head, smiled tightly. "Thanks. I think I'll just go. I'm tired, too. See you tomorrow."

"Or whenever," he said, trying to keep it light.

She nodded, lifted a hand to wave at the people at the bar, and gripping to the shoulder strap of her bag, began weaving through the increasingly rowdy pub crowd, heading for the door.

Tessa stormed back to Homicide, and her car, furious. She'd thought she was breaking through Steve Hayden's reserve, but the phone call had crueled all that. Worse, she'd been about to tell him about Brady Mumm, but it was obvious that he now thought that all her nervy stupidities of the last few days had been because of Brett.

What kind of unprofessional idiot does he think I am?

Tell him about Mumm tomorrow.

I'd rather die.

She was angry with herself, with Steve, and with Brett. The internal dialogue raged all the way home. It wasn't until she was halfway up the stairs of her apartment building that she realized she'd forgotten to check the backseat of the car. She'd forgotten to check the shadows in the garage.

Sobered, she let herself into her flat. It was still, silent. The table lamp cast black shadows. The answering machine was blinking red.

She listened to her messages. Brett, saying he hoped she was okay, and that he'd try her on her mobile. One of Brett's work colleagues who obviously wasn't up to speed on Brett's present accommodation arrangements. Someone ringing to say the shirt she'd ordered was now in stock. And the sound of someone breathing, then putting the phone down.

He knows where you are.

The flat was too quiet. Tessa turned on the television set for company. Then she found an apple, cut herself a couple of pieces of cheese, poured herself some water, and sat down at the dining room table with her case notes and photographs.

Marty Mayhew. Peter Grogan. Tracey Fernandez. Lloyd Greely. She stared at the four photographs, then put the one of Peter Grogan aside, and concentrated on the remaining three. There was something about them, something, that had made the killer strike. What was it?

The Thursday night movie pounded on towards its climax. An ad break, then a news update about the serial killer: "A police spokesperson admitted today that there are so far no leads as to the identity of the serial killer who is now believed to have claimed three victims in three days. Police are appealing for any information . . ."

Tessa took a notepad and drew a line down the center. On the left side of the pad she wrote "Similarities," on the right, "Differences."

She scribbled away for a minute or two. The "Differences" column grew very long. On the "Similarities" side there was only "age group (mid-late twenties)."

My age group. So young to die.

No one wants to die.

She tapped the pen on the paper, racking her brains. The three hadn't shopped in the same place, attended the same church, gym, hairdresser, doctor, or dentist. There was no common organization, political party, or group that had been discovered. They didn't even use the same bank.

She stared at her useless list. The almost blank left side tormented her. Wasn't there anything except age group these people had in common?

They're all dead. Murdered.

It was stupid, but she wrote it down. She'd found before that even the silliest ideas could start a chain of ideas that led somewhere.

They were all killed by the same person.

She wrote that down, too.

Their deaths are all being investigated by the same team.

This was one time, it seemed, when her chain of ideas method was failing. But fortunately there was no one present to witness it.

She pulled another set of photographs from the file. Dee's photographs of the dead bodies. Peter Grogan, in his skeleton costume, slumped in the ghost train car. Tracey Fernandez, sprawled on the carpet, long red ponytail streaming. Lloyd Greely, surrounded by hanging sides of beef and lamb.

All the deaths were colorful.

She wrote it down, then crossed out "were colorful" and wrote "looked dramatic."

She studied her list. The left-hand side was longer now. But it was silly and meaningless. The similarities were all about the victims' deaths, not their lives. They were about the investigation of, not the prelude to, murder.

That might be the point of it all. The investigators, not the victims, might be the point of it all.

The thought jumped up at her, grinning at her shock.

What did Lance Fisk say? "We seem to be determined to keep you busy."

No! I won't think of that! That way lies madness. Galloping paranoia. Think of more similarities . . . free-associate . . .

Slowly she wrote: "Every case featured symbols of birth, babies, children." And added, "very pointed symbols."

The birthday cards, the children's rubber stamp marks, the knife plunged into the place where the umbilical cord attached the babies to their mothers. Cutting the cord again. All the deadly symbols the killer had left on the bodies of his victims, and in their homes, were about birth, children, motherhood. Like a series of horrible jokes.

Birth, babies, children, birthdays . . . fathers and mothers, dads and mums . . . mumm . . .

Mumm got out on Sunday.

Tessa threw the pen down and jumped up, panicky and suddenly breathless, stifled. She almost ran to the windows, and pulled the curtains back. Then she tugged at the windows themselves, opening them as widely as she could. Humid, traffic-smelling, but fresher air streamed into the room. She breathed it in gratefully. The night city, glittering lights, separated by black and secret spaces, lay spread in front of her.

He chooses his victims . . . He is making a pattern . . . Everything is a message for us . . .

Not a message for us, but a message for—me?

A homecoming plane rumbled across the spangled sky, drowning out the sound of the TV set. You hardly noticed the planes when the windows were closed. That was why Brett hadn't liked them opened, day or night, even though they were screened. The noise drove him crazy.

Tessa looked up at the plane. It seemed so isolated, so safe up there in the sky—a small, brightly lit world where people spoke in low voices, and stayed in their places, and were fed small, neatly contained meals by courteous attendants in carefully varied versions of the same uniform.

If only things were as quiet, organized and predictable on the ground.

Tessa turned away from the window and glanced at her watch. It was 10:30. She wondered if she dared to try to sleep.

The computer screen glows. The room is silent. The typist is at work again.

". . . Maybe you saw me, and you have decided I am not what you wanted. I mean, not what you expected. If so, please just let me know, and I won't bother you any more . . .

Love from Baby."

At eleven, at the airport, Jasmine Ho refused a drink and said goodbye to the other attendants on the international flight from which she'd just disembarked. Some of the others seemed intent on making a night of it. But for Jasmine, as usual, the idea of going straight home was much more attractive. Besides, Jasmine's landlord was visiting for a routine check of his premises at 9 A.M. on Friday.

Jasmine wanted to be up and around well before he called.

She liked her spacious Eastern Suburbs flat, and wanted to keep it. She'd been away from home for ten days. There would be dusting to do, and junk mail to be removed from the letterbox, before the landlord came.

She picked up her small and shining red car from the airport carpark and drove home. It didn't take too long at all, at this time of night on a weekday.

As she arrived at her building, she noted with pleasure, as always, the cleanness of its lines as it rose from its landscaped grounds. She noted with annoyance, as always, the heedless clutter of visitors' cars that crowded the paved apron in front of the underground security carpark. She never complained, but it made entering the garage very awkward.

She nosed her compact car through the parked vehicles, and pressed the remote control device that would allow her to enter the carpark. While she was waiting for the barred shutter to complete its slow climb, she thought how glad she was to be home. She liked her job, but it was very tiring. Her feet were swollen, her legs and back ached. She had started to wonder whether she would have to give up flying. It would be a shame, but she could find a ground job somewhere else in the company for sure. And after five years, she'd really had enough traveling.

She lugged her suitcase from the car boot, set it precisely on the little wheels that enabled it to be pulled instead of carried, carefully checked that the car was locked, and left the garage through the door that led to the lifts. The door, as usual, failed to close completely after her. She had to push it till she heard the lock click into place. She should ask for the door to be fixed, she thought. That was one thing about which it would be quite proper to complain. A lot of people didn't bother to make sure the door locked behind them, and this was supposed to be a security building.

The basement foyer was hushed, and the lift doors gleamed, opening straightaway as she pushed the button, closing on her again for the silent trip upward.

At the eighth floor, the lift doors opened with a discreet chime. Jasmine stepped out and started down the empty hallway, trailing her suitcase after her. Its little wheels made tiny squeaks as they rolled over the carpet. She made a mental note that the wheels needed a drop of oil. Or perhaps the device needed replacing. It had done good service over the last few years.

Her key was already in her hand as she reached her door. She thought pleasurably of tea in a fine cup, of a warm shower and her own bed, of a few days of pleasing herself instead of ministering to the needs and whims of others.

She turned her key in the lock. The door swung open to stuffy darkness. The flat was always airless when she arrived home. But she'd open all the windows. It never took long for everything to get back to normal.

She stepped inside, pulling her suitcase after her. She closed the door and turned on the light. Then the phone began to ring.

Thirteen

Jasmine Ho's landlord knocked at her door, as agreed, at nine on Friday morning. He received no reply. The door remained firmly closed, and inside the apartment there was no sound.

The landlord was a busy man, he had given fair warning of his visit, confirmed by letter, and he had no time to waste waiting for Miss Ho to return from wherever she had gone. Nor was he willing to postpone his visit.

The landlord had thought Jasmine Ho seemed a responsible, careful, and tidy young woman who would cause him no trouble. But all the same, it was odd that she'd broken their appointment, and it was with some slight trepidation that he opened the door with his own key. During his early years as a budding capitalist, he had had several unfortunate experiences with tenants. One chap had painted the walls of the bathroom black. Another had mounted a very large three-dimensional collage on the living room ceiling, puncturing the pristine white with eight huge expandable screws. Then there was the woman who had seemed so normal but, it turned out, had been breeding angora rabbits in her bedroom.

Jasmine Ho, he soon realized, had not despoiled his apartment's paint, furniture, or fittings. But she had sadly let him down in another sense. She was about to cause him a great deal of trouble.

A suitcase on wheels stood near the phone table. Jasmine herself lay dead beside it, her small, heart-shaped face hideously swollen and blackened. The landlord never admitted to anyone, even his wife, that, following the initial shock, his first coherent feeling was one of relief, because the steak knife plunged into his tenant's stomach had not caused her to bleed on the carpet.

There was no doubt that Jasmine Ho's death was the fourth in the series. An unsigned birthday card, this time featuring a teddy bear in a party hat, stood on the chest of drawers in Jasmine's bedroom. A koala stamp stained the pale gold skin on the back of Jasmine's hand. The steak knife in her navel matched the rest of the set. She had been strangled with a pair of tights of the same size and type as those in her room.

One of the neighbors had heard the phone ring in Jasmine's flat—after eleven and before midnight, definitely, though she couldn't be more specific than that. She had heard nothing else. She was in her own living room at the time. The phone was answered, she said, after about three rings. Other than thinking that people were very inconsiderate to be calling at such an hour, she had paid little attention to what was going on next door, being totally preoccupied by the bad attack of indigestion which had gotten her out of bed in the first place, and which she described to them at length.

The neighbor on the other side was asleep by 10:30. The phone didn't wake him. Careful Jasmine, unwilling to cause a nuisance, always turned the bell down to a dull buzz when she went away.

But they hardly needed the neighbors' testimony. The room in which Jasmine Ho lay dead told its own story. Her suitcase had been left halfway between the door and the phone table. Marks in the fine film of dust on the table showed that the phone had been dragged slightly out of its accustomed position. The receiver, also dusty, bore only Jasmine's fingerprints, and, overlaying them, glove smears. The landlord, using greater discretion than might have been expected, given some of his later actions, had used his own phone.

As clearly as though she'd been in the room, Tessa could see what had happened in the last few minutes of Jasmine Ho's life.

Jasmine came into her flat, dropped her suitcase, walked

straight to the phone, picked up the receiver. She was then attacked from behind. The phone was dragged out of position as
she fought for her life, and lost. It wasn't surprising that the indigestion sufferer had heard nothing. Jasmine was a small,
fine-boned young woman. Easy prey. Afterwards, her killer,
wearing gloves, put the phone back on the hook, and completed his ritual.

Everything was clear. Everything but the killer's name, face,
identity. The carpet, despite its dusty surface, defied all Lance
Fisk's efforts to isolate footprints, partly because of its rough
weave, and partly because the landlord, waiting for the police
to arrive, had not regarded their instruction to touch nothing as
precluding his tramping through every room, presumably with
a view to reletting the apartment as soon as possible.

But Jasmine Ho, well-organized and tidy in all she did, was
eventually to provide the police with their first genuine lead.
An hour after the landlord had put through his emergency call,
Steve Hayden was leafing methodically through the gold-
edged pages of Jasmine's slim, black address book. He reached
the section headed "F." And there, right at the top, in Jasmine's
small, clear handwriting, was the name, address, and phone
number of Tracey Fernandez.

"They knew one another! This is—" Tessa broke off, and
snatched at Jasmine's appointments diary, slim and black to
match her address book. They'd already checked the last
couple of weeks, seen she'd been out of the country, seen her
note about returning Thursday evening, her note about the
landlord's visit early Friday. But they hadn't yet examined the
rest of the book in detail.

Tessa leafed through the diary in growing excitement. Jasmine Ho and Tracey Fernandez weren't just acquaintances—
they were friends. Tracey's name was sprinkled regularly
through the diary pages. "Coffee, Tracey, Cafe Royal 11 A.M.,"
"Lunch, Tracey, Peppino's, 12:30," "Tracey, Fairview, 2 P.M.,"
"Ring Tracey re ballet"—and on it went.

"They always saw each other in the daytime," Steve
commented.

Tessa thought she knew why that would be. But she didn't feel like telling him. After last night she was unwilling to betray knowledge of the difficulties involved in living with an opinionated man, one of them being, in her experience, that somehow he never liked your friends.

But a phone call to Guido Fernandez soon confirmed her suspicions. Guido was obviously very hung over, and was feeling morose. But in between musings on mortality, the cruelty of fate, and his loss, he managed to raise the strength to make it completely clear that he had indeed had no time for Jasmine Ho.

He and, by association, his wife, were out of an air hostess's intellectual league, he implied. Or should have been. But the two girls had been at school together, and Tracey insisted on keeping up the friendship. What she found to talk about with a glorified, overpaid flying waitress she should have grown out of under Guido's guidance, heaven only knew. Jasmine didn't come round to the house, thank God. She bored Guido stiff. But she and Tracey talked on the phone, or went out together, when Jasmine was in town.

"This can't possibly be a coincidence, can it?" Tessa asked, after she'd hung up. "They were friends. They went out together all the time. And they're both dead."

Steve reached for the diary, started flicking through it again. "It could be a coincidence. Weirder things have happened. But I reckon we'd better act as if it isn't. Make a start by checking all the places in the diary. The places they met."

"Working on the theory that the killer saw them together somewhere. Or even met them." Tessa was being very careful today to be logical, rational, and downbeat. Steve's misunderstanding at the pub had angered her. But her thoughts of last night had frightened her. She hadn't thought she could be so irrational, so paranoid.

The discovery that Jasmine and Tracey had known each other provided a way out. A new theory was stirring, and she wanted to follow it up. That was far preferable to dwelling on the other insane idea that kept intruding on her consciousness, and that had kept her awake for most of the night.

Steve was nodding. "That's it. The diary doesn't always say where exactly the places are, or what they are, so it'll take awhile, but . . ."

We haven't got awhile. It's Friday. Sometime, somewhere, someone today . . .

"We could—" Tessa interrupted loudly before she could stop herself. He paused, and looked at her inquiringly. Deliberately, she lowered her voice. "We could try a shortcut. Spend an hour testing out a theory. Might lead nowhere. But if it works . . ."

"What theory?" He'd distanced himself again. He towered above her, dark and uncommunicative.

She took a breath. "Maybe if the killer saw *two* of the victims together in one place, he saw *all* of them at the same place."

He said nothing.

"Why not?" she asked passionately. "Look, Marty Mayhew's the key to this, He's the victim that got away. We'll have to show him Jasmine's photograph anyway, won't we?"

"He didn't recognize any of the other photographs."

"No. But we'll have to ask him about Jasmine just the same. So why not make that extra bit of effort and get him to go through the diary with us, to see if he's ever been to any of the places where Jasmine saw Tracey?"

"It's a matter of time, Tessa."

"It could save us a lot of time. I'll see him at Funworld. I'll go on my own. You don't have to be involved."

Steve didn't argue any more. Maybe he thought she had something. Maybe he'd just decided to let her have her head so she'd fall on her face. In the mood she was in, and after another almost sleepless night, she didn't particularly care either way.

Marty Mayhew said the same thing about Jasmine as he'd said about Tracey Fernandez and Lloyd Greely. He thought he might have seen that face before, it looked vaguely familiar, but he couldn't swear to it. He wasn't great with faces. And he saw so many people every night at Funworld . . .

He was bemused, at sea, sitting on his narrow bed in the hot little room behind the ghost train. He had obviously just begun to grasp the extent of the disaster that he had so narrowly escaped.

"This is the fourth one," he said, blinking at Tessa with those glorious, sultry eyes that looked so deceptively sophisticated. "I was saying to Val, this guy's a looney. A real looney. I mean, poor old Pete was just the start, wasn't he?"

Tessa pulled the chair out from under the table and turned it to face him. Then she took Jasmine's diary from her bag. Marty eyed it nervously. What now?

Tessa explained what she wanted from him. He nodded, and sat up a little straighter, as though this would help him to concentrate.

Starting at January, Tessa began leafing through the diary, looking for Jasmine's references to Tracey and reading out the names of the places where the two women had met. The art gallery, various cafes, movies, dress shops, furniture shops, theatre matinees, department stores . . . there were dozens of meeting spots. Tracey and Jasmine had seen each other every few weeks.

Month gave way to month as the pages of the diary turned. And Marty's face remained blank. His head shook monotonously, helplessly. He hadn't been to any of these places. He'd never seen any of those movies. He liked Westerns, Val liked adventure-type things. He'd never been to a play. He'd never heard of the cafes Jasmine mentioned.

He wanted to help. He really did. But nothing rang a bell.

This is a waste of time.

Keep going.

Sighing inwardly, Tessa turned the page. They were well into the second half of the year by now. " 'Blackies, 10:30.' Blackie could be a person. Or it could be another cafe." Again, that shake of the head. Marty was shuffling his feet, kicking his heels against the vinyl floor. He was getting restless.

Another couple of pages. August gave way to September. On Tuesday the 9th, Jasmine had had another appointment with Tracey. "Tracey, Fairview, 3 P.M."

"Fairview," read Tessa, "whatever that is." She prepared to turn the page.

"Fairview's a house," Marty said slowly.

Tessa glanced up at him quickly. He nodded, and jerked his thumb towards the promenade.

"It's here. Just up the cliff road a bit. One of those old houses, where you pay to get in and look around. You know, full of antiques and that. Some rich guy whose wife wrote poems used to own it. I've been there." He sounded almost un-believing, as though he had thought it impossible that the two glamorous-looking women in the photographs he'd seen could actually have trodden the same ground as he had.

Tessa's stomach was turning over. "You've really been there?" she asked, just to be certain. A visit to a stately home seemed unlikely entertainment for a guy like Marty.

He nodded again, looked down at his hands. He had red-dened. She realized he must have caught her tone and cursed her insensitivity.

"Just thought I'd like to have a look," he mumbled. "The furniture and that. When you've got afternoons off you can't sit round looking at yourself all the time, can ya?" He glanced up at her. "They let anyone in as long as they pay," he added.

Tessa bit her tongue to stop herself from floundering into stammering apologies which she knew could only make the situation worse. "Can you remember when you were there?" she asked crisply. "Was it sometime this year?"

He stared at her. "Yes," he said. "In September. On my birthday. In the afternoon."

Tessa gripped the little book in her hand. She cleared her throat. "Your birthday . . . ?"

"The 9th," he said. "September the 9th."

He'd been there on the same day as Jasmine Ho and Tracey Fernandez. The very same day.

Could still be a coincidence.

It couldn't.

Marty was scratching his chin. "I might have seen those two chicks there, you know," he said slowly. "Now I come to think about it, I can sort of see it. I think they *were* there. I saw them on the veranda, at the side. The Chinese-looking one was wearing a pink dress. The one with the long red hair had a hat on."

He beamed, his face transformed by relief and excitement. "This'll help, won't it?" he said. "It'll help."

"Should do," said Tessa, containing her own excitement with extreme difficulty. "Listen—did anything unusual happen while you were at Fairview? Did you see anyone acting oddly? Was there any sort of argument, or fight? Did you speak to anyone?"

He shrugged, the excitement dying out of his face, leaving it rather sad. "Nothing happened," he said flatly. "There weren't many people there. No one acted funny. No one looked sideways at me. Except the old duck at the desk where you pay. She looked down her nose. But she took me money, all right. It was good enough for her, even if I wasn't. No one else come near me. I just hung around for a few hours, looked at some stuff— it was sort of interesting, I s'pose, in a way—and then come back here."

His shoulders slumped and he looked down at his hands.

She left him sitting on his bed, and went outside to call Steve.

Fourteen

Mrs. Freda Sparrow was a little uncomfortable. Her earrings were pinching, and her new shoes (navy blue, elegantly plain except for a tasteful gold bar across the toe, perfectly matching the navy blue of her jacket and skirt) were the tiniest bit tight. She secretly eased her heels out of the binding leather and felt immediate relief.

It would have been wonderful to take the shoes off completely, but of course she couldn't do anything so unprofessional. The antique desk at which she sat in the Fairview reception hall provided no cover for such an action. And she couldn't have visitors to Fairview confronted by her swollen feet on their arrival. As Mrs. Sparrow, president of the Fairview Volunteers Committee, always told new recruits, Fairview was a sacred trust in more ways than one. This little play on words was always well received at meetings.

The Fairview Trust had come into being on the death of Fairview's owner and lifelong inhabitant, the poet Marianne Fairley-Harper. She was born in the house to Ada and Frank Fairley, lived in it with them throughout her childhood, and refused to leave it even upon her marriage, at thirty-five, to Victor Harper. Victor, a banker, had happily, it seemed, moved in with her and her father (her mother having died attempting to bear another child when Marianne was ten), saying that the house was quite big enough to accommodate three.

Would that men were so easy to manage these days, Mrs. Sparrow sometimes thought with a sigh. Victor must have very much loved Marianne (Mrs. Sparrow always called her Marianne—she thought of her as a friend) though, judging by the several portraits that hung about the house, the poet had not been a particularly beautiful woman. She was rather plain in fact, tall and rawboned, with very large, melancholy eyes. Windows on her sensitive soul, Mrs. Sparrow always thought romantically.

Some said knowingly that love had nothing to do with it. Marianne's family was extremely wealthy, and the banker was after the loot. Publicly, Mrs. Sparrow always protested vehemently against this cynicism. But in her heart she sometimes wondered. Victor and Marianne had after all had separate bedrooms, some of Marianne's later poetry bewailed the faithlessness of men in quite strong terms, and there hadn't been any children. At these moments Mrs. Sparrow would comfort herself by considering, with secret, spiteful glee, that if Victor had indeed been a fortune-hunter, his plans had come undone. Despite the fact that Marianne was five years older than he was, he died twenty years before her. In the end, it was Marianne and Fairview who benefited from Victor's money, not the other way around.

The Trust had had considerable assets when it was first established, though conservative investment had eroded its value somewhat, and several times the trustees had had to appeal to the government for assistance, or obtain a bank loan, to keep the house in order. There were those (Mrs. Sparrow had actually met them) who thought the money poured into the place year by year could have been better spent. Who thought that just because Marianne's poetry (verse, they called it) was no longer in print, being rather too romantic and wordy for present public taste, her home should not be honored.

But Mrs. Sparrow, who loved the poetry, and loved the house even more, felt the opposite. Marianne's father's money might have paid for the home's luxurious appointments, but it was Marianne's taste that had made of the house a palace of gentle harmony. Many of her original manuscripts, illustrated in the margins with her own delicate watercolor flowers and birds, lay in glass cases in the rooms. Her own hand had embroidered the samplers on the bedroom walls, and the covers on the cushions of the dining room. She herself had directed the gardeners to create the wisteria arbor, the fish pond, and the rose walk.

And this is what Mrs. Sparrow meant by "sacred trust." She and her volunteers owed it to Marianne to ensure that visitors to her home, even if they came by tourist bus, had from beginning to end a tour that was elegant and unspoiled by clamor or amateurish behavior.

Not that every volunteer took this stricture seriously. One young woman, doing her first day's work, on a Sunday, had even manned the reception desk wearing denim jeans and a singlet top. Of course this had only happened the once. The ladies on duty serving the Devonshire Teas that day had rung Mrs. Sparrow and told her as soon as they arrived home, and Mrs. Sparrow had spoken to the young woman the very next day. She'd been extremely tactful, in her opinion, but the young woman hadn't taken the criticism well, had been extremely rude about it, in fact, and had resigned on the spot.

The incident had upset Mrs. Sparrow. As she told members of the Committee later, she always put these things behind her, but wasn't accustomed to being shouted at. Most of them were suitably shocked and sympathetic. But Helen Carr, who really had never quite fitted in, had drawled in that rather offensive way of hers that it wasn't so easy to find volunteers for the reception desk on the weekends, when the visitors were so much more numerous, and maybe Mrs. Sparrow had been a bit rash.

Thinking about this made Mrs. Sparrow grow quite warm. She'd given ten years' faithful service to the Fairview Volunteers, had been their president for four of those years, and if she didn't have the right to insist on high standards, who did?

She noted the garishly dressed middle-aged couple who'd come in only half an hour before drifting out of the house, and her mouth tightened with disapproval. Half an hour! No one could appreciate Fairview in that time. Mind you, she'd known when they came in that they weren't the sort of people who would do the house justice. The woman was wearing tight red trousers, her hair was a tousled mass of dyed black curls, and her leathery brown neck was hung with gold chains. Mutton dressed up as lamb, thought Mrs. Sparrow. Her husband, if husband he was, was wearing shorts and an appalling tropical shirt stretched tightly across his flabby belly.

Ten years ago, people like that simply didn't come to Fairview. The trustees had encouraged this sort of invasion by placing advertisements in the tabloids, and putting a hoarding up on the promenade, showing where the house could be found.

They claimed this was necessary to encourage income, because the house was expensive to maintain, but Mrs. Sparrow's own opinion, frequently expressed to trustees and volunteers alike, was that it was folly to lower the tone. A peaceful and tasteful ambience, created as much as anything by the type of visitor wandering the beautiful old rooms, was essential to maintain the famous Fairview grace. Not to mention the difficulties inherent in preserving the treasures of the house from the depredations of the wrong sort of people, who might stoop to thieving, or vandalism. But no one would listen to her.

She was, in fact, sorely tried, and irritability lurked behind her lipsticked smile as she greeted the two young people entering the house. But the young people looked the right sort—at least they were dressed properly, if a little soberly for the time of day—and Mrs. Sparrow knew her duty.

Heroically she forced some warmth into her expression, slipped her feet fully forward into the biting shoes, and pushed the leather-bound visitors' book invitingly forward on the desk as they approached. At the same moment, to remind them that they had to pay, she discreetly indicated the polished mahogany donation box standing at her right hand. It still bore the notice, "Donations," though (most unfortunately, in Mrs. Sparrow's opinion) it these days also bore information on the exact "donation" required, plus the note that children under twelve and pensioners were admitted half price, and children under five were admitted free.

The wooden box had been retained for the look of the thing, but because in the past so many visitors had been left fumbling for the correct change while an impatient line formed behind them, the trustees had provided a vulgar metal cash box always kept, at Mrs. Sparrow's insistence, and despite the inconvenience, in the reception desk drawer.

"Welcome to Fairview," she said, with exactly the right note of polite condescension, perfected over a decade. As she always told her ladies, it was important for guests to realize that they were privileged, as well as welcome.

"Mrs. Sparrow . . ." the young man said, noting, as few people bothered to do, the neat brass name badge on her lapel.

He reached into his jacket pocket and drew out a slim wallet. Mrs. Sparrow readied herself to open the drawer and remove change from the hidden cash box, but to her confusion the visitor simply opened the wallet and showed her an identification card.

"Pensioners half price," she said firmly, startled at the thought that these days you just couldn't tell who was who.

But he was speaking at the same time, and, astonished, through the sound of her own voice, she heard his deeper one saying the words "detective" and "homicide." She focused on the identification card, and discovered that, astounding as it seemed, Fairview had received a visit from the police.

Mrs. Sparrow pulled herself together as best she could, told them her name, and, despite her fluster, managed speedily to establish herself as being the person in charge, the longtime president of the Fairview Volunteers, on duty Tuesday to Friday without fail (Fairview being closed on Mondays) and entirely *au fait* with Fairview procedures.

That having been established, they asked her if they could look at the visitors' book. They were interested in a particular day in September. Just, they said, a matter of routine.

She demurred at first. She told them that she really felt the book was confidential. That the visitors wrote down their names and addresses in the book because they were asked to. That guests did not expect that their privacy would be invaded by officials. That she didn't feel she should take the responsibility. But it was soon clear that the detectives weren't going to be put off. The young woman in particular (it seemed the young woman was also a detective) became rather pert, and asked for a contact number for the head of the board of trustees.

In the end, Mrs. Sparrow felt it was best to let them see the book. She didn't want the trustees brought into this. They might use the incident to attempt to remove her from her position. A recent meeting had been rather uncomfortable. One trustee, frustrated by her strong opposition to the plan to allow visitors to use the inside bathrooms as well as the discreet but now rather inadequate outside toilet block, had actually called her obstructive.

Having carefully marked her place in the book with the slim, royal-blue ribbon attached to the spine, she began to turn back to the date the detectives required. She took her time, being careful not to mark or crease the pages.

She could feel their impatience. The young woman, Detective Vance, was simmering with it. This gave Mrs. Sparrow a perverse pleasure. They could wait. She was in charge here, and she was going to ensure everything was done properly.

She reached September and slowed down even more, pretending to check the dates carefully penned in the margins. But as the dates drew closer and closer to September the 9th, she suddenly tired of the game and started turning the pages more rapidly.

"You've passed it, I think," said the young man, his voice, which was rather nice, betraying not a trace of impatience or reproach.

Mrs. Sparrow looked quickly down, saw August dates in the margins, laughed lightly and apologized, flipped back a page, and stared. Honestly, she told one of the volunteers afterwards, her heart leaped into her mouth.

The book had been vandalized. A page had been torn out. You could see its fragments poking raggedly from the gutter. Most of the names and addresses for Saturday the 6th and all the details for Sunday the 7th and Tuesday the 9th were missing. She turned to Tessa and Steve, mouth agape, and said the first thing that came into her head.

"I didn't do it," she gasped. "Honestly I didn't."

*   *   *

White under her makeup, Mrs. Sparrow dithered over the photographs of Marty, Jasmine, and Tracey, unable to say whether she remembered seeing them at Fairview or not. She thought she had, but she'd also seen the pictures of Jasmine and Tracey in the paper, and wasn't sure if that was why their faces seemed familiar.

She was most definite, however, that nothing unpleasant or unusual had happened at Fairview on the 9th of September. If it had, she would have remembered, she said. Fairview wasn't a place where unpleasant or unusual things happened. Also, Tuesdays were always slow. Visitors were few, in comparison to later in the week, and at the weekends, when the famous Fairview Devonshire Teas were served.

She would have noticed anyone acting strangely, she said. Except for visits to the staff ladies' room, and at tea and lunchtime, when the girl from the office stood in for her, she stayed at her post in the reception hall at the front of the building all the time. As much to watch people leaving, as to take their money on entering, she said. Most of the valuable objects were in glass cases. But you couldn't be too careful.

It stood to reason, then, Steve suggested gently, that if anything happened in one of the other rooms, especially upstairs, or out in the garden, Mrs. Sparrow wouldn't know about it, unless there was noise involved. Crestfallen, Mrs. Sparrow had to admit that was true.

Tessa left them and began wandering through the house, reading the brochure Mrs. Sparrow had pressed upon her, looking around to establish the layout of the house in her mind, and thinking. The fact that the relevant page of the visitors' book had been torn out was proof positive that whatever Mrs. Sparrow thought, whatever Marty Mayhew had said, something had happened at Fairview on the 9th of September. But what *had* happened?

Whatever it was, it was nothing to do with Brady Mumm. He was still inside, then.

Yes.

At last she could admit, and face, the grotesque theory that had crawled into her mind last night and frightened her so much. That list of similarities between victims—all to do with their deaths, and the investigation of their deaths, rather than their lives—it was meaningless after all.

However Brady Mumm felt about her, whether or not he was tormenting her with nuisance phone calls, he wasn't behind these killings. They hadn't been a message for her in particular. It had been insanity to think they were.

You knew that, really. That was the problem. You thought you were going nuts because you even considered it.

She visited sitting room, library, dining room, study, summer room, and kitchen, glanced briefly into the garden, where several visitors were walking, then returned to the reception hall. Steve and Mrs. Sparrow were still talking. The woman was pointing to a closed door behind the desk. The office, Tessa guessed.

Anxious to finish her tour, she hurried up the grand stairway to the floor above.

There were six bedrooms, each with different-colored wallpaper, each with its gleaming fireplace, its made-up bed, its polished chest of drawers with starched embroidered white runner, its marble washstand with flowered ewer and basin, its carefully arranged tokens of antique domestic life—frilled nightgowns, nightcaps, shawls, ropes of beads, dried flowers under glass, dolls, books, warming pans. Discreet silk ropes with tasseled ends fenced off the beds—presumably so that the coverlets would not be disarranged or spoiled by curious hands.

A few visitors were wandering around, examining the samplers on the walls, staring blankly at the furniture, murmuring to each other. They seemed always to grow uneasy as Tessa entered the rooms they occupied, and after a moment would slowly drift away, as though she had invaded their privacy, or they felt that they were invading hers.

Or maybe it was the ghosts of the house who were being invaded. Tessa couldn't rid herself of the feeling of intrusion. She found the atmosphere unsettling. Everything was so perfect, and so dead. A house trapped in amber. But the people who had lived here—how would they judge this sanitized version of their lives, and the gaily dressed people from another century tip-toeing through their strangely silent rooms?

She entered the sixth and smallest bedroom, which was separated from the others by short passage. Whatever it had been used for in the past—storeroom, nanny's sewing room or maid's room, perhaps, it was now set up as a child's room—a small girl's room, without question, because the walls were papered in pink. A mat, pink with a border of bluebirds, lay on the polished floor. The high, narrow bed, with its feather mattress and white cover, was pristine. A child's dressing-gown, pink (of course!) with a hood, hung on the bedpost. A tiny porcelain tea set was arranged on the chest, where a few rag books also lay. In one corner of the room there was a small cane chair on which was sitting a charmingly ancient teddy bear.

Like the other bedrooms, the walls this one was decorated with samplers and embroideries, almost all signed MF or MFH. Marianne Fairley-Harper had loved sewing (so the brochure said), and she'd obviously had a lot of time on her hands over the years. But several of these embroideries featured cutesy dogs, kittens, ducklings and rabbits, alphabet blocks and dolls. They had obviously been made for a child. The child Marianne never had, perhaps.

The thought made Tessa feel gloomy. She turned to go—there was nothing more to see up here, and the attics, the brochure said, were closed—and then something caught her eye.

It was the cross-stitch embroidery hanging over the chest of drawers—less pastel and more interesting than most of the others. Painstakingly detailed pictures of traditional children's toys—trains, balls, blocks, teddies, rag dolls and soldiers—had been worked on the broad band of linen between the frame and a plain blue internal border. And inside the blue border, embroidered in red, were some familiar words—the lines of a verse Tessa remembered from her own childhood. She drew closer, till she was standing against the silk barrier cord, read the words again, and felt a cold thrill run from the top of her head to her feet.

Monday's child is fair of face,
Tuesday's child is full of grace,
Wednesday's child is full of woe,
Thursday's child has far to go,
Friday's child is loving and giving,
Saturday's child works hard for a living,
But the child that is born on the Sabbath day
Is bonny and blythe and good and gay.

Birth day, death day.

Her hands gripping the silken rope, Tessa thought it through. Making sure.

Monday's child—Marty Mayhew, extraordinarily good-looking. If anyone could be described as "fair of face," he could.

Tuesday's child—Tracey Fernandez. A dancer. Full of grace.

Wednesday's child—poor Lloyd Greely, terribly unhappy since the death of his wife. Full of woe.

Thursday's child—Jasmine, the flight attendant. Far to go.

The symbols of childhood, birthdays . . .

The rhyme fitted. It fitted perfectly.

Everything is a message . . .

The killer, Tessa knew, had stood right here in this place. Had read the rhyme, as she had done. Had remembered it, perhaps, from long ago. Here, bizarre as it seemed, was the place where it had all begun.

"Tessa?"

It was Steve, calling in a low voice from the hallway. He'd climbed the stairs silently, but he'd learned better than to come up behind her, soft-footed.

She answered him.

"You right?" he asked, coming into the little room.

Tessa almost laughed. She turned to face him, still holding the silken rope.

"What's up?" he exclaimed, the expression on her face alerting him to the fact that something had changed.

She told him. He listened, and didn't interrupt. His eyes

flicked from her face to the verse on the wall. He was fascinated. But she could see that he was struggling with it.

"It fits," he said, when she'd finished. "But . . ."

"What?"

"It's—it's bloody insane."

She just looked at him.

He ran the back of his hand across his mouth. Trying, she thought grimly, to find a way out. "The descriptions are pretty general," he said at last. "You could make every one of them fit thousands of people. Why would he pick the targets he did? You're not saying they were really born on those days of the week, are you?"

Tessa shook her head. "We'll have to check, I guess, but I wouldn't think so. He's just choosing people to match the descriptions in the rhyme."

"If you're right, there are three more deaths to come."

"And we've got descriptions of the victims."

Steve looked again at the verse, letting this sink in. "Friday's child—loving and giving," he murmured.

"Could be a charity worker, or a priest."

"Could be a nurse, a nun, a Salvation Army major, a nice, kind bank manager, or my mum!" Steve ran his hands through his hair. "Could be anyone, Tessa. And look at the others. Saturday's child—works hard for a living. Ah, right. Easy. Homicide detective. Watch your back. Sunday's child—bonny and blythe and good and gay. No worries. A happy, good-looking homosexual. I'll put the word out."

Tessa smiled. For once she was unthreatened by his cynicism or his objections. She knew he thought she was right.

"I was born on a Tuesday," she said. "What about you?"

"No idea," he said absently. "Wednesday, probably. I always draw the short straw."

"I wonder what Thorne is."

"With any luck, Thursday. The further he goes, the better."

She laughed, and he grinned back at her. Just for a moment a feeling of warmth and camaraderie flowed between them.

I've missed that so much.

Have you considered that he might have missed it too?

"Yoo, hoo!" a high, slightly nasal voice called from the hallway. "Detective Hayden?"

"Yes?" called Steve.

Feet thumped briskly down the short corridor, and then a young woman came bustling a little breathlessly into the room, carrying a folder. She had a plump, rosy face, and her eyes were magnified enormously behind strong, wide-framed glasses.

"Mrs. Sparrow said you wanted to see me," she chattered excitedly. "I work in the office downstairs? I was just out getting some morning tea when you were there before. I thought I'd just pop up now, because Mrs. Sparrow wants to have her own morning tea in a minute, and I'll be on the desk, and anyway, I wanted to—"

"Fine," Steve cut in smoothly, to break the flow. "Thanks for coming up. We appreciate it. This is Detective Tessa Vance. And you are . . ."

The girl pointed to her brass name badge, giggling. "Oh, sorry," she said. "That's me. Bonnie Gay."

Tessa and Steve glanced at one another, and back at the name tag. Bonnie Gay. This time, the coincidence was too great even for Steve to swallow.

They both knew, without doubt, that they were looking at Sunday's victim.

Fifteen

Bonnie was leaning forward, half whispering. She was telling them that *actually*, the reason she'd particularly wanted to catch them before they came downstairs was because, well, obviously a murder inquiry was *incredibly* important, and if you had information you shouldn't care about people's *feelings* and so on, but there was something she'd rather Mrs. Sparrow didn't hear. Mrs. Sparrow was *so* upset already.

Tessa nodded encouragingly, and saw Steve doing the same. At this stage neither of them wanted to alert Bonnie to her possible danger. The more she could be encouraged to talk, and think rationally, the better. Frightened out of her wits, she could freeze up or, worse still, start inventing things.

"Mrs. Sparrow says you wanted some visitors' names and addresses, but when she looked, the page had been torn out of the visitors' book." Bonnie smothered a laugh with her hand. "I shouldn't laugh, but *honestly*, you'd think holy writ had been desecrated, the way she's going on. She takes it all so *seriously*."

She put her head on one side and sparkled at them roguishly. It crossed Tessa's mind that Bonnie could prove to be a little wearing in large doses.

"The thing is," whispered Bonnie, glancing over her shoulder conspiratorially and then bending even closer to them, "All the names and addresses in the visitors' book are also on my computer!"

She saw their faces change, and clapped her hands. "I *knew* you'd be pleased," she giggled. "But Mrs. Sparrow wouldn't. So I came up here, and—"

"You're saying that you have all the names and addresses of

the people who were here on the 9th of September?" Steve interrupted.

Bonnie nodded eagerly. "As long as they signed the visitors' book," she said. "And they all *do* sign. Mrs. Sparrow won't let them in otherwise. She wants to make sure the book is a true record, she says. But I think that *actually* she wants it as proof of how many visitors come. In case the trustees think she's embezzling the donations box."

The idea of what the self-important pouter-pigeon matron downstairs would say if she knew her subordinate was gaily discussing the possibility of her pilfering the Fairview funds even made Tessa smile.

"Not that she would," Bonnie hastened to add, seeing the smile.

"Why do you transfer the names and addresses to the computer without Mrs. Sparrow knowing about it?" asked Steve bluntly. "She's your boss, isn't she?"

Bonnie flapped her hands in mock horror. "Oh, *no!*" she said. "Mrs. Sparrow's the Volunteers. I'm office. I report *directly* to the Board of Trustees. *They* asked me to put the names and addresses on the computer. But they said not to mention it to Mrs. Sparrow. She wouldn't approve at *all*. They're trying to build up a mailing list. So they can write and hassle people for donations, I guess. Or maybe even sell the list, for all I know. They need all the money they can get. This place costs a *fortune* to run."

She pulled a sheet of paper out of the file she was carrying.

"Anyway, here you are," she said happily. "I printed out all the entries I had for September the 9th. They're not in alpha order or anything. I'm just typing straight from the book at the moment. But that shouldn't worry you. There aren't very many. Only thirty-two. Tuesdays are like that, unless we get a tourist bus."

She handed the list to Steve, who told her she was wonderful. "It's lucky that what you wanted was so long ago," she beamed as he glanced at the paper, while Tessa waited in an agony of impatience. "I'm not quite up to date. I only work

here two days a week, you know, and I have to transcribe from
the visitors' book in my last hour, when Mrs. Sparrow's gone."

She craned her neck to look around his shoulder at the
names on the list in his hand. "Is that what you wanted?" she
asked, hungry for more praise.

"It's great," Steve said casually. "Thanks very much. We'll
let you get back to work now."

"Oh. Don't you want to ask me anything else?" asked
Bonnie, her magnified eyes surprised and disappointed.

"Not just for now," said Steve. "We'll drop in and see you on
our way out. Okay?"

"Oh—sure." Bonnie smiled brightly. She was someone,
Tessa thought, who had grown used to snubs and who protected herself by pretending not to notice them. "See you then,"
she caroled, and walked rather self-consciously from the room.

Steve stood motionless as her footsteps died away. Then he
passed the list to Tessa without comment.

Tessa ran her finger down the listed names, checking
quickly. Marty Mayhew was there, about halfway down the
list. That would be right. He said he'd come in the afternoon.
Tracey Fernandez was there, not too far behind him. Directly
under her was Jasmine Ho. But none of them was the name she
was looking for.

It won't be here. Too good to be true.

It will. It has to be.

And then she saw it. In black and white. "Lloyd and Joy
Greely," and the Greelys' home address.

Lloyd Greely, Wednesday's victim, had been at Fairview on
the same day, and at approximately the same time, as all the
other victims. Tessa looked up, biting her lips to stop herself
from exclaiming in triumph. Steve raised his eyebrows.
"You're not surprised," he said, matter-of-factly.

"Not really," Tessa said, keeping her voice as low-pitched as
she could, while her heart thumped with excitement. "I thought
it was possible Lloyd was here, given that all the others were,
and that Bonnie Gay works here. He must have been on holidays, or had a day off or something. Okay. That means—"

"That means we can stop talking about coincidences," Steve

interrupted soberly. "Not that you ever were. I was the one talking coincidences. But I'm convinced now. Something happened in this place on the 9th of September. That, or our killer just came in here one fine Tuesday, saw the rhyme, had a rush of blood to the head, and chose his future victims from the crowd available."

"It can't be that," Tessa muttered. "How would he know what Jasmine Ho did, for example, just by seeing her around?"

"He might have talked to her. He might have talked to them all."

Steve moved to the door. He was anxious to start moving. Tessa took a last look at the rhyme, and followed.

"It doesn't quite work, you know," she said as they negotiated the narrow corridor, and entered the broader hallway. "Lloyd Greely wasn't full of woe on the 9th of September. His wife was still alive then."

Steve stopped and tapped the list she was still holding in her hand. "Look, we just don't know the whole story. Right? But what we do know is that these people were here on the 9th. We've got to get going. You take Bonnie back with you. Take your time. Pick up some sandwiches for lunch on the way, maybe. You do the interview with her. I'll brief Thorne, get some help, and go through these names like a packet of salts. Locate every one of them."

"Today's victim, and Saturday's, must be on here," Tessa murmured, looking at the list. Her skin was crawling at the thought.

So little time. So little time.

"Yeah." Steve's lips tightened. "And the name of the merchant who's planning to kill them, too."

Bonnie Gay was sitting at Mrs. Sparrow's desk when they arrived back downstairs. She was pleased to see them, pleased not to have been forgotten, thrilled to be asked to accompany Tessa back to Homicide to make a statement.

She talked all the way to the car, and all through the following journey. Tessa learned that Tuesday and Friday were Bonnie's Fairview days. Mondays, Wednesdays, Thursdays, and Saturdays she was a receptionist for an optometrist who had two practices in different parts of the city.

She enjoyed both her jobs, Bonnie said. Not the office work, particularly, but the contact with people. She was a *people* person, she said. On her breaks at Fairview she always went outside to have her cup of tea. She often chatted with the visitors. They could see by her name badge that she was a staff member, so they tended to come up to her and ask her things—where the toilets were, and so on. She didn't mind. It was all part of the job. And Mrs. Sparrow wasn't exactly *approachable*.

Bonnie was twenty-four. She worked six days a week because she was saving to go overseas. Sunday was her day off. She enjoyed her Sundays, too. She lived alone in a rented flat. Her father and mother were divorced, she said. Just one of those things. She saw both of them as often as she could, but of course her life was very busy. She had two younger sisters, Terry, twenty, and Rachel, seventeen. They still lived at home with her mother. She adored them both, though Rachel was going through an awkward stage at the moment.

She'd love to buy a unit of her own when she came back from overseas. By then, maybe, she'd have found someone to share with—not necessarily a man, a *love interest*, she said earnestly, though of course somewhere in the world there was someone for everyone. But a friend. That would be nice.

The unbroken flood of confidences, all communicated in that falsely cheery, nasal tone, was exhausting. Negotiating the more than usually chaotic city traffic, while Bonnie talked on and on, Tessa found herself intensely irritated, and at the same time filled with pity.

Bonnie reminded her of a girl she'd known at school. A girl who seemed never to have any close friends, but hung around the peripheries of one group or another. Always bright, always cheerful, she would latch on to any newcomer to the school, taking them round, talking to them at recess or at lunch. They would at first be grateful, and relieved that they had so easily found a friend. Then, inevitably, even the shyest and quietest of them would find their feet and slowly, awkwardly drift away from her.

Tessa had been sorry for that girl. But not sorry enough to spend much time with her. It was a matter of survival. There was something about her that set your teeth on edge. And once encouraged, she clung.

It was with some relief that Tessa noted Bonnie quieting as they drew up outside the grand old building which housed Homicide. By the time they got into the lift, Bonnie had become completely silent. Perhaps she was affected by the strangeness of the place, overawed by the surroundings. Or maybe she could feel, as Tessa could, the charge of suppressed urgency in the air.

Steve would have briefed Thorne by now. The wheels would be turning. A team would be going through the list Bonnie had given them. Tessa was restlessly impatient to know what was happening. She deposited her charge in the interview room, and left her there sipping tea and eating sandwiches, looking brightly around the bare walls through her enormous spectacles.

Steve wasn't at his desk, which was cluttered with files and messages. The office had an abandoned air. It was warm, and filled with a heavy, funereal scent rising from a florist's delivery lying on Tessa's desk.

Tessa stared at the bulky, cellophane-wrapped bunch of white lilies, temporarily paralyzed. The flowers, thick yellow pollen already spilling onto the purity of their petals, glared up at her through their transparent covering. The perfume was almost overpowering.

A florist's card was pinned to the yellow and white ribbons that tied the bunch, but it was blank.

Tessa snatched up the phone and rang the florist's number. The woman who answered was effusive, but entirely unhelpful. The flowers (gorgeous, aren't they?) had been ordered and paid for anonymously. An envelope slipped under the door. Lilies, white lilies, nothing else, had been especially requested. They, all of them at the shop, had thought it was wonderfully romantic. A secret admirer. Everyone would love to have one of those, wouldn't they? They all hoped Tessa would like the flowers. And sorry, no, they hadn't kept the note.

Tessa thanked her, and hung up. She found she was shaking. She grabbed the lilies and stuffed them into her rubbish bin. The petals crushed, the strong stems bent, but wouldn't break. She pushed at them with all her strength, wanting to destroy them, remove them from her sight.

He knows where you are . . .

Steve and Thorne came in. Steve looked at her blandly, noting the ruined flowers, her trembling hands.

He thinks Brett sent them.

Thorne frowned.

Tell him about Mumm.

"Bonnie Gay?" he asked crisply.

"In the interview room, having some lunch," said Tessa. She could hear that her voice sounded high and stressed. She concentrated on keeping her hands still.

Thorne let his gaze wander over the rubbish bin, then glanced at his watch. "Well, Tessa, when you've finished arranging your flowers, you could take her statement," he said politely. "What do you say?"

The interview room was a little world of its own. No sense of the atmosphere outside penetrated, and Bonnie Gay became loquacious again, once she got started.

She remembered nothing particularly special about the 9th of September. She was certainly at Fairview on that day, she said, but even looking back at her diary, which she obligingly did, failed to remind her of anything special that had happened. As far as she was concerned, Tuesday September the 9th had been a day like any other.

Shown photographs of Tracey and Jasmine, she put her head on one side and said she *did* remember them, actually. How absolutely *awful* that they were dead. She couldn't really take it in. She'd seen them a couple of times around the house during the afternoon. They seemed to be very good friends. The Asian one was very small and fragile-looking. The other one, the one with the long red hair—dyed, of course—you could tell it was dyed—laughed a lot. She was wearing a hat that she kept pulling off, then putting on again. If Bonnie'd tried to do that with a hat, her hair would be sticking out everywhere and she'd look *ridiculous.*, she added, with a flash of her old vivacity.

She didn't notice them talking to any men. They could have done, of course, while she wasn't around. She would have been in the office a lot of the time.

She thought she remembered Lloyd, though she couldn't be sure. And she'd certainly seen Marty. He looked like a film star, she said, though he had a tattoo, and it was obvious that he was a bit "rough." Still, she'd heard that film stars often were.

Tessa left her alone again and sought out Thorne. He was in his office with Steve.

"Do I tell her she's in danger?" she asked bluntly. She had herself too tightly under control to bother with the niceties.

Thorne eyed her over his spectacles. "I wouldn't, just yet," he said. "She's safe enough for the moment, according to your theory, isn't she, Tessa? She's the Sunday victim. Safe till midnight Saturday."

He makes it sound like a game.

"If it wasn't for her name, I'd pick her for Saturday's child," Steve commented. "Working in that place with that Sparrow woman's working hard in anyone's language."

Thorne laughed. "She'd probably agree with you. You ask anyone if they work hard for a living and they'll say yes, harder than anyone they know."

It's not a game. Not something to joke about.

Everyone copes differently. You know that.

"Why don't we keep her around here for a while till we're ready to come clean?" Steve suggested. "Put her in one of the offices. Ask her to wait till her statement's typed up, or something. I don't reckon she'll object."

"How many of the people on the list have you contacted?" Tessa asked.

"The tally was eighteen when I came in here," said Steve. "It's turned out to be fairly easy tracking. A lot of them are retired or unemployed or shift workers or whatever. That's why they were at Fairview on a Tuesday afternoon, and why they're at home now. Four of them we haven't actually spoken to. German tourists, left the country six weeks ago. That's confirmed. We spun the other fourteen a line. Didn't tell them anything, just checked them out."

"Are any of them known?"

"None have a record so far. Not on the names they're going by, anyhow. We'll get them all in eventually, check them out properly, but the one we're particularly interested in just at this moment is . . ." he consulted a note in his hand " . . . a woman called Rosemary Mackintosh. She's at work, but one of her housemates was in when we called. We've sent a car for her. We want her in here."

"Why her?"

"She was at Fairview in the afternoon, when Marty and the others were there. She's a child-care worker . . ."

Friday's child is loving and giving.

"And she's twenty-eight years old. Same general age group as all the victims. All the other people we've contacted so far have been middle-aged or older."

"The killer could be—"

"Any age. Of course," Thorne interrupted. "We're not letting Dolf Hermin's profile run us, Tessa. But we've decided to concentrate on possible targets for the moment. Safety first. Time marches on. And Hermin's pretty well convinced that the age group of the victims is important, especially given this birthday rhyme thing."

Tessa nodded. Fair enough. Age was the only thing the victims so far had more or less in common, except their resemblance to characters in the "Monday's child" rhyme. And of course anyone likely to be a target should be protected.

"Glad you approve," said Thorne. He was being sarcastic, of course, but it was gentle sarcasm. And he did smile.

The detective who had stood next to Tessa at the task force briefing came in with a scribbled note, which he handed to Thorne. He was still sweating, Tessa noted. In fact, he seemed still to be wearing the same shirt.

"Lindsay Cramer, twenty-five," he said. "Got onto him just

now. He works from home. He's in the Eastern Suburbs. He's driving himself in in about an hour."

"What does he do?" snapped Thorne.

"Time and motion expert. Consults all round the traps. Own business. Sounds like he could be a goer."

Saturday's child works hard for a living.

"How many still to contact?" Steve asked.

"Only five, now. Not counting the dead ones," said the sweating detective idiotically. He was obviously overtired. Tessa warmed to him.

Thorne stared after him as he left the office, and seemed to suppress a sigh. But before he could say anything, his phone rang. He picked it up without haste, and listened.

"Hold her there. Vance and Hayden will be right with you," he said, and hung up. He looked up at Tessa and Steve over his glasses. "Rosemary Mackintosh is here," he said. "What are you waiting for? You're on."

Sixteen

Rosemary Mackintosh was dark-haired, gentle-eyed, soft-voiced, and tense. She was taller than average and very slim. Her shoulders were slightly bowed and she had a defenseless, used-up look. As she was escorted to the interview room, she apologized several times for her clothes—a dark red shirt and jeans on which here and there small, clutching fingers had smeared traces of paint, Vegemite, and peanut butter.

She must have been curious as to why she had been brought to Homicide, but seemed too timid actually to ask. She sat on the edge of her chair, her large, big-knuckled hands twisting in her lap as she spoke.

She worked 7 A.M. to 4 P.M. four days a week at the child-care center, she told them. She had Tuesdays off.

"Bet you're glad you're not on the full week," Steve said, grinning at her. "Must be hell looking after forty screaming kids all day."

She smiled back. "Oh, no," she said, in that gentle voice with the country drawl. "I miss the center, really, when I'm not there."

She paused. "I come from the country," she added finally. "My family's all there. Mum and Dad. My grandparents. Four younger sisters and a little brother. I really miss them. And I miss the place. You know?"

"Yeah." Steve nodded slowly. "I come from the bush myself. Know how you feel." He tugged at his tie, as though its tight grip on his neck had suddenly become unbearably irritating.

"The center's nice. Like a big family," the dark-haired girl went on impulsively. "The kids are lovely. They drive you crazy, in a way, and it's hard on your back hauling them round, but you get to love them, especially the littlies. Some of the ones who've left to go to school still write to me. Send me pictures and things. I love that."

She was obviously sincere. Tessa felt a wave of relief flow through her.

She's the one, Friday's child. We found her.

You don't know that.

She's the one. She must be.

Asked about Fairview, Rosemary said she went there just for something to do. Questioned further, she said, shyly, that she was writing a children's book, and usually spent her Tuesdays doing that. But sometimes, in the afternoons, if her back ached and she knew she shouldn't sit in front of the computer any more, she went out for a walk. She lived in a house she shared with five others quite near Fairview, she said, and on her walks she'd often gone past the place, and wondered what it was like inside. That Tuesday afternoon, and she was taking their word for it about the date, she went in. She knew it didn't cost a lot to get in to places like Fairview.

Asked if anyone had talked to her, or if she had witnessed anything unusual while she was there, she said no. But though her eyes were dark with the growing awareness that something was very wrong, she still didn't ask them why they wanted to know.

She's a natural victim.

She's safe now. He can't get to her now.

After the interview, they asked Rosemary to stay while her statement was typed, and put her into an empty office down the corridor from Bonnie Gay, with a mug of weak black tea and a uniformed constable to keep her company.

Checking the progress, they found that three more people on the list had now been contacted. They were all women. Two were in their eighties, one was sixty-two. They had been dismissed from contention, as suspects and as targets. And Lindsay Cramer had just arrived in reception.

"This is like a French farce," Steve complained. "Hustling people out one door while other people come in the other. Hiding people away in separate rooms. The whole thing's crazy."

He was eyeing Tessa, frowning, as though somehow the

situation was her fault. As though things like this hadn't happened before she turned up.

Like in a medieval village when the pig died and the old woman with the wart on her nose got blamed and burned at the stake.

You can talk. You were thinking the whole thing was happening because of you for a while. Because of . . .

"We can hardly just let Rosemary Macintosh walk out of here. She's Friday's target," Tessa said aloud.

"We don't know that. Friday's child might be one of the two people we still haven't contacted. We've got no idea how old they are, and the Sparrow can't help us."

"Rosemary's a target," said Tessa positively. "She's vulnerable, and she's the right age."

"She might be. But how do we know she's Friday's child, and not Saturday's? She works hard for a living, whatever she says."

But they met the contender for Saturday's child next.

Lindsay Cramer exactly fitted Tessa's impression of what a time and motion expert should look like. He was neat and well-groomed in a dark gray suit, pale blue shirt, and tie covered in blue and gray triangles. His carefully cut, pale brown hair was already thinning at the temples. His high forehead was lightly corrugated with exactly parallel lines that leaped into prominence when he raised his light eyebrows, which was often. As if prepared for any contingency, he was carrying a large briefcase which bore his initials in gold.

Unlike Rosemary Mackintosh, who had been too timid and eager to please to ask questions, he quietly insisted on knowing why his working day had been interrupted by the call to Homicide. Steve told him a version of the truth: that they were trying to establish the movements of a wanted person who was known to have been at the house that afternoon. He accepted this without comment, simply nodding. Tessa decided that he was intelligent, but totally lacking in imagination.

Despite his lined forehead, receding hair, and the gray shadows under his eyes, Lindsay didn't look much older than his twenty-five years, but in personality he could have been fifty, so settled and ordered were his thought processes and actions. He made Tessa feel like a feckless teenager.

He lived alone, he told them, in his own townhouse, one room of which doubled as his office. When asked about his visit to Fairview, he snapped open his briefcase to reveal a triumph of organization: various-sized compartments containing lap-top computer, phone, folders, diary/address book combination, business cards, a pad of paper, pens (all with tops). It was an office in miniature. Tessa was fascinated.

Lindsay took out his diary and found the reference to Fairview, which he had planned and diarized. He had two appointments in the area on the 9th of September, he explained, but unfortunately it had been impossible to group them quite conveniently. Rather than waste the time in between engagements, he'd decided to spend the intervening hour at Fairview. He was interested in antique furniture. His late father had owned a furniture business. Cramer's Furniture—the detectives might have heard of it.

They both had. Cramer's Furniture was a large chain. Involuntarily, Tessa glanced at Steve, whose face remained expressionless.

Does he see it? The guy must be rolling in money. He's not Saturday's child. He doesn't have to work hard for a living.

Wait. Listen.

The interview was heavy going, though Lindsay was a good witness in some ways.

Fairview had been slightly disappointing, he said, as most of these places run by amateurs tend to be, but he'd stayed in the house two hours, and visited every room. He remembered the layout clearly. He'd noted the visitors' book, and the fact that the cash box was kept in the reception desk drawer, which made speedy change-finding awkward. He remembered the girl with glasses who stood in for Mrs. Sparrow during her absences from the reception desk. She was the one, in fact, who had been at the desk when he came in. She had been pleasant and efficient.

But he hadn't paid attention to the actions of the visitors. He'd noticed nothing unusual whatever about the behavior of any of them. There had been no one else in the small sixth bedroom when he saw it. Visitors to the house were few.

"Tuesdays must be slow," he said, with the first spark of genuine interest he'd displayed so far. "Restaurants and cinemas have the same problem. The trustees should drop prices on Tuesdays, and open Mondays to take advantage of public holidays. Mind you, with that system they've got at the front desk, they couldn't cope with a big crowd."

"You like your work?" Steve asked casually.

Lindsay stared, as though Steve had asked something very strange.

"My work's my life," he said earnestly. Suddenly he seemed very young indeed.

Steve grinned, and stretched, as though the formal part of the interview was over. "I would have thought that with your background you'd be in a position to take it a bit easy."

Lindsay stared again, this time coldly. "I don't want to take it easy. I like what I do. My mother's well off, certainly. My parents helped me to buy my house. But that hasn't got anything to do with it. I've built up my own business—"

"But eventually, when your mother dies..." Steve persisted.

Lindsay lifted his chin. "She's dying now," he said bluntly. "She's in hospital, in the last stages of cancer."

There was a brief moment of awkwardness. Then Steve was murmuring that he was sorry, and the man across the table was nodding, brushing the apology, the condolences aside.

"It doesn't matter how much money I inherit," he said. "I'll never stop working. What else do you live for?" A slight smile crossed his face. "Can you imagine me hitting the high spots in Monte Carlo?"

It was the first touch of humor he'd shown. Self-deprecating, wry, it made him seem very much more human.

"You look tired," said Tessa softly. "Is that because you've got a lot of work on, or because of your mother?"

Again, he smiled. "It's the combination," he said. "If you organize your work, don't waste effort, avoid double handling, and so on, most jobs can be done in reasonable time. But the visits to the hospital, and feeding her cat, watering her plants, and so on, are taking up my leisure time. And of course that's not so good. It's important to take time to relax. It makes you work more efficiently."

"That's a good theory. Must tell the boss," drawled Steve.

Lindsay's brow creased as he raised his eyebrows and leaned forward. "It's not a theory, it's fact," he said earnestly. "People work far more efficiently when they're happy and relaxed. Too many employers forget the human element. They treat their workers like numbers, or machines. Then they wonder why they don't get loyalty, why there's absenteeism and so on."

Tessa watched him, fascinated. His voice had strengthened. His whole face was alive. Talking about his work, he was a different person.

My work's my life.

He's Saturday's child. He's the one.

Steve wasn't so convinced. Tessa knew that, because after Lindsay had finished speaking, Steve asked him, less casually than before, if he could see his diary.

"He could be the Saturday target. I'm not sure." Steve was thoughtful. He'd been disconcerted by Lindsay Cramer. By the young man's apparently calm acceptance of his mother's condition, by his dry, thoughtful delivery, by his total absorption in his work.

"Could be the killer," said Thorne. "Thought about that?"

"Course. I checked his alibis for the relevant times. He didn't really have any. He was at home, alone, working. But he didn't seem like serial killer material to me," said Steve. "What about you, Tessa?"

She couldn't remember that he'd ever asked her opinion before. She was momentarily confused, then heard herself saying, "He doesn't fit the profile."

"We can't go by the profile," said Thorne. "That mistake's been made before. But I don't see why you say he doesn't fit, anyway. He's a young, middle-class white male."

"He's just not—"

"How do we know if he was abused as a child or tortured animals or any of that other claptrap!" Thorne snorted. He immediately realized that he'd let his irritation overcome his usual care in choosing his words, and became even more irritated as a result. "He's got no real alibi for the times of any of the murders—"

"He's got a mobile phone," Steve put in.

"The killer hasn't been using his own phone," Thorne said briefly. "The calls to Fernandez, Greely, and Ho have been tracked. All of them were made from a phone belonging to some old—elderly—woman in Greendale who didn't even know it had gone. She can't even say when or where she lost it. It just wasn't in her car when she looked."

I knew it. This killer's too clever to—

Thorne was settling down. "But in fact I think Cramer's safe," he said. "Dolf Hermin's here. He watched the interviews from the video room. He's seen the Marty Mayhew video too. He agrees with you. Not just on Cramer, but on Mayhew, Mackintosh, and Gay as well. How he can be so certain I wouldn't know. But he is certain, and he's the expert."

"He's given them all a clean bill of health? On the basis of one interview?" Steve looked disbelieving.

Thorne shrugged. "Clean bill of health as far as being a psychopathic serial killer is concerned. It's not much of a compliment. He says they're all capable of murder. Mayhew might kill in anger, or revenge, or to get something he wants. Cramer might kill for gain, or jealousy, or to protect his reputation. Mackintosh has a lot of repressed anger, could snap and lash out, or might kill to defend herself or someone she loved. Gay ditto on the repressed anger, the jealousy, and maybe the gain."

He permitted himself a smile. "Makes you edgy at the idea of being around the lot of them, frankly."

"With those descriptions, it makes you edgy at the idea of being around anyone," muttered Steve. "He's really saying anyone's a potential murderer."

"He is. Strange man."

"Maybe he just faces facts," said Tessa. Only as they glanced at her did she realize she'd spoken aloud.

Thorne stood up from his desk and went to stare out the window. "We're going to have to come clean with the three we've got in here. We can't keep them forever with no explanation. Cramer won't stick it, anyway, even if the women will. But if we let them go and they get themselves killed, there'll be hell to pay. We'll have to give them protection."

"I think Rosemary Mackintosh is the genuine Friday target," Steve said. "If we keep this quiet, we could stake out her house. If our friend with the knives and the birthday cards has been stalking her he'll know she gets home at about 4:30, and the first of her mates doesn't get home till 6:30 on Friday nights. He'll try to get her in the two hours she's alone. We've got a chance of grabbing him."

Thorne, staring out the window, nodded slowly.

It's hours till 4:30. And what if . . .

"We set it up," said Steve. "Put a substitute for Rosemary in the house. Keep Rosemary here."

Thorne turned to face him. "And the others," he said. "For the afternoon at least. So they don't get a chance to gossip and blow the whole thing. All right. Steve, send a car for Mayhew, will you?"

Steve picked up the phone, punched in some numbers.

They've got it all worked out.

Say something.

"I don't think we should risk waiting till 4:30. There are still two people we haven't contacted. We've got no idea where they are, or how old they are," Tessa murmured to Thorne as Steve spoke into the phone. "What if while we're waiting for the killer at Rosemary Mackintosh's house, he's attacking one of them? I mean, till we find them we can't be sure Rosemary *is* Friday's target. She's just the best prospect we've got so far."

"I quite agree," said Thorne drily. "Do you have any suggestions for pinpointing the killer in the next few hours?"

Tessa lifted her chin. "Yes," she said.

He raised his eyebrows. "Well, don't keep it to yourself."

"Something must have set the killer off on the 9th of September," Tessa said. "An argument, something he saw or heard—*something*. Something made him decide that members of this group were going to be his targets, anyway."

"It might just have been seeing the embroidered rhyme in the bedroom," said Thorne. "It might have made him think of something out of his past. Then he noticed Bonnie Gay's name—and bingo!"

"Maybe." Tessa shook her head. "But I still think something must have happened. Some little thing . . ."

"So what are you driving at?"

"We're trying to keep all this quiet, so as not to alert the killer. Fine. But we've got to tell Bonnie, Rosemary, and Lindsay what's been happening. And Marty Mayhew's going to find out too. He'll have to be told—that's why you're bringing him in. And we want to keep Rosemary, at least, under protection. So why not take them all to Fairview?"

Thorne smiled thinly. "And what do you think that will achieve?" He glanced at Steve, who had finished his call, and was now listening to them, his hands plunged deep in his pockets.

"It's hard to remember things out of context," urged Tessa. "If we take them back there—well, someone's memory might be jogged. One of them might remember some little thing. Something that will lead us to the killer more quickly."

Thorne raised his eyebrows and turned to Steve, inviting comment.

"Waste of time," drawled Steve. "That sort of shortcut stuff only works in the movies. Plus, keeping it quiet's going to be impossible. Killer's going to get wind of it, get scared off, and go into smoke. We've got a good chance of getting him tonight. We don't want to blow it with a whole lot of pointless fireworks."

"There's no reason why he should find out, if we're discreet," Tessa argued. "And look at it the other way. If the stakeout leads nowhere because Rosemary Mackintosh isn't Friday's child—"

"Yeah." Thorne rubbed his chin. "She's right, Steve. If we get another death while we're mucking round watching the Mackintosh house, there'll be hell to pay."

"You reckon the targets will cooperate quite happily, do you?" asked Steve grimly. He could see that he was losing this argument. Thorne wanted a bet each way.

"I think they will, once we've explained to them," said Tessa. "They'll be safer together, and with the police, than they'll be on their own, won't they? They'll want to help catch the guy. It won't be dangerous. They'll have police protection."

"And despite what I said about profile—and I meant it—" Thorne put in, "—one thing we do know is that we're dealing with an obsessive individual. If Tessa's right about the birthday rhyme—and however wacky it is, Hermin thinks she's spot on—the targets have to be killed in order. Bonnie Gay should be safe, because she has to die on a Sunday. And Lindsay Cramer will theoretically be safe, too, till midnight tonight. It's only Friday's child—Rosemary Mackintosh or whoever—who's in real danger."

"So what happens now?" Tessa was fidgeting, glancing at her watch.

"You get back to the targets. Keep them sweet till Mayhew arrives, and I'm ready to talk to them. I'll get the Fairview thing set up."

Steve wasn't happy. "You don't want me at Fairview, do you?"

Thorne shook his head. "It's Tessa's baby. She can look after it."

"Right. I'm going after the last two on the list," Steve was saying. "Concentrate on them."

He thinks we should both be doing that. He thinks I'm endangering the stake-out.

It was Thorne's decision.

"If we can cross the last two off the list, the stake-out's looking good," said Thorne. "The reenactment thing—well, you never know. And it'll keep the targets busy for a while. Stop them climbing the walls."

Keep Tessa out of our hair. Help her shoot herself in the foot. What's wrong with you? You got what you wanted.

They think I'm unstable. Those flowers . . .

Forget it.

Seventeen

The stage was set for the reenactment, compliments of Inspector Thorne, by the time Tessa arrived at Fairview with Lindsay Cramer and Rosemary Mackintosh in the back of her car, and Bonnie Gay in the front. The grand wrought-iron entrance gates were locked and hung with a sign noting that the house was closed for urgent repairs, and apologizing to thwarted visitors for any inconvenience. As instructed, Tessa drove around to the back, where some far less grand wire security gates swung open to receive her car.

Glancing in the rear-vision mirror, Tessa saw the plainclothes policewoman who had opened the gates push them shut behind the car and click the padlock in place. Thorne's orders had been precise, it seemed. His attention to detail was impressive.

Tessa parked in a brick-paved courtyard where four other cars already stood. One car was small, white and gleaming. Mrs. Sparrow's, no doubt. The other three were the unmarked police cars that had brought in Marty Mayhew and the rest of Thorne's troops. Around the edges of the courtyard were an aluminum toolshed, several garbage bins, a wheelbarrow, and a huge pile of mulch. A line of poplars screened the area from the rest of the garden.

"There used to be stables here," Bonnie chirped brightly as she scrambled out of the car. "But they burned down. Kids set them on fire, apparently. Isn't it awful?"

Tessa murmured something appropriate. Rosemary and Lindsay said nothing. They slid from the car themselves and hovered beside it, as though unwilling to move away from its protection.

Thorne, calm, succinct, and surprisingly sympathetic, had briefed them before they left for Fairview, and Bonnie had been talking compulsively almost from the moment he finished. Most people would be sobered by hearing that they were almost certainly a serial murderer's target. Lindsay Cramer and Rosemary Mackintosh certainly had been. Lindsay stiffened, and the shadows under his watchful eyes grew darker. Rosemary pressed her hand to her mouth to stifle her small, horrified, protesting exclamation.

But after a single moment's stunned silence, Bonnie Gay rallied, and the flow of irrelevant chatter began.

She's as scared as they are. It's her way of coping, Tessa told herself. But Bonnie's determination figuratively to whistle in the dark was playing havoc with everyone's already raw nerves.

Tessa ushered her charges through the back entrance. It led to a dark little scullery where no doubt years ago a succession of miserable teenage kitchen maids had spent dreary hours washing up after the Fairley dinners. Now it was cluttered with bright-blue plastic buckets, cleaning rags, and damp, stiffening mops.

"Straight through," said Bonnie, taking charge with the pleased condescension of the only aficionado in a group of helpless amateurs. She led them past a huge old kitchen now equipped with the needs of the Fairview Volunteers ladies who served the Devonshire Teas on weekends, through a maze of corridors and on to the front rooms of the building.

In the marble-paved reception hall, small, murmuring knots of people and two isolated individuals awaited them.

Dee Suzeraine was there with her video camera, chatting with a couple of female police officers—one Asian-looking, in a pink dress, one with long red hair, wearing a hat. They were the closest approximations to Jasmine Ho and Tracey Fernandez that Thorne could come up with in the time available. Another couple of constables, a man and a woman who were supposed to represent Lloyd Greely and his wife, stood looking at one of the paintings.

Ghosts.

Very much apart from the police presence, Mrs. Sparrow,

looking very ruffled, was sitting stiffly behind her reception desk, no doubt to reinforce her official position and to separate herself from the intruders. Closing Fairview to the public on one of its officially open days must have been anathema to her, Tessa thought, and having the place invaded by the police, and by a group of dubious characters who had had the bad taste to get themselves involved with a murderer, was painful.

Just as isolated, though in bizarre contrast, was Marty Mayhew, who was leaning against a wall, tattoo well in evidence, looking tough, brooding, streetwise, and unconcerned. Out of his element, his sweetness and simplicity were well hidden. He nodded and half smiled when he saw Tessa, but his eyes moved quickly from hers to flick over the faces of her companions.

"There he is," Bonnie whispered piercingly and unnecessarily.

Tessa led her group over to where Marty stood and introduced them to him. Marty and Lindsay shook hands with masculine mutters. Rosemary smiled anxiously and murmured that she was pleased to meet . . . then stopped abruptly, as if realizing the situation was inappropriate to conventional greetings. Bonnie looked up at Marty with her head on one side, and giggled coyly. She was plainly thrilled by this gorgeous, dangerous-looking boy, so different from most of the men she bumped up against in her daily life.

These were people who never otherwise would have met. They'd been thrust together by circumstance, like people trapped in a lift, or passengers on a hijacked aircraft. All were gripped by a terrible tension that manifested itself in different ways, but was so palpable that it made the air difficult to breathe.

There was an awkward silence.

"Well, what happens now?" Bonnie asked, adjusting her glasses as if preparing for action.

Indeed.

This is Tessa's baby.

It's not how I imagined it.

"The idea is to just do what you did on the afternoon of the 9th of September," Tessa said carefully. "Bonnie, that means you're at the desk for some of the time, and outside for a while. But mostly you're in the office."

Bonnie wrinkled her nose comically, and stole another look at Marty.

"Rosemary, Lindsay, and Marty, you come in from the front and pretend to sign the visitors' book. Rosemary first, Marty second, Lindsay third. Then all you have to do is wander around like you did that day."

"I'm not sure I can remember exactly what I did," murmured Rosemary apprehensively.

"It doesn't matter if you don't remember your movements exactly. Just do your best. Try not to take any notice of the video camera."

"Hey, we're going to be film stars. Could be your big break." Marty winked at Bonnie, who giggled.

"The people over there will be walking round with you. They're dressed a bit like—like other people who were in the house when you were. If you remember where they should be at any particular time, tell them. If you think of anything, anything at all—anyone you saw in any particular room, anything anyone did, you say so straightaway, and they'll make a note of it. All right?"

Lindsay nodded.

"It's cool," said Marty, sticking his hands in his jeans pockets and looking around impassively.

Bonnie nudged Tessa. "You'd better word up Mrs. Sparrow before we start, Tessa," she whispered, with the air of one giving timely advice to a forgetful colleague.

Tessa controlled her irritation. "Yes," she said. "Come on then. Everyone ready?"

You sound like a kindergarten teacher.

They trooped over to where Mrs. Sparrow was sitting and Tessa did another round of introductions.

Mrs. Sparrow was very much on her dignity. She was aloof with Bonnie Gay, whose betrayal over the visitors' book had not been forgotten, and whose unexpected leap into prominence she seemed to resent. She allowed herself to be introduced to Marty Mayhew, so obviously not out of the top drawer, with barely concealed distaste. She patronized Rosemary Mackintosh till even Rosemary showed signs of restlessness. But when she heard Lindsay's name, her eyes sharpened till she looked like her namesake bird darting after a dropped breadcrumb.

"Lindsay Cramer! For heaven's sake, you must be George and May Cramer's son . . . Cramer's Furniture!" she exclaimed.

"That's right," murmured Lindsay. He turned away slightly, but Mrs. Sparrow wasn't going to be put off so easily.

"I had no *idea* you'd been to Fairview. I would have shown you around myself," she enthused. "Your mother and I worked together on a Red Cross committee at one time. Not long before your poor father died. I was *devastated* when I read he'd passed on. What a tragedy that was for you, dear."

Lindsay admitted that it was.

She lowered her voice. "And now you're mixed up in all this. How dreadful for you. I'm finding it terribly stressful myself."

Mass murder was not the sort of thing people of their sort were used to, she implied. As opposed, presumably, to others less gently brought up.

Lindsay, obviously extremely uncomfortable, aware of Marty Mayhew's cynical regard and Bonnie's avid interest, murmured politely again, and glanced at Tessa with something like desperation.

"I think we should start," Tessa said, rising to the occasion. She marshaled the waiting troops, and the reenactment began.

Bonnie went into the office behind the reception desk. She closed the door behind her, but every now and then the door would open a crack as she peered out. Tessa thought of trying to stop her, but decided there was no real point.

Rosemary moved self-consciously to the desk and pretended to write in the visitors' book while Mrs. Sparrow sat staring into space and smiling thinly. Rosemary then drifted away, looking anxious and somewhat at a loss.

Marty slouched forward to take his turn, his thumbs tucked into the pockets of his jeans. Mrs. Sparrow went on staring into space. Marty waited a moment, then walked back over to the windows.

The moment he was gone, Bonnie Gay emerged from the office and attempted to take Mrs. Sparrow's place at the desk. She and Mrs. Sparrow then had a murmured argument, during which they both smiled, but neither would give way. Tessa intervened, explaining that the reenactment was naturally not expected to be accurate as to time. Only order.

Mrs. Sparrow huffily left the desk and went into the office, closing the door behind her with an indignant snap. Lindsay Cramer came up to the desk. Bonnie greeted him with an arch smile and a "Welcome to Fairview," and pushed the visitors' book invitingly towards him. Lindsay stood awkwardly for a few seconds, then moved away, heading for the dining room.

Bonnie smiled broadly in Marty's direction. He levered himself off the window wall and strolled towards the stairs.

This isn't working.

What did you expect?

After half an hour, Tessa was in the grip of an increasing sense of anticlimax. Lindsay, Rosemary, and Marty were self-consciously wandering around the house, obviously entirely discomposed, noticing nothing except their observers. Only Bonnie Gay seemed to have any real recollection of where people had been, or what they'd been doing, but she had been in the office for much of the afternoon, and the details she did manage to point out were trivial.

Lindsay, Rosemary, and Marty had been to the small sixth bedroom, but none of them had been there at the same time as anyone else. None of them remembered anything at all of note. As the minutes slipped by Rosemary looked sicker, Lindsay grew more and more tight-lipped, Marty more watchful.

"Bit of a washout," Dee said, grimacing in a friendly way as she passed, on her way to the dining room in pursuit of Rosemary, who had just come downstairs.

A waste of time.

Steve had said it would be. He was right. Tessa thought about him for the first time in a couple of hours. She wondered if he'd had any luck in tracing the last two people on the list.

Not letting herself think too carefully about it, she took out her phone and punched in his number. She turned away from the sight of Mrs. Sparrow, who was once again sitting disapprovingly at the reception desk, and fixed her eyes on the side windows.

"Hayden."

"It's Tessa, Steve."

"Hi. What's up?"

"Nothing. I mean, nothing's happening here. Like you said. How're you going?"

"Making progress." The voice at the other end of the phone was brusque. "I'll let you know when I've got something definite. Okay?"

"Okay."

Steve cut the connection, and Tessa was left listening to the dial tone.

He's got better things to do than talk to you.

The sound of running feet behind her. A call.

"Tessa? Tessa!"

It was Bonnie Gay. Her eyes were dilated with terrified excitement. "You'd better come. Something's wrong with Rosemary."

Tessa's heart gave a great thud.

"What is it?" called Mrs. Sparrow from the reception desk. Her chair scraped on the marble as she stood.

There were shouts from the dining room. The sounds of a scuffle.

Tessa ran. Bonnie ran with her, panting, chattering in her ear. "She started acting really weird. Now she's having some sort of fit. She's—"

Friday's child . . .

Rosemary Mackintosh was bent over a chair in the Fairview dining room, breathing strangely and muttering to herself. The red-haired policewoman in the hat was holding her by the shoulders, asking her what was wrong, asking had she eaten anything, what had she eaten? Lindsay Cramer stood looking on, horrified. As Tessa came into the room, Rosemary shouted, and threw the policewoman off, with surprising strength.

She was like a different person. Her glazed eyes stared at Tessa, recognizing nothing. Her mouth worked soundlessly.

"Call an ambulance," Tessa heard herself saying to the policewoman.

"Done," the woman said crisply.

We sound so calm.

"What is it?" puffed Mrs. Sparrow from the door.

Rosemary stumbled, fell to her knees. Her bag tumbled from her shoulder to the ground and some of the contents spilled out onto the rug. A battered wallet, keys, a hairbrush, two disposable hypodermic syringes . . .

Drugs . . .

Rosemary crawled, growling, among her belongings, her hair, wild and tangled, hanging over her face.

Marty, coming in, swore eloquently. Lindsay edged away from him.

"What's wrong with her?" squealed Bonnie, staring in repulsion.

"She needs sugar," snapped Mrs. Sparrow. "She's diabetic."

"Are you sure?" Tessa heard herself say.

"I've seen it before. Bonnie, get out of the way! Get some orange juice. Quickly!"

Bonnie darted from the room and pounded off towards the kitchen.

"She should be carrying something. They always carry something." With surprising agility, Mrs. Sparrow threw herself down beside the shoulder bag and emptied it completely. Pens, diary, another syringe, some tubes of medication, and a handful of small golden sweets twisted in cellophane scattered on the floor.

Mrs. Sparrow scooped up a sweet, tore off its wrapping, and in a second was kneeling beside Rosemary's crawling figure, trying to get the sweet into her mouth. "Have this, dear," she coaxed. "Your barley sugar. Come on. You know you have to. Into your mouth. No, that's naughty. Come on . . ."

Rosemary mumbled, shook her tousled head. "Someone hold her!" ordered Mrs. Sparrow. Tessa sprang to hold Rosemary's twisting neck and shoulders.

"Here we are, dear," said Mrs. Sparrow firmly. "You know you need it. Good girl." She forced the barley sugar between Rosemary's lips. "That's right," she cooed, holding the jaw firmly closed with her perfectly manicured, plump little hands. "Now you'll be right. Now you'll be right."

Bonnie came thundering in with a tall glass of juice. She pushed excitedly past Lindsay Cramer, Marty Mayhew, and the others gathered by the door, lurched forward, and managed to pour most of the juice over Tessa's shirt before getting it into Mrs. Sparrow's hand.

"Dear oh dear," clucked Mrs. Sparrow.

Dear oh dear.

The paramedics had come and gone. Rosemary, pale and shaky but back to her senses, thanks to Mrs. Sparrow, had refused further medical help, saying she was fine. Now she sat with her feet up on one of the Fairview couches, swathed in the bright blue tartan rug from the back of Mrs. Sparrow's car, blinking worriedly at the people gathered around her.

"I'm terribly sorry to have caused all this trouble," she said in a low voice.

"You gave us such a *fright*," babbled Bonnie, patting her arm with clumsy gaiety. "Wasn't it *lucky* that Mrs. Sparrow knew what was happening and fixed you up? How did you know, Mrs. Sparrow?"

"My husband was a diabetic," said Mrs. Sparrow, primming her lips and raising her chin as though being compelled by social obligation to admit something slightly shameful.

"Well it's lucky for Rosemary he was!" exclaimed Bonnie with astounding insensitivity. "I didn't know *what* to do. I was scared to *death*, Rosemary. I thought you were having a *fit* or something."

Rosemary's pale cheeks suffused with color. Marty grinned foolishly. Lindsay moved uneasily in his place by the door, and stared at Bonnie with dislike.

Bonnie continued, oblivious. "You were crawling round growling and—"

"We should let Rosemary have a bit of privacy now, don't you think?" Lindsay cut in, glancing at Tessa. "She should rest."

Bonnie stared at him resentfully.

"Oh, no, I'm okay now. Really," said poor Rosemary, trying to smile. "It was all my own fault. I just—I was so rattled today I forgot to eat when I should have."

"Silly girl," reproved Mrs. Sparrow. "You must look after yourself."

Rosemary nodded, swallowing. "I usually manage really well. My mother has diabetes. I inherited it from her. Two of my sisters have it too. We know how—we can manage it. Usually." She turned her head towards Tessa. "I'm really sorry," she said again. "I messed everything up."

"It doesn't matter at all," said Tessa honestly.

"Your shirt's all stained with juice. I'm really sorry—"

"Stop *apologizing*!" exclaimed Bonnie, smiling and tapping Rosemary's arm again. "You can't help having an illness, can you? I mean, you inherited it. It's not your *fault*, is it?"

Rosemary murmured something indistinguishable.

"I mean, look at me," Bonnie went on, beaming around. "I'm in the same boat. My mum and dad have always worn glasses. They're both *terribly* shortsighted. So I never stood a chance of being normal, did I?" She laughed, and looked up at Marty, adjusting her spectacles kittenishly.

"What did you get from your parents, Marty?" she dimpled.

"I wouldn't know," Marty drawled. "Never met 'em." He glanced at Lindsay Cramer challengingly, but Lindsay stared straight ahead of him, refusing to react.

Bonnie's face took on an expression of sickly sympathy. "Oh, that's so sad," she crooned. "That's awful! Oh—well, there you are, Rosemary, see? There's always someone worse off than you."

Lindsay made a small, disgusted sound, which Bonnie pretended not to hear.

"It doesn't matter how you're born, I always think," said Mrs. Sparrow in haste and with a sublime disregard for the truth. "You're what you make yourself, I always say."

"Except if you're Lindsay Cramer and inherited lots of lovely money," Bonnie said archly, looking at her fingernails.

"Just because my family has money, it doesn't mean I have," said Lindsay, with dry dignity. "All I inherited from my father was flat feet and maybe a bad heart. My father died of a heart attack. Statistically that means I'm a heart risk."

"Look on the bright side, mate," Marty murmured beside him. "The serial killer might get you first."

Bonnie giggled. Mrs. Sparrow looked shocked.

"Thorne's here," Dee muttered in Tessa's ear. "Being briefed. Out the back."

Tessa nodded. Absently she brushed herself down. Not that it really mattered how she looked. What mattered was Thorne's now almost certain knowledge that the reenactment had not only been a complete waste of time, but had nearly ended in genuine disaster.

"Will we be able to go now?" asked Lindsay quietly.

"We can't just go home," Bonnie objected. "I mean, we're *targets*, aren't we?"

"If you wouldn't mind just waiting here a minute . . ." Tessa made her escape. In one sense it was an enormous relief to leave that tension-filled room, but she wasn't looking forward to what was ahead of her.

She found Thorne standing in the old stables courtyard with a couple of plainclothes police. No doubt he'd been speedily briefed on what had occurred. He saw her and beckoned. Tessa began walking towards him, bracing herself for an explosion.

But there was no explosion. Just an icy calm, which was worse. "No new information, I gather," he said as she reached him.

"No, sir. Do you want . . . ?"

He held up a hand. "I'll expect your written report in due course—no point in wasting time talking now. I've got the gist from the others. Is Rosemary Mackintosh well enough to travel?"

"I think so."

"Is it your opinion that she's likely to take action against us for putting her under undue stress?"

"No, sir."

"Hope you're right. I'm taking the four of them back to Homicide. I'd suggest you—" his eyes flicked over her stained clothes "—go home and change. As quickly as you can, please."

"Yes, sir. Sir?"

"Yes."

"Marty Mayhew won't want to go back to Homicide. The ghost train's reopening tonight. He's rostered on at six."

"He'll be there. It's only Mackintosh I want to hold. I'll put her in sick bay." He glanced at his watch. "We've got the stake-out from four-thirty, unless Hayden comes up with anything new in the next hour."

"He still hasn't found the last two—?"

"Not that I've heard. All right. Anything else?"

Tessa hesitated. There *was* something she wanted to say. She just couldn't find the right words.

Thorne didn't wait. He turned on his heel and strode towards the back door, the plainclothes police walking in a gang behind him like a motley bodyguard.

Tessa slid into her hot car and started the engine, feeling more alone than she'd ever felt in her life. She looked back at the house, basking in the afternoon sunshine. It seemed, from this view, blank and secretive.

Get going.

But Tessa sat, tapping her fingers on the wheel, staring. The reenactment had been a washout. A total washout. Why, then, did she feel that something *had* happened in there? Something important?

Rosemary could have died.

That wasn't it.

You're kidding yourself. You can't accept that you blew it.

The gates were standing open. Tessa drove her car out into the back street. Totally preoccupied with her own thoughts, she failed to notice the old blue car parked farther along the road. Neither did she notice, as she turned for home, that it was pulling out from the curb, and following her.

Eighteen

Steve strode into the Homicide building looking at his watch. Mission accomplished, he was in a confident state of mind. They were closing in on their killer. He knew it. He felt the familiar tingle of excitement.

As he got into the lift, he realized that he hadn't rung Tessa Vance back, and swore softly under his breath. He should have rung her back. Just to show a bit of solidarity. So the reenactment was a fiasco. So what? It was worth a try. Anything was worth a try. And like Thorne said, it kept the targets from climbing the walls. Steve felt differently about the whole thing now. Less threatened. He could afford to be generous.

He'd called Thorne to tell him he'd located the last two on the list and they were out of it. But he'd forgotten to call Tessa. He grinned wryly to himself as the lift climbed. She'd be miffed now, probably. She was obviously used to more attention and hand-holding than he was providing. And she was in a mood to think all men were insensitive bastards anyway, thanks to the boyfriend.

This thought changed his mood. The girl was her own worst enemy, he told himself. She could be okay. She could certainly come up with the goods. But she had emotional problems. She let her personal life get in the way. She was erratic. She expected everyone else to put up with her moods, and gave nothing back.

By the time the lift doors opened he was ready for a brawl. What right did Tessa Vance have to get miffed, anyhow? What did she think he was, her lady's maid? At her beck and call? She'd rung him at a bad time. He couldn't talk to her in front of that poor old woman, could he? Then he hadn't thought to ring back. He'd had enough on his plate. So what?

Thorne and Dee were standing talking near the doorway to the office. There was no sign of Tessa.

Thorne looked up. His eyes were glittering with energy. His whole body was taut. You could almost see adrenaline dripping from his fingertips. "Steve! Good. So we're on our way."

"Looks like it."

"It's all set up." Thorne glanced at his watch. "Nearly three-thirty now. We should leave here in thirty minutes max, so we can get settled in. Won't be a long haul. The killer's window of opportunity is from four-thirty, when Mackintosh usually gets home, till just before six, when her mates start trailing in. That's when he'll make his move, if he follows his pattern. And that's when we'll get him."

"Where's Tessa?"

"Home changing her clothes," said Thorne curtly. "Reenactment ended up in a bun-fight. Mackintosh got sick. Did you know she was a diabetic?"

"Never said a word. What happened?"

Thorne flapped a hand dismissively. He plainly didn't want to go into details.

"Reenactment didn't give us anything, then?" Steve persisted.

"Nothing. Complete waste of time."

"It was worth trying," Dee put in. "You never know."

Thorne didn't dignify that platitude with a reply. "We'll be keeping Mackintosh here," he said to Steve. "She's agreed to swap clothes with our substitute."

"Who'd you get?"

"Young constable. Lyn Barnstable. Not a bad match, either. Younger than Mackintosh and a tad taller, but not so you'd notice from a distance. Same sort of hair. She's keen. Volunteered."

"Who'd volunteer to be bait? Likes to live dangerously, does she?" chirped Dee.

Thorne gave her a cold look. "She can look after herself, but she'll be wired. We're not taking any risks."

He looked at his watch again. "Vance should be here by the

time we leave. If she isn't, we go without her. This is time-critical." He moved towards his office, then turned back. "Thought I'd let Mayhew, Cramer, and Gay go as long as they stay put where we can keep tabs on them. Any objections?"

"They don't know about the stake-out, do they?"

"Course not. Only Mackintosh knows."

"Fair enough."

"Right. I'll get them away now." Thorne wrinkled his nose. "This place smells like a funeral parlor," he remarked. He went into his office, closing the door behind him.

Dee sniffed. "It does, you know," she said. She looked around for the source of the smell, and saw the flowers crushed into Tessa's bin.

"Gross," she said, peering at them. "Where'd they come from? Must have cost heaps. Why did Tessa chuck them?"

Steve shrugged.

Dee unashamedly fossicked in the bin. Cellophane crackled, and the cloying scent of the dying lilies rolled through the office in waves. "Hey, there's a card here," she exclaimed. "But there's nothing on it. That's weird. What kind of looney'd shell out for flowers like this and not claim the credit? Same creep who hangs up when you answer the phone, I guess."

Steve frowned slightly. And for the first time, he started to wonder.

Tessa parked her car and ran up the stairs to her flat, her keys ready in her hand, her head filled with thoughts of Fairview, punctuated by nagging demands for haste. Her hair was limp and sticky, she was enveloped in the faint smell of rotting oranges, but she wasn't aware of it. She wasn't aware of the carpet under her feet, or the blandness of the stairwell walls either. And she wasn't aware of the stealthy tread behind her.

There was something. Something I should have—

Hurry. They'll be waiting for you.

She reached her own front door, stuck the key in the lock, opened . . .

Something happened.

Her phone rang. She dragged it out of her handbag and answered anxiously, shouldering her way into the stuffy flat, sticking her key into the inside lock with her free hand.

Hurry . . .

The door was still half-open. She pushed her foot back against it, to close it.

No time . . .

"Tessa, it's Steve Hayden. Where are you?" The voice, strangely formal, came over the line.

"Home. I had to get changed. What is it?"

"Just ringing to say you'd better get a move on . . ."

The door hadn't closed. It was jammed on something. Tessa began to turn, and in that split second a shape out of her nightmares was bulging through the half-open door, her head was being wrenched to one side by a hard, gloved hand clasped over her mouth, and with terror she was feeling the cold pain of a knife point at the side of her neck.

The voice on the other end of the phone, thin, distant was still speaking. " . . . When can you get here? I'll wait for you, if—Tessa are you there?"

The door swung shut, and clicked. Locked. Deadlocked.

"You're busy, darling," said a voice in her ear. It had been five years, but the voice hadn't changed.

The knife point pushed a little harder into her neck. Stinging pain. Liquid warmth trickling down to her collar. The hand loosening from her mouth, taking the phone from her hand.

The voice again. Rough, husky, seductive. Hot breath on her cheek. "Tell him you're busy, Tessa." The phone held up so that she could speak, but he could hear what Steve said.

Tessa cleared her throat. Tears of pain stung in her eyes. "I'm busy, Steve," she whispered.

"What d'you mean busy? Speak up, I can hardly hear you." The voice at the other end of the phone was angry, disbelieving.

"I'm—busy. Can't talk . . ."

"Look, don't give me that!" Steve was really angry now. He was shouting. "You get over here fast or Thorne'll have you for breakfast. We're leaving for the stakeout in ten minutes. This is it, Tessa. Rosemary's definitely the Friday target. I finally tracked down the last two on the list. They were in the right age group, it turns out, but they're out of it. They're dead. So—"

"Dead?" Tessa gasped out the word. The shock was so great that for a second it overwhelmed her fear. She felt dizzy. It was as though the world had turned itself over.

Doesn't he know what that means?

"That's it," Steve's voice snapped. "Car accident and suicide. Statistics. Out of it. Nothing to do with this. Get over here, Tessa."

"Steve, no—" Tessa began. She broke off, gasping with pain. The knife point had jabbed. Just a little, just to remind her . . .

Brady Mumm laughed softly.

There was a moment's silence from the phone. Then Steve's voice came back, coldly angry. "Forget it. I'll handle it." Then there was nothing but the sound of the broken connection, and Brady Mumm was laughing again as he switched the phone off and tossed it onto the table, out of her reach.

Steve slammed down the phone, fuming. "Tell him you're busy, Tessa." And she'd done it! Then that low, intimate chuckle. Did she think he hadn't heard it? Did she think Steve wouldn't realize she had Brett with her? And in what circumstances? Her voice was enough. Did she have any idea how she sounded? How breathless and trembly? It was obvious what was going on. What did the silly girl think she was doing?

He was intensely uncomfortable, as well as angry. The phone call had made him feel like a Peeping Tom. An Eavesdropping Tom, more correctly. He didn't like it. He was heartily sorry he'd tried to help the stupid bitch out.

Thorne came in with Marty, Bonnie, and Lindsay in tow. They were leaving.

"You're going straight home, right?" Thorne said to Lindsay.

Lindsay nodded, swallowing.

"You can stay here if you like. Sure you don't want to change your mind?"

Lindsay shook his head. "I've got work . . . I'd rather be home."

"All right, then. I've told you that's fine. We've checked your place over. The locks have been changed. Everything's secure. Take it easy. Just keep yourself locked in. Any problem, you know where to call. We'll ring you every hour on the hour. Your guards will arrive later on tonight. They'll have identification on them. But you don't have a problem till midnight, theoretically. You do understand that, don't you?"

Lindsay nodded again. He understood. Only too well, it seemed. He was collected, but tense and pale.

"Hopefully all the precautions will be unnecessary," said Thorne, with an air of finality. He turned to Steve. "Take them down the fire stairs, will you, Steve? Let them out one at a time."

"It's like a spy movie," giggled Bonnie.

Thorne smiled blandly. He looked around. "Tessa not back yet?"

"No."

"How long does it take to change your shirt?"

Steve had no answer for that. He wasn't going to put Tessa Vance in, but neither was he going to defend her. She was on her own from here on in.

He took Bonnie, Marty, and Lindsay to the fire stairs and led them down. Their feet clattered on the concrete, echoing against the hard walls of the stairwell.

"I might come and see you at Funworld sometime," Bonnie said flirtatiously to Marty as they neared the bottom. "You're just down the road, and I *love* ghost trains."

"Anytime, babe," he said, winking at her. "I've got a room round the back. Come round and see me. Before six. I'll make sure you get a free ride."

It was automatic innuendo, as meaningless to Marty, Steve thought, as a comment on the weather, but Bonnie tittered, apparently thrilled.

A couple of cars were waiting. Marty walked out from the fire stairs and got into the first. As it sped away, Bonnie waved.

"Isn't he *awful*," she said.

"You going home, Bonnie?" Steve asked.

"No. Back to Fairview. To help Mrs. Sparrow clean up and everything. I told Inspector Thorne. He said that was *quite* okay, because I'm not in danger till Sunday. I just have to keep in touch, and not tell anyone, and someone will come and get me tomorrow." She laughed piercingly. "Oh, doesn't that sound *awful*. I mean, someone from here will come. They've changed my locks and given me new keys. Isn't that *marvelous*? I didn't have to pay for it or anything."

Lindsay's phone rang. He jumped, fumbled for it, finally managed to answer.

"See you tomorrow, then," whispered Bonnie to Steve. She tripped out into the street and climbed into the waiting car as though she didn't have a problem in the world.

"Yes, right. Yes, I see. Thanks," Lindsay was muttering. His face seemed grayer as he cut the connection. Steve saw that his hands were trembling. "The hospital," he said, in a strangled voice totally unlike his usual one. "My mother's sinking, they think. They want me to come. She's very restless. She's asking for me. I didn't expect . . ."

Confusion, shock, and fear were etched on his face. Sweat had broken out on his forehead.

Steve murmured some conventional words of sympathy, but he was surprised. Lindsay had been expecting his mother to die. Not so soon, maybe, but in the near future. And he hadn't seem particularly attached to her. Only in a conventional sense. Maybe, underneath, he wasn't such a cold fish as he seemed.

Lindsay glanced at him, obviously embarrassed to have so exposed his anxiety, and struggling to regain control of his emotions. Finally he took some deep breaths, and straightened his shoulders.

"What do you suggest I do?" he said, in an almost normal voice. "This couldn't have happened at a worse time. I should go to the hospital. I really have to go, don't I? It would look so odd if I didn't. And I should be there—when poor Mum goes. But—will I be safe?" He wiped his damp hands on his trousers and cleared his throat. "What if I have to stay for hours? Even all night? With this—this killer on the loose. Looking for me. What about the arrangements to protect me?"

He wasn't thinking of his mother's danger, but of his own. Self-preservation, Steve thought. The basic instinct.

"What do you suggest I do?" repeated Lindsay.

Steve thought rapidly. Until midnight, at least, Lindsay would be as safe in a hospital room as at home. Possibly safer, despite the changed locks. He was so scared that he could be trusted not to go wandering around the grounds unescorted, or anything like that. And with a bit of luck everything would be over in a couple of hours anyway.

"Hospital number? Ward?" he asked.

Lindsay gaped at him. He didn't understand the point.

"I want to check it's not a fake call," said Steve patiently.

Lindsay gave him the number, looking frightened again, and Steve rang. After a couple of transfers he was speaking to a tired sister, who confirmed that yes, she had just spoken to Mr. Cramer, and yes, Mrs. Cramer was sinking. They didn't expect her to last out the night. He thanked her and cut the connection.

"You can go, Lindsay," he said. "You'll be as safe in hospital as at home. Is your mum in intensive care?"

A shake of the head. "Just an ordinary private room. She told them she didn't want—heroic measures, they call it, don't they?"

"They'll let you use your mobile, then. We'll ring you on the hour, as planned. Nothing to worry about. Just don't leave the hospital without telling us. Agreed?"

Lindsay swallowed, and nodded. Already he was recovering his normal poise. Steve watched him into his car, then turned and took the fire stairs two at a time.

Thorne, with a face like thunder, was at Tessa's desk punching in a number while Dee watched uncertainly from the door.

Steve raised his eyebrows. Dee slipped over to him. "Tessa. Not here yet," she muttered. "Why didn't you call her, get her to get a move on?"

"I did. She's playing silly buggers," Steve muttered back.

Scowling, Thorne crashed down the receiver. "Vance is not

answering her home phone, and her mobile's turned off!" he said, in a dangerously low voice. "She's on duty! We need every bloody hand we have. It's appalling incompetence, or worse!"

Since this was Steve's opinion exactly, but it was against his code to say so, he said nothing at all.

Thorne looked at his watch yet again. "I'm going," he said. "You take your own car and meet as discussed. I'll deal with Vance later. Constable Suzeraine? You're coming with me, aren't you?" He stormed out of the room, leaving the air quivering behind him.

"Tessa doesn't seem to me the sort to play silly buggers," Dee hissed to Steve. "If she's not here, there's a good reason."

She hurried after Thorne, leaving Steve to think about it.

Steve glanced at Tessa's desk. Like his, it was piled with memos, files, notebooks, photographs. Days out of the office had resulted in their both losing the paper war. On an impulse, he walked over to the desk. He stood looking down, taking everything in. The top drawer was partly open, a newspaper jammed inside it. Beside the desk, in the bin, the lilies wilted in their cellophane.

The flowers with no identified sender. Why hadn't the boyfriend signed the card? Why had he sent white lilies, unrelieved by any green? Why had Tessa stuffed them in the bin, if she was going to make up with the guy only a few hours later? Women were unpredictable—Tessa Vance particularly so, in his limited experience with her, Steve thought ruefully. But could they change their minds so fast?

Why did the boyfriend—this Brett—hang up when she answered? He hadn't hung up when she answered in the pub. And hadn't she seemed surprised that it was him? She'd been embarrassed, sure. But hadn't she seemed just that—embarrassed? It was nothing like the grim silence with which she'd greeted the hang-up calls.

He reached for the folded newspaper stuck in the desk drawer. She'd kept it. Why had she kept it?

He pulled it out and scanned the outside pages—the pages she'd been reading when she folded the paper and put it away.

Stories about banks, about water pollution, about a little kid who was lost and found in a shopping center, about some politician spouting from the safety of his cushy office about law and order, about the release of Brady Mumm—that was an ironic juxtaposition if ever there was one.

Brady Mumm was guilty as sin. Everyone knew it. It wasn't Steve's division who'd gotten him, but the word had gone round. Mumm's defense was smart, though. He'd conned the jury, and the judge was sympathetic. What hope did law and order have if merchants like him killed when they felt like it, and got five years?

Tessa had doodled on the margin of the page near the Mumm story. Triangles. Question marks. She'd been reading it. Steve looked at Mumm's picture. Smiling.

Still staring at it, he rang Tessa's mobile number again. One more time. Recorded message. Her phone was switched off. Still switched off.

"Tessa doesn't seem the sort to play silly buggers to me," Dee had said.

And in a way, she wasn't. He could see that.

Steve wasn't used to introspection. It wasn't a thing he generally found useful. But now he found himself thinking— if he hadn't heard all the gossip, all the stories . . . if Tessa Vance hadn't been so young, so—well—beautiful looking . . . if Tessa Vance had been his partner for a long, long time, a person he respected, who had a track record—how would he have interpreted the way she was behaving?

He would have thought there was something wrong. Badly wrong.

Not a just broken relationship. God knows, Homicide was full of them.

Something else.

If he'd heard a breathy, trembling voice at the other end of the phone, obediently repeating, "I'm busy," and someone laughing . . .

He scrabbled among the papers on the desk. Fortunately the woman was even untidier than he was. He was sure what he was looking for would still be there.

Nineteen

Tessa was living her nightmare. Brady Mumm had found her gun in her handbag. He'd dropped it through the living room window, into the bushes below.

"Don't want you getting any silly ideas," he said, nudging the knife into her neck.

He'd backed her through the flat—slowly, slowly—fingering her furniture, her possessions, her clothes. He'd laughed when Thorne rang and left a curt message on the answering machine. They'd been through every room.

He invades their most private places . . .

He's going to kill me.

Talk to him.

But he was talking to her. Telling her how he'd waited for this. How he'd thought about it for five years. In jail, where she'd put him.

Don't say he deserved it.

"It wasn't only me," Tessa whispered.

"You're the one I remember." His breathing was faster now. She could feel it, hot, on her cheek. "The babe in uniform. Little Miss Perfect. You'd made up your mind about me. That was so obvious. Bitch! You wanted my balls on a plate. I promised myself. She'll learn. One day, I'll have her screaming."

"You're free now, Brady," she said, in as level a voice as she could manage. "You're out. Think about what you're doing. You kill me, and you're history. I've told people about your calls. And the flowers. People know."

The knife moved across her neck, cutting the skin a little more. She winced in pain. Mumm laughed.

"Come up in the world, haven't you? Out of uniform. Homicide now, isn't it?" he said, in that soft, husky voice. "Might have taken me a bit of time to track you down, except for seeing you on the box Monday night. All dolled up, but I would have known you anywhere, bitch."

They were back in the living room now. He pushed her against the wall, enjoying her fear. Out of the corner of her eye she saw her mobile phone lying on the table. Just out of reach.

You could distract him. Get to it.

It's turned off. Would take too long to . . .

"You've got a serial killer," crooned Mumm. "Bit of luck for me. He's been keeping you on the hop, hasn't he? Running you round. It's all been in the papers. Made it really easy to keep an eye on you. Seems like this bloke's got the right idea. He puts a knife through their stomachs, right? I like the sound of that."

I'm going to die.

Talk. Talk him out of it.

"That isn't all he does. You don't think that's all he does, do you?" Tessa said, thinking rapidly, keeping her voice level. "You know the police always keep things back. There were lots of things you could never duplicate."

He blinked at her lazily, smiling.

"You think I'm going to try a copycat? Think I'm that dumb?"

She had thought so. She floundered, not knowing what to say.

He laughed, relishing her confusion. "Your detective boyfriend was dark with you, wasn't he?" he sniggered. "The boss, too, by the sound of it. They've given up on you. They're going to some stake-out. So we've got lots of time. And no one's going to find you till tomorrow."

"They'll know it was you, Brady," Tessa said, keeping her voice level.

"How could it be me? I'm home right now, asleep upstairs in my dear old mum's house. She's drunk as a skunk and wouldn't know if her ass was on fire, but she'll swear blind I was there."

"They'll investigate. They'll go straight to you. Because of all the people I've told. But if you go now, I won't tell anyone. Not a soul."

He laughed, his face close to hers.

"I want to do it slowly," he said.

Distract him. Break his grip. Get away. Down the hall. Lock yourself in the bathroom. Scream out the window. Do it!

Never make it to the bathroom. Front door closer.

Distract him. Break his grip. Get to the front door.

Front door deadlocked.

One second to unlock. Do it. Got to do it. That or die.

Distract him . . .

The house phone rang, shrill. Startled, Mumm half turned. The knife hand relaxed.

Now!

Tessa twisted down, around. Still in his grip she hurled herself at the table, stretching out her free arm, her fingers scrabbling for the mobile phone.

"We can't come to the phone right now . . ." Absurd, disembodied, her own voice mocked her from the answering machine.

Mumm was hauling her in, grinning, snarling.

She yelled savagely as swung her free arm around and slammed the phone into the side of his face with all her strength.

He roared, staggered, half fell, clutching at his eye and nose. His grip loosened . . .

Go!

She was tearing herself free, running for the door, turning the key, pulling. She had the door open. He was stumbling towards her, blood oozing from his nose, his right eye half closed. He was choking with pain and fury, already grabbing for her.

Out! Run!

One second more.

She was turning the key in the lock again, to deadlock. She was wrenching the key free. He had the hem of her jacket in his clutching fingers. But she was out, out, through the open door, the key in her hand. She was slamming the door behind her, locking him in.

Got you, you bastard!

Did she scream it, or think it? She'd never know. She tried to run, and couldn't move. Her jacket was holding her. The hem was jammed in the door, pinning her to the wood that was shaking and reverberating with his pounding, howling, cursing from inside.

She struggled out of the jacket and left it hanging limply, upside down, empty arms trailing to the floor.

Call for help. Call Steve.

No one home in the flat opposite. She ran down the stairs, fruitlessly pushing buttons on the phone in her hand, trying to get a connection. Static. Tiny lights flickering.

I've killed it.

It died for you.

She started to laugh. No one home downstairs. Her right arm was numb to the elbow. She reached the ground floor and ran outside, punching at her phone, shaking it. Finally, a static-filled connection. She gasped the address. Urgent! Urgent! She ran to the fence-line, snorting with laughter. She wasn't hysterical, she told herself. Not really. Just so glad, so glad to be alive. But Steve—she had to get Steve. Or Thorne. Or someone. She had to tell them . . .

A police car passed Steve, sirens blaring. Behind it was another. Unconsciously he speeded up as soon as they'd passed. The sirens made him uneasy. He saw the cars make a left-hand turn a block ahead. It crossed his mind that he must be very near Tessa's place now. In fact, the cars had turned into what could be her street.

The sirens stopped. He felt tension growing in his chest. He pushed his foot down, straining his eyes to read the sign ahead. Adamson Avenue. It was Tessa's street. He rounded the corner, tires squealing.

The police cars had stopped in front of a block of apartments. Police were running to where a small, bedraggled figure sat on a low wall.

Tessa. What . . . ?

Steve pulled up, and leaped out of the car. Tessa hadn't noticed him yet. She was focused on the cops. Her neck was bleeding. Blood had soaked into the collar and breast of her shirt. He could hear her voice, high and clear. " . . . Brady Mumm. Locked in my flat. Thirty-five. Third floor. Too high to jump," she was saying crisply. "Clear the building. Get help. He's violent, dangerous. He's got a knife."

Three of the police ran for the building. The one that remained, a beefy sergeant, started speaking rapidly into a radio phone.

Tessa looked up and saw Steve. Her eyes widened and she seemed to go into fast-forward. She jumped up and thrust a door key into the sergeant's hand. "I've got to go," she gabbled. "Sorry. Tell them it's forcible entry, assault with a deadly weapon, attempted murder."

She rushed up to Steve. "Where have you been?" she snapped. "Where's Thorne?"

He couldn't believe it. Was she crazy? She looked it—tousled, bloody, wild-eyed. She must be in shock.

"Thorne's at the stakeout," he said. "What's been going on here, Tessa? What's happened to you?"

She was shivering, despite the heat. She'd lost her jacket somewhere, and her stained shirt was hanging out over her skirt. He pulled off his own jacket and put it round her.

The beefy sergeant finished on the phone and came lumbering towards them.

"Where's Rosemary Mackintosh?" Tessa demanded.

"Safe. In sick bay at the station," he said. "Tessa—"

"Come on. We have to go," she cried desperately. "Where are your car keys? Oh, just wait while I get my gun."

The sergeant came up to them, frowning suspiciously. "You can't go anywhere at this point, Miss, I'm sorry," he said. "Could you show me some identification, please?"

She ran her hands furiously through her sticky hair. "My wallet's in my jacket upstairs, and the jacket's jammed in the door," she said. "I'm Senior Detective Tessa Vance. You'll have to take my word for it."

Then she was off and running, plunging into the shrubbery beside the apartment block.

Steve showed the sergeant his own identification. "I can vouch for her," he said. "She's my partner."

"Crikey," said the sergeant eloquently.

Tessa emerged from the bushes in a shower of leaves. She had a gun in her hand. She beckoned to Steve and began pelting towards his car.

"I'll have to go with her," said Steve urgently, already starting to move.

Tessa tucked the gun into the waistband of her skirt and leaped into the car. It roared to life.

"Better you than me," the sergeant said.

Steve ran. By the time he reached the car, Tessa had turned it round. He pulled her door open.

"Get out," he said firmly.

"We've got to—"

"I'll drive." No way was he going to trust her with his car or his life, in the state she was in.

He half expected her to object, but she didn't. She slid out of the car and ran round to the passenger side. Steve got behind the wheel himself with some relief.

"Where are the others?" she demanded as she climbed in. "Bonnie, Marty, Lindsay? Have you got them somewhere safe?" He noticed that as she buckled up her seat belt she favored her left hand.

He decided it was best to humor her. She was all vibed up, and she was in the mood for asking questions, not answering them. He drove to the corner and waited to turn right. "Bonnie's back at Fairview. Marty's at Funworld. Lindsay's at the hospital. They rang to say his mum was dying."

"What? Oh, Steve—"

"It's okay. I verified it. He's scared to death but he'll be safe enough there, poor bastard. I'm calling him every hour. Oh, speaking of which . . ." Steve glanced at his watch. It was three minutes to five. Briefly he thought of the stakeout. Had anything happened yet? He hoped it hadn't. Not yet. He wanted to be there.

He passed his phone to Tessa. "It's a bit early, but call him now, will you?" he said, and gave her the number.

*   *   *

Lindsay Cramer sat unmoving in the quiet hospital room and stared into space. The double-glazed window faced west, and the yellow curtains had been drawn to shield the air-conditioned room from the fierceness of the lowering sun. The curtains glowed, and they, like the windows, were warm to the touch, but the rest of the room was a twilight world, neither dark nor light, neither hot nor cool. And his mother lay in the bed at its center, neither dead nor alive.

She lay still, very still, on her side. Her shallow breathing hardly moved the stiff white sheet that covered her small, thin body. She looked almost like a child. Her hair was still dark. Even her face seemed smoother than it had for years. A monitor above her head registered her heartbeat with thready lines, but it made no sound. She was lying almost flat. They did that with the dying. He remembered reading that somewhere.

She'd been semiconscious when he arrived. Her head was moving from side to side on the pillow, and she was mumbling fretfully. It was hard to hear exactly what she was saying. They said she was saying "my son." But he thought maybe she was just saying "the sun," because the strong light from the window was shining in her eyes. They preferred the more touching explanation, but he noticed that they drew the curtains anyway, just after that, and she seemed to settle. But she'd seemed to take comfort, too, from holding his hand, and shortly afterwards she'd drifted into this state that should have looked like sleep, but didn't.

Since then he'd just sat and waited. He felt he was in suspension. As though he was outside time. He had never liked just waiting. But there were times when waiting was all you could do. And he felt safe in the golden-dim room. He vaguely remembered the fear that had gripped him not so long ago—in that gray stairwell at the police station. It seemed foolish now.

He glanced at the peaceful figure in the bed. He felt he should be feeling more. He should have more of a sense that something momentous was about to occur in his life. He'd thought he would feel more, when the time finally came. But somehow he didn't. It was strange.

Almost certainly he would, afterwards. Human beings weren't machines, as he often told his clients. You couldn't always predict their emotional reactions accurately. And sometimes it took months for stressful events to be reflected in their behavior.

He glanced at his watch. Wearily he stood up, picked up his phone, and went outside, into the wide, vinyl-smelling corridor with its cheery mass-produced paintings on the walls.

He suspected they'd forget to ring on the hour. That they'd get tied up, or excited over something, and just forget. Ring at ten past, twenty past, or whenever they remembered. The thought filled him with a mixture of panic and irritation.

But they rang early. The trill of the phone made him jump. It seemed so loud in the silent corridor. He answered.

It wasn't Steve Hayden. It was the woman, Tessa Vance. She was in a car. He could hear the sound of the motor, and traffic. She was asking if everything was okay.

"Yes, thanks," he said. "Yes, I'm at the hospital. I'm fine. . . . No, there's no change. . . . At six. All right. Thank you."

She said goodbye and cut the connection. The sounds of the outside world snapped off. He was alone again.

"He's fine. But I can't understand how you could have him go off on his own. Him or any of them," Tessa said, biting her lip. "I mean, why did you?"

"Why not? That was always the plan. You know that," Steve muttered, concentrating on the road. The traffic was heavy.

"It's so risky. Putting all our eggs in one basket." Her face was puckered with anxiety. "Where are you going? You're not going to the stakeout, are you? We should go to the hospital. Or—Lindsay's okay, so maybe we should go to Fairview first. Pick up Bonnie, then—"

"What are you on about? Of course we're going to the stakeout. We were supposed to be there half an hour ago."

"Call Thorne and tell him—"

"I can't call. Radio silence. And there's no point. No point in chasing after the others. It's Rosemary who counts. It's Friday.

It'll be Friday till midnight, right? And it's only just after five now. Rosemary's the only one under the gun." Suddenly Steve had had enough. "Look, you're the one who was so keen on that bloody rhyme," he said, through gritted teeth. "You're—"

"But that's all changed now, hasn't it?" she interrupted impatiently.

He was almost overwhelmed by a wave of hot anger. Recklessly he pulled the car over to the curb and screeched to a halt.

"Why?" he demanded, turning in his seat to face her. "What's changed? What's wrong with you, you bloody maniac?"

She stared at him.

"Didn't you tell me those last two people you traced were in the right age group, but dead?" she said blankly.

"Yes," he said. "But that was months ago. Car accident. Suicide. That's got nothing to do—"

"It's got everything to do with it. Lloyd Greely's wife had an accident, too, remember? An electrical accident at home. And she was in her twenties."

"So?"

She ran her fingers through her hair. "Don't you *see*?" she exclaimed, her voice rising. "At Fairview on the 9th of September there were a total of ten people who were in their twenties. Only three months later, *six* of those ten are dead. And it would have been seven, if Marty hadn't taken his girlfriend out instead of working. Seven out of ten, Steve. Three to go."

Steve leaned over the wheel, staring through the windscreen. His assumptions were doing somersaults. He hadn't thought about it that way. He honestly hadn't. Nor had Thorne. Why hadn't he seen it?

He knew why. He'd been too busy working at crossing the last two people off the list. Too pleased when he managed to do it. Too taken up with plans for the stakeout. Wanting action. An end to it.

"You're saying the deaths are all connected," he said slowly. "The accidents, and the suicide, were homicides that weren't picked up. And the serial killings . . ." He turned to look at her.

She nodded, simmering with tension. "That's it. We've been conned. The serial killings aren't real serial killings at all! The whole Monday's child rhyme thing's a fake. You always said it was dodgy—because you could make almost every line of the rhyme relate to just about anyone. Well, you were right. That's why the killer chose it. He chose his targets, and then he found a way to link them. The rhyme at Fairview and Bonnie Gay's name probably gave him the idea."

"It's crazy."

"That's the point, Steve. It's crazy—but the killer isn't. Not in the usual sense. The killer's just using all the serial killer trappings to fool us, put us off the scent. We listen to Dolf Hermin's profile, we look at all the signs and symbols. Eventually we work out about the rhyme. We run round looking for a psychopath. But the killer's not crazy. Not crazy like that, anyway. He's got a reason for what he's doing, Steve. He just wants all these people dead."

He banged his hands on the wheel. He couldn't cope with it. "Why would anyone want to kill ten unrelated people who went to Fairview on a certain day, for God's sake?"

"Because they saw something? Heard something?"

Steve shook his head. "It can't be that. You know it can't. It's only people in their twenties who've been targeted. It's out of the question that something happened and only people of a certain age saw it."

They stared at one another.

"Well, I don't know what the reason is," Tessa said finally. "All I know is, the order they die in doesn't really matter. It never mattered. And that means that all of them are in danger. Right now. And we're just sitting here . . . Will you drive, please?"

Steve swore, put on his indicator, and waited for a gap in the traffic. "Listen. We've got to think this through logically," he said as calmly as he could. "I see what you're saying. You could be right—okay, okay, you probably are right. It's a matter of what we do about it." He saw an opportunity and swung out onto the road again.

"We go to Fairview—"

"We don't. We go to the stakeout."

"Steve!"

He held up a hand to silence her. "Just listen. We don't have to panic. This merchant's only faking the serial killing thing. Right. But he doesn't know we've caught on to that, does he? So he's going to go on according to plan, acting the part, killing the targets in order, isn't he?"

He glanced across and saw that she was biting her lips, but slowly nodding.

"All right," he said. "So he's still going to go after Rosemary Mackintosh today. And that means the stakeout will trap him. Right?"

"Yes." Tessa was calming. "Yes. Right. Okay. We go to the stakeout."

Twenty

Tessa let herself sink back into her seat. Steve's logic had settled her, drained away her panic and sense of urgency. But her strength seemed to have gone down the plug-hole with everything else. Suddenly she felt as limp as a rag doll. She became aware of her throbbing arm, and rubbed it, wincing. She looked down at her shirt. It was stiff with blood and orange juice. She remembered the events in her apartment almost with surprise. "I'm a mess," she said ruefully.

"Listen, why didn't you tell me about Brady Mumm?" Steve demanded abruptly. "No wonder you've been jumpy. You should've had protection."

She shrugged and looked out the window. "I didn't want to cry wolf. I wasn't sure there was a problem."

"That's no excuse. You still could've told me. We're supposed to be partners," he snapped.

She swung round to face him. "You haven't been acting like we were partners," she said tightly. "You've been acting like I'm some addle-brained idiot who's been foisted on you and who you don't like and don't trust."

This was so uncomfortably close to the truth that Steve could find nothing to say.

"And this afternoon you just hung up on me." Her voice was dangerously quiet now. "Why did you do that, Steve? Why didn't you come straight over? Surely you could tell there was someone with me?"

He hesitated for a second too long. She lifted her chin and stared straight ahead of her, a dark red flush staining her cheeks.

"You didn't come because you thought the man with me was Brett," she said. "I know that's what you thought. Don't bother to deny it. But don't start preaching to me about being partners, either. All right?"

She bit her lip and turned her head to look out the side window again.

There was a short, deadly silence. Finally Steve cleared his throat. "I won't deny it," he said, his eyes on the road. "I did think that. For a while. But then—I changed my mind."

He glanced at her. Rigid shoulders. The tousled back of her head. Was she even listening?

"I changed my mind," he said more loudly. "All right? Why do you think I drove over there? For the good of my health?"

No answer.

"I could've gone straight to the stakeout. Thorne *told* me to go straight to the stakeout. But I didn't. I rang Bridget Murphy. She told me about Mumm. Then I was worried about you. I had to see if you were okay. Look, so I made a mistake. You can hardly blame me, the way you were going on. Can you?"

"Yes," she said. "Anyone who knows me—"

He lost his temper. "Well, I don't know you, do I, Tessa? I've known you less than a week. And I'm not a bloody mind reader."

"Don't shout at me!"

"I'm not shouting. You're shouting. Look, I've apologized. That's all I can do. Take it or leave it."

Again, silence hummed between them.

Arrogant pig.

No, he's not. You're the one being arrogant. Why should he take you on trust?

If I'd been a man he would have.

That's life.

It's not fair.

Nothing's fair.

She glanced at him. He was frowning, staring at the road. He wasn't going to speak again. She could see it in the set of his mouth.

Your move.

"Thank you for apologizing," she said primly. "I appreciate it. And I'm sorry I didn't tell you about Brady Mumm. It was a mistake."

He acknowledged the words with a nod. She hadn't expected more. But she noticed his mouth relaxed slightly, and the hands on the wheel lost their white-knuckled look.

She laid her head back and closed her eyes. Her left arm throbbed. The hum of the car engine filled her ears. Smooth, comforting. The nightmare that had been Brady Mumm had proved real, and been defeated. She didn't have to think about it, or fear it, or keep silent about it any more. Relief rolled through and over her in a soft, warm wave.

At the stakeout, they'd catch the killer. Maybe, even now, he was in custody. The targets were all safe. Friday's child, Saturday's child, Sunday's child. Safe. Everything was going to be all right.

When Steve next looked at her, she was asleep.

The rambling old two-story house that Rosemary Mackintosh shared with four others was already deeply shadowed by the massive cypresses that stood between it and the sun. A white van decorated with lilac daisies was parked across the road. A man sat in the driver's seat, his head lolling back, his cap tipped over his eyes. In the back of the van, Thorne, Dee, and two uniformed constables listened to amplified chinking and clattering and the chirping of small birds.

A young woman wearing a tracksuit and carrying two shopping bags walked along the footpath towards the van. When she reached it, she put down her bags and flexed her cramped hands. At the same time she spoke. Her low voice drifted through the ventilation grille. "All quiet so far, sir. No one's been in or out."

"He's in the house already, then. He must be," said Thorne.

"What's he waiting for?" muttered one of the constables.

"Have you sighted Vance or Hayden?" said Thorne in the direction of the grille.

"No, sir," came the soft reply.

Thorne swore under his breath.

The young woman picked up her bags again, and moved on.

In the kitchen of the house, her ears alert to any sound, Lyn Barnstable was making tea. Lyn Barnstable never drank tea or coffee, believing caffeine to be a poison she could do without, but Rosemary always had tea when she came home, and just now Lyn was Rosemary.

She'd opened the window, and the sounds of sparrows floated into the room. Otherwise, the house was silent. She stood at the window, dunking the tea bag up and down in a mug of hot water, being Rosemary, and waiting for the phone to ring.

The kitchen was spacious and inconvenient, in the old style. There was little bench space, and a lot of floor. Six mismatched chairs stood carelessly around a wooden table scattered with newspapers, toast crumbs, empty mugs, teaspoons, pens, a half-full ashtray, and jars of jam, honey, and peanut butter with the lids only half–screwed on. The ancient round-shouldered refrigerator had been painted green. and reminder notes, printed notices about garbage, and cartoons cut from magazines clung to it, held down by fridge magnets advertising real estate agencies, a vet, and a hardware chain.

The people who lived in the house presumably liked the kitchen the way it was, but it wasn't to Lyn's taste. It smelled of cooking and tobacco smoke. The clutter irritated her. The lifestyle it indicated—unstructured, casual, disorganized, self-indulgent—was the reverse of the one she found congenial.

The phone was on the table, with all the other mess. Its long cord trailed away, tangling, across the floor to the point on the nearest wall. It had to ring soon. She knew it. She wasn't afraid, but her stomach was knotted with tension as she took her mug to the table and sat down with her back to the door. This was her first real taste of police work as she'd imagined it. Everything else so far had been routine. She wanted to make a good job of it. Do it perfectly.

As a sign of her commitment she took a sip of the weak black tea. The sparrows chirped in the cypresses outside the window. She stared at the phone. Waiting.

*   *   *

Marty Mayhew was struggling into his skeleton costume in his room behind the ghost train, when his phone rang. He cursed in frustration. He didn't have time to take a call.

He'd nipped out to the promenade after the cops dropped him off at Funworld. He wanted to see Val, and there were a few things he needed anyhow. He'd thought seeing Val would make him feel better, but it hadn't. She'd been in one of her moods. He'd gotten back just before five, only to find that Laurie, the new guy Jacko had dug up to replace Pete Grogan, had pissed off without finishing his shift, and Jacko was off his face because the punters weren't getting their final thrill. Soon as he saw Marty, he yelled at him to change and get inside, as fast as he could.

Marty didn't want to do it. He wasn't supposed to start till six. He'd been looking forward to a few quiet moments, after the day he'd had. But he knew he had to oblige. He wasn't management's favorite boy at the moment. It was only because of Jacko that Marty still had a job. He couldn't risk getting Jacko offside. Not that he expected to work on the ghost train forever. But for now, without this job, this place, he'd be stuffed.

Why did the bloody phone have to ring now?

It didn't occur to Marty just to ignore it. The phone rang, you answered it. That was the way it was. He pushed his hands hurriedly through the tight wrist-bands of the costume, and snatched up the receiver.

The voice on the other end of the line was something of a surprise. Not an unpleasant surprise. He hadn't expected it, that's all.

"G'day," he said. "Yeah, I've just come in. How'd you get this number?"

He listened.

"No—'course I don't mind. I was going to call you, as a matter of fact. Soon as I found out *your* number."

Again he paused to listen.

"Yeah," he said, after a moment. "But I wasn't sure if you . . .

Yeah. How about that? . . . Yeah, that'd be good. But I have to work now. . . . Yeah, so did I. But I have to start early."

The person at the other end of the line spoke again. Marty thought for a moment.

"Yeah, why not?" he said finally. "Come over. Give me— half an hour. Yeah. Five-thirty. Behind the ghost train. There's a back path that'll take you straight here. You can get onto it just behind this ride called Go-Go Jalopies. You can't miss it. Door'll be unlocked. Make yourself at home. I'll work a bit, then nick out and see you. . . . No—I want to. No—it's okay. . . . No, 'course I won't. Who'd I tell? You neither. Don't want to get the sack, do I?"

He hung up, feeling quite daring and pleased with himself. He didn't usually make quick decisions. He liked to go into things slowly and carefully. Things tended to go wrong if he didn't. But he couldn't see a problem with this.

He grabbed the skull balaclava and pulled it on, full of anticipation.

Rosemary Mackintosh lay down on the camp stretcher in the Homicide sick bay, pulled the soft blue blanket up to her chin, and turned on her side. She didn't close her eyes. She couldn't sleep, even if she'd wanted to. She already felt as though she were dreaming. Awake, in a nightmare.

She felt like a hospital patient, or a prisoner. Locked in, though the door wasn't locked. The unfamiliar clothes she wore were slightly too big for her, and smelled of another woman's soap and talcum powder. She felt quite cold, despite the blanket, but she knew the room was warm because the last policewoman who came in to check on her had asked if she was too hot.

The room was dim because the venetian blinds were closed, shutting out the light. She didn't mind the darkness, anyway. There was nothing to see in the little, bare room. A table. Some paper cups. A jug of water. A phone. A metal cupboard from which they'd taken the blanket. She supposed a prison cell wouldn't be much barer than this. Except they wouldn't give a prisoner a phone.

Her thoughts drifted. That girl, Lyn Barnstable, was in her house right now, wearing her clothes, living her life. Or pretending to. Lyn Barnstable looked a bit like Rosemary, they'd said. Enough like her to stand in for her at the house, anyway. But all they had in common was hair color and basic build. In every other way they were opposites. Two sides of the same coin, maybe. Positive and negative. How did people get to be as confident and brave and self-assured as Lyn Barnstable?

In the dark, Rosemary smiled sadly. Did Lyn Barnstable ever wonder how people got to be as timid and apologetic as Rosemary Mackintosh?

Rosemary's thoughts drifted on. Lyn was in her house. The kitchen was a mess. Lyn Barnstable would probably think that was awful. But you couldn't be worried about that. It would be idiotic to worry about a thing like that now.

The luminous numbers on her watch told her that it was ten past five. The earliest parents would be starting to arrive at the center by now. They'd be packing up the little cases and the brightly colored backpacks, admiring the day's collection of paintings of rainbows, suns, and people with long legs and tiny heads, and the decorated ice cream container bristling with pasted-on paper patty cases and painted macaroni that had been started yesterday, finished today, and now could be taken home. The children would be saying goodbye. They'd be waving and kissing, calling "see you tomorrow" in high, piercing voices, or just trailing away, glad to be going.

They probably wondered where she was. Little Jamie would have missed her. And Alicia. Tailin, too. No one to hold Tailin's hand at sleep-time today. The others wouldn't have had the time, and they thought Tailin should learn to go to sleep alone anyway. But Tailin missed her mother more at sleep time than at any other. Rosemary understood that. Being on the edge of sleep made you vulnerable. Made you afraid. Made you think of things you'd rather not think of. It was the time you needed company, if you could get it. The right sort of company.

Friday's child is loving and giving.

They'd decided she was Friday's child. But they'd never asked her what day she'd actually been born. In fact it *was* a

Friday. She'd always been Friday's child, loving and giving. She'd always felt she was, from the first time she heard the rhyme as a tiny child. Her grandmother used to say it to her. Used to say it fitted her perfectly.

Sometimes she wondered if that rhyme had actually molded the way she thought about herself. If somehow it had been a self-fulfilling prophecy. She'd always thought of herself as a giver rather than as a receiver. But it hadn't been a cause of self-congratulation. It had been more like a sentence. She'd love, and give. Endlessly. But no one would ever feel they needed to love her, or give to her. Mildly affectionate, an affection that cost them nothing, because she asked for nothing, they'd take her for granted, lean on her when required, then go off and live their lives.

Like the kids at the center—they loved her, depended on her. While they were with her she was as close to them as a member of their own family. Then the time would come for them to go to school, and they'd leave. Over the next few months she'd get a letter, two letters, maybe, from her favorites, telling her of their doings, signed in huge letters, with kisses that filled the page. Sometimes they'd even come back to see her. Then after a while there'd be no more letters, no more visits. Like Puff the Magic Dragon in the song that always made her cry, she'd be forgotten.

Sometimes, when she was very tired, like now, she wondered if one day the well would dry up, and she'd have nothing more to give. Then what? Nothing coming in, nothing going out. Emptiness.

There was a click from the door. Rosemary closed her eyes. A crack of light glowed pinkly through her eyelids. Huddled under her blanket, she breathed evenly. The door softly closed again.

Mrs. Sparrow came bustling into the Fairview office and gave a little shriek.

"Oh! I thought you'd gone," she said. "I heard you in the ladies."

"I had a few things to fix up first." Bonnie Gay smiled

cheerily and went on applying fresh lipstick. "Did you want something in the office? Can I help?"

"I was just going to lock the windows." Mrs. Sparrow was flustered.

"I've done it," said Bonnie. She looked at her own face in the mirror of her powder compact, and smiled more widely. She thought she knew exactly what Mrs. Sparrow had been going to do in the office. She was going to look through the files. Try to find out if there was anything else the trustees hadn't told her about their administration of Fairview. It had been a big shock to her to find out about the visitors' book computer list.

You'd almost feel sorry for Mrs. Sparrow, Bonnie thought, if she wasn't so stuck-up and so bossy. The other Fairview Volunteers couldn't bear her. They were just too scared to stand up to her, and too scared not to vote her in as president every year. She'd made this place her own personal kingdom—queendom, Bonnie corrected herself, giggling—and she was absolutely determined to keep it.

The trouble was, she was living in the past. She was a sort of dinosaur. Just because her husband had been a judge she thought she was better than other people. Look at how she'd fallen all over that wimp Lindsay Cramer. Just because his father had money, and his mother served on committees, that didn't make *him* anything special.

Bonnie's own father was an electrician. Her mother worked part-time in a bank, and the only committee she'd ever served on was for the school fête. But that didn't make Bonnie any less important than Lindsay Cramer, whatever Mrs. Freda Sparrow might think.

Bonnie hummed to herself, putting away her lipstick and checking her face once more in the little mirror. She was pleased to see how good she looked. Her eyes were shining behind her glasses. Her cheeks were pink, and that wasn't just blusher. It had been an exciting day, and it wasn't over yet. She snapped the compact shut and glanced up to see Mrs. Sparrow eyeing her suspiciously.

"You aren't going to do anything silly, are you, dear?" said Mrs. Sparrow.

Bonnie laughed.

Twenty-one

Steve cut the engine and Tessa woke up, startled. They were parked in an unfamiliar street. "Are we there?" she asked stupidly.

"It's around the corner," said Steve. "You all right to walk?"

"Of course I am. Where's Thorne?"

"In a florist's van opposite the house. Unless it's all over." Steve got out of the car, slammed the door, and stood waiting for her.

She tucked in her shirt and pulled his jacket around her to hide the gun and some of the blood, and scrambled out of the car herself. "I'm a bit conspicuous," she muttered, joining him on the footpath.

"No one'd take you for a cop, anyhow." Steve grinned, looking her up and down. "Here," he said, "this'll fix it." He put his arm around her shoulder and drew her close to him. "We'll walk like this. We're a loving couple. Put your arm round my waist. Lean up against me. It'll hide the blood on your neck."

She did as he said. She could see it made sense. She knew it was just professional. But as they started walking she was conscious of his warm skin underneath the smooth fabric of his shirt, and the strong arm around her shoulders. It was . . .

Don't think like that.

She could hear his heart beating.

He'll get blood on his shirt.

It doesn't matter.

On the corner, a man in overalls and a hard hat was crouched over a hole in the pavement.

"Anything happened yet?" murmured Steve, as if he was commenting on the weather.

"Nup," said the man laconically.

They turned the corner and started pacing towards the florist's van parked about halfway along the street.

Something should have happened by now.

"We check in with Thorne. Let him know we're here. That's all," Steve whispered into her hair. "Don't try to tell him you think the serial killer thing's a blind. Not till after."

"Why not?"

"Too hard to explain in a couple of words. We'll only have a few seconds. He won't get it. It'll just confuse him."

They walked, slowly, clinging together, murmuring. She was taking two steps to his one. From a distance they looked like lovers, totally absorbed in one another. But they were talking about death, not love.

"If the theory's right, if we're right, what's the motive?" muttered Steve. "Whoever the killer is, he doesn't know the targets personally. Bonnie, Lindsay, Marty, Rosemary all saw the list of visitors. None of them recognized any of the names. The only victims who even knew *each other* were Jasmine Ho and Tracey Fernandez, and Lloyd Greely and his wife. Why would this merchant want to kill a whole lot of strangers just because they were in their twenties and just happened to be at Fairview on one particular afternoon?"

He's right. Why would anyone want to kill a whole lot of strangers just because they . . .

Tessa stiffened, stopped. Suddenly she'd seen a possible reason.

"Maybe he didn't want to kill them all," she said in a low voice. "Maybe he only needed to kill one. He only had one enemy. But he didn't know which."

She felt the arm around her shoulders tighten, then push slightly, urging her on. She started walking again, but her heart was beating fast in her chest. And so was Steve's. She could feel it.

"He's willing to murder ten people to get just one?" Steve's voice was grim. "You're saying he was being blackmailed or something?"

They'd almost reached the florist's van. Her thoughts were racing.

"That could be it," she said rapidly. "He didn't know who the blackmailer was, but somehow he knew they were in their twenties. He was told to leave a payment hidden somewhere at Fairview that afternoon, then leave. But he knew the blackmailer would be there to pick it up."

"He'd hang around, see who took it."

"Maybe he tried, but it didn't work. There were lots of people of the right age there. He got distracted. He would have been hiding somewhere. People got in his way, maybe. Anyway, somehow he missed seeing the pickup. So later he broke in and stole the page out of the visitors' book. Then he did what we did. Traced every one of the names. Found out who was in the right age group. And one by one . . ."

"Tessa—"

"Can you think of a better idea?"

They'd reached the van. "Vance and Hayden," murmured Steve in the direction of the ventilation grille.

"Where have you been?" came the angry reply. "It's five o'clock."

"Had a few hassles. Have we missed anything?"

"No. She's in there, but nothing's happened. Get moving."

They walked on. They passed a man clipping a hedge who glanced at them curiously, but didn't speak. Tessa couldn't tell if he was a police officer or a gardener. If he was an cop, he was making a surprisingly good job of the clipping, but he'd nearly finished. He'd have to find something else to do if he didn't slow down.

There was a bus shelter ahead. They walked towards it, taking their time. When they reached it, they sat down. Tessa tucked herself into the corner, where she could sit in the shadow. Steve stretched, and looked casually at his watch. He could have just been checking how long they had to wait. And in a way, he was.

"Five-fifteen," he said. "You'd think he'd have made his

move by now. He would have known when she got home,
When the others got home. Chosen his time, like with all the
others."

He watches them.

A figure was standing in dimness, gloved hands raised. They
brushed the hangman's noose, setting it swinging, but the
figure paid no attention. There was a scratching sound, as a
lightbulb was turned, loosened, and pulled free from its socket.
Relief. Satisfaction at another step successfully accomplished.
Now there would be no light to flood the room with exposing
glare, and in darkness the victim would not see the noose, or
the shadow of death approaching. The plan, so newly born, still
damp and tender such a little time ago, was hard and strong
now. Everything was moving, falling into place. The timing
was perfect.

Then—a soft tap on the door. The figure in the room stiffened. What. . .?

Slowly the door began to open.

In the bus shelter, Tessa moved restlessly. "I've been
thinking about the blackmail motive," she murmured. "It
doesn't feel right. The Fairview thing happened three months
ago. But a blackmailer always comes back for more. A blackmailer would have gotten in touch again by now. Maybe two or
three times."

"It's probable. So?" Steve was leaning back, eyes half-
closed, watching the cypresses that screened the Mackintosh
house.

"Well, that means that since the 9th September the killer's
almost certainly had two or three more chances to work out
who the blackmailer is. Why go on killing people who were at
Fairview?"

"I don't know, Tessa. If blackmail's not the motive, what
is?" Steve was weary of talking. He was edgy, wanting action.

If blackmail's not the motive, what is?

"Dolf Hermin said everything in the murders was a clue—a

message for us," Tessa murmured. "Everything the killer does has a reason. Conscious or unconscious."

"If this guy isn't a real serial killer, Hermin's been up a tree all along," muttered Steve. "The profile's shot, everything's shot. Killer could be anyone." He glanced again at his watch and frowned. "It's getting too late. We're kidding ourselves. He's not going to show."

With controlled anger he banged his hands on the bus seat. "Taking the targets to Fairview for that reenactment was a big mistake, Tessa. The killer found out about it. It scared him off."

"I don't see how he could have found out about it," whispered Tessa defensively. "We were incredibly careful. Hermin was in on it. Thorne organized the whole thing down to the smallest detail. No one knew about it, or about the Monday's child thing, except the people who were there."

She saw his face change, tighten. He'd realized something, and the sickening knowledge struck her at the same moment.

How could she not have made the connection? Steve had spelled it out himself, just now. The killer wasn't a genuine serial killer. So Hermin's profile was meaningless. So the killer could be anyone. Male or female. Young or old. Psychopath or not.

The killer hadn't turned up to kill Rosemary Mackintosh as predicted. But no one knew the police were onto the plan except the people at the reenactment.

Steve rubbed his hand over his mouth, and put it into words. "It could be one of them," he said.

Tessa sat rigid with tension.

You organized the reenactment. You introduced them to one another. If the killer's one of them . . .

"There are only six steak knives in the set!" The words burst out of her as she swung round to face him. She forgot to speak quietly, forgot to keep the blood on her neck and shirt hidden.

A teenage boy riding by on a bike rode by, glancing covertly in their direction, and speeded up.

Steve pulled his jacket around her, warning her with his eyes to remember where they were. His jaw was set. He was refusing to panic. He was fighting the logic, looking for a way out.

"Listen," he said quietly. "I'm going to call them all, one at a time, all right?"

She nodded, swallowing.

"Who first?"

"Rosemary."

Steve punched in numbers. Spoke casually, breezily. "Monica? Steve Hayden. Just checking on the patient. All well? . . . Fine. No, that's okay. Don't disturb her. Thanks, Monica. Bye."

He turned to Tessa. "Fast asleep," he said. "Next?"

"Lindsay Cramer."

"You spoke to him yourself at five."

"Ring anyway."

Tessa watched as Steve made the call. Watched as, his face remaining expressionless, he cut the connection.

"He's got his mobile turned off," he said reluctantly. "That figures. He's sitting with his mother. He wouldn't want her disturbed. He probably won't turn the phone on again till six, when my next call's due."

"Go through the hospital switchboard."

"Tessa—"

She clenched her fists in frustration. "I'd do it myself if my phone wasn't wrecked," she hissed. "Can I help it if—"

"All right, all right." He punched in more numbers. Finally got through to the right ward. Asked the question. Waited. Then he thanked the person on the other end of the phone and again cut the connection.

"He's not in his mother's room," he said flatly. "They think he's probably gone to the cafeteria."

"Try Bonnie."

But the Fairview phone was answered only by Mrs. Sparrow's recorded voice, painfully correct, stating opening times. And Bonnie's home phone wasn't answering either.

"She's probably in between work and home," Tessa muttered. "Marty? He should be in his room. He wasn't rostered on till six."

Again Steve made the call. Again with no result. Marty Mayhew's phone rang out, unanswered.

Tessa ran her hands through her hair. "We'll try them all again in ten minutes," she said.

Steve looked at her. Her face was white and tense. The cut on her neck, the scarlet rivulets of drying blood that had run into her shirt, looked black in the mellow, deepening light.

"Tessa," he said gently, reasonably, "we're going too fast. We're not thinking. This theory of yours—about all the deaths being connected—about the serial killings being faked up—it's not necessarily true. Coincidences do happen, you know."

She shook her head violently.

"Think about it," he persisted. "If the same killer was responsible for all the deaths, if he wanted to kill all ten people in that age group at Fairview that day, why take time over three of them—setting them up as nicely spaced accidents and suicide and so on—setting them up so well that no one suspected anything—then suddenly start committing consecutive murders, trying to knock seven off in one week? Why the panic? What's the rush?"

What's the rush? Why take time over three of them, then . . .

Tessa suddenly saw it. The pattern. "The accidents were taking too long to set up," she said slowly. "The killer started running out of time. The killer's working on a *deadline*."

"Deadline? *What* bloody deadline?"

Tessa stared at him.

Deadline.

A wild, ugly idea flew into her mind. She examined it fearfully, from a distance. Moved closer . . .

Nothing in this sort of crime happens by chance. Everything is meant, consciously or unconsciously. . . . Everything is a message for us.

Consciously or unconsciously . . .

"The killer could have chosen anything to make the last murders look like serial killings," she said slowly. "But the choice was the birthday rhyme. The knife in the navel. The birthday cards. The children's stamp. The motive's there, in those symbols."

She knew. The mad, mean sum of all its parts, the answer squatted grotesquely before her, filling her with sick horror.

Steve shook his head. "God, Tessa, you can't have it both ways. Either this merchant's an obsessive serial killer or he isn't. If he isn't, the symbols are part of the act. Part of a conscious decision. The rhyme was at Fairview. Bonnie Gay's name fitted. So—"

"That was the rationalization. But why choose something so complicated, unless you were attracted? Unconsciously attracted . . ." Tessa stood up. "We have to get back to the car," she said. Her voice was thick, choked. He was still shaking his head. She cleared her throat and tried again. "Steve—nothing's going to happen here. We've got to go. We've got to hurry. Steve—please."

Either he was too exhausted to argue any more, or the anxiety in her eyes, the urgency in her voice, prevailed. He took her arm. "All right," he said roughly. "Come on."

It seemed hotter, instead of cooler, by the beach. The salty, humid air hung motionless, clinging around the buildings, pressing down on the promenade. The water, sulky at low tide, slopped onto sand strewn with pimply kelp, cigarette packets, and half-buried plastic bags. Up on its clifftop, Fairview stood dim and silent. Many of the houses around it were already gleaming with light, but its working day was over. Now only ghosts were left to inspect its perfect, polished rooms, and to brood on its past, in darkness.

The shops and cafes on the promenade were preparing themselves for Friday night. Some by pulling down iron shutters, others by refurbishing tables, lighting candles, putting out inviting blackboard menus.

The Funworld entrance gates loomed garishly at the end of the street. The glamour of darkness was still far away. The shrieks and the endless rumble of machine-driven rides that floated from the gates and over the perimeter fence had an automatic sound. In the twilight the colors were lurid and the lights were yellow and depressing, like house lights turned on too soon in a sad house.

Tessa and Steve hurried through the entrance and pushed forward towards the ghost train, through the last of the daytime customers aimlessly milling, wondering whether to stay or go, and the first of the nighttime groups moving in, smiling and eager, but secretly wondering whether they had made the right decision in coming at all.

Ahead was the ghost train, Jacko presiding. He was drumming up custom, selling tickets, impersonally grinning and wheedling, running an automatic line of chat. Tessa watched him helping people out at the end of their ride, tucking the few awkwardly waiting customers into their places, sending empty cars on to complete another futile circuit, as though this was the normal practice. He'd been doing this for forty years. Forty years of guile and salesmanship and cynicism, of working at others' play, of seeing people at their silliest and their most vulnerable.

Forty years . . .

They came up to the platform and shutters seemed to come down over Jacko's small, sharp eyes as he saw and recognized them. He stuck his thumbs in his belt. "What can I do for ya?" he asked.

"Is Marty inside?" said Tessa, raising her voice over the noise. "Is he working?"

Jacko nodded.

"Are you sure?"

Without comment, the old man turned as a car burst out of the exit doors, the girl wide-eyed and giggling, the boy looking bored.

"See the skeleton, did ya?" he leered, heaving the girl out onto the platform.

The girl nodded, still giggling. The boy shrugged and sneered, clambering out after her, ignoring Jacko's hand. "Pathetic," he said.

"There y'are," said Jacko over his shoulder, ushering two more customers into the vacant places.

"It might not be him," Tessa whispered. "Last time—"

Steve nodded. Together they moved past the ghost train, past the laughing clowns who yawned, wagging their heads slowly from side to side, waiting for customers. The brown-faced, blond-haired woman who stood in the booth made no attempt to hail them. She'd seen them before, and knew what they were. She'd been interviewed on Monday night.

If the earliness of the evening meant that customers on the other rides were few, the reverse applied to Go-Go Jalopies, which was in full swing. Preschoolers solemnly clutched the wheels of the primary-colored cars, which sailed around their sedate circle suspended on stiff metal arms, while parents waved or took flash photographs. A respectable queue of adults and jiggling, jumping children stood waiting between the parallel rails that made a path from ticket box to entry point. The children's faces were alive with anticipation. Their minders were doting, tolerant or simply resigned, depending, presumably, on whether their charge was their first child, their second, or the last in a long line.

The ride stopped, and the changeover of riders began. Confusion. Excitement. No one noticed Tessa and Steve moving past the ride towards the back path.

That's how it was done.

The concrete path that ran behind the laughing clowns and the ghost train was shadowy. Steve took out his flashlight. The pencil-thin beam guided their way as they moved along the narrow space in single file. They reached the staff toilet block and rounded the corner.

Marty Mayhew's room was closed. No light showed under the door. But the back entrance to the ghost train was open a crack, leaking flickering green light and muffled wails into the dimness of the courtyard.

Someone is here. Someone is watching us.

"Steve—" she whispered.

"I'll go in and talk to him," said Steve. "You wait—"

He broke off, as if listening. But if there had been a sound, it had stopped. The little yard seemed unnaturally silent. Tessa's spine crawled.

Someone is watching us.

"I think there's someone here," she breathed.

Steve drew his gun and flicked the torchlight quickly around the courtyard. Corners, shadows—and suddenly, against the barrier fence, behind a tangle of woody shrubs, a gleam.

A broken bottle.
Too high.

Steve moved towards the fence, holding the flashlight high. Tessa was behind him. She heard him swear softly under his breath. She saw his gun-hand drop slowly to his side. She moved around beside him, and saw.

The torchlight shone full on a tangle of twigs and leaves, and behind it the paleness of a face—a nightmare, swollen face, tongue protruding, and huge spectacles, gleaming in front of popping, unseeing eyes.

Twenty-two

Bonnie Gay was dead—dead, strangled, propped against the fence with a steak knife in her stomach and a birthday card between her lifeless fingertips. Poor, silly, lonely, harmless Bonnie Gay, who'd blithely come down from her clifftop seeking excitement, and had found death instead. Sweat broke out on Tessa's forehead as nausea twisted her stomach and gripped her throat.

Bonny and blythe and good and gay. Poor, silly girl. Poor, silly . . .

She half sobbed. She couldn't help it. Steve looked at her, his face impassive.

"Looks like you were right," he said. He straightened and moved away from the body, back into the center of the courtyard. Tessa followed him. He handed her the flashlight and pulled out his phone.

Then they both heard it. A furtive sound. From inside Marty's room.

Tessa's breath caught in her throat. Her stomach knotted.

Could be a mouse, a rat, a cockroach, the breeze from the window blowing . . .

No.

Silently they moved to the door. Steve lifted his gun. Rock steady. Then he was reaching for the door, pounding on it with the other hand, the hand that held the phone, calling a warning. She hardly recognized his voice.

No reply from behind the door. Absolute silence.

"Ready?" he murmured.

"Yes." Her fingers, sweating, were clutching her own gun

now. The flashlight beam was wavering as she struggled to force her stiff left hand to do her will.

Ready. Ready . . .

This is it.

"Police!" Steve called again, and threw open the door. Tessa was right behind him, reaching for the light switch.

No light. But in the dimness, luminous bones gleamed. The torchlight picked out a horror-movie scene—an animated skeleton crouched over a sprawled body. A knife blade gleamed in a bony hand.

Serrated blade. Wicked point. Steak knife.

The skull face flashed upward, staring for a split second, then, as Steve yelled again, the skeleton was finally abandoning its prey, springing forward, as careless of danger as if it were indeed immortal, driving its head into Steve's stomach, slashing at his arms with the knife, making for the door, tossing Tessa aside as if she were a doll. She fell, crashing against the doorjamb. The gun flew from her hand. Then the apparition was gone, flinging itself through the opening, onto the veranda. Its feet pounded on boards. A door slammed shut. It had fled into the ghost train.

Steve was doubled up, gasping, bleeding. He was falling to his knees beside the body on the floor. The body of Lindsay Cramer.

"Steve!" Tessa screamed, grabbing the rolling flashlight, struggling to her feet. But then she saw that he was all right. He was bending over Lindsay, feeling for a pulse in the livid neck. He was bending to start mouth-to-mouth resuscitation, scrabbling at the same time for the phone inside his jacket, careless of the blood dripping down his arm.

Staggering, confused, Tessa looked around frantically for the gun which had flown from her hand when she was pushed over. The torch beam jerked and wavered, picked up a gleam of metal. The gun was there, on the floor near her foot. She bent and grabbed it. As she straightened the torchlight fell on Marty's clothes cupboard. The door yawned open. Inside, sports coat, trousers, and in front, two empty hangers. Something was missing—the gleaming bones of the second skeleton costume, the skull balaclava hanging lopsided from the hanger.

Steve was speaking into the phone, sounding impossibly calm. He was cutting the connection and bending again, rhythmically breathing life back into the man on the floor.

Tessa ran. After the killer. Into the ghost train.

She threw open the door and plunged into the groaning, screaming darkness. Cars rattled on the rails, every second one empty. Green and blue light flashed, illuminating the nests of snakes, the vast spiderwebs, the mummies and monsters— every phony horror in the maze providing possible concealment for the real horror lurking in the shadows.

He's hiding.

No. He'll try to get out. Make a break for it. Find the exit.

Tessa took a turn, then another, and stopped, confused. The torch was almost useless. She'd lost her bearings. Somehow, things didn't look the same. Suddenly she had no idea where she was.

Around another corner . . . and there, ahead, the glimmer of bones. Tessa's heart lurched. She'd been on the right track after all. Why had she thought she was lost? The skeleton man skulked in his usual spot by the exit. Moving only very slightly, turning a little towards her. No sign of panic or disturbance. An empty car rattled past Tessa, paused, rattled on, past the skeleton man, slowly, and out.

The second skeleton suit wasn't there.

The gun cold in her right hand, the flashlight wavering in her left, Tessa moved forward. "Marty!" she called softly.

No reply. Yet he must have heard her. He was facing her now. She could see the grinning teeth, the bony eye sockets. He looked taller here in the dark.

She called again. Very slowly he started turning away. And still he didn't answer. Her spine crawled. She ran towards him, shining the torch full in the dreadful face and then, with a cry, flicking the beam upwards.

The rope around the neck stretched to the rafters. The body hung heavily, swinging very slightly, turning this way, that way, seeing nothing, hearing nothing, knowing nothing . . .

But as soon as she touched it she knew. It wasn't Marty Mayhew, dead, hanged. It was the dummy—the hanging man dummy, moved from its usual spot, dressed in the skeleton suit. That was why she had lost her bearings, moving through the ghost train.

The thoughts flashed across her mind in a second, a millisecond. That was why she thought she was lost. The hanged man that had frightened her once before had been missing. It had been moved. It was here.

It isn't him. Where is he then? Where is—?

And then, hands were around her throat. Warm, gloved hands. Incredibly strong. Unbeatable. Implacable.

Hiding. Waiting for me . . .

The hands around her neck tightening. Choking.

No air. I can't . . .

The darkness had become scarlet, as she fought to breathe. The torch dropped to the ground, rolling away, illuminating the gaps between black-painted partitions and real spiderwebs. The gun discharged, uselessly, into the air.

The train . . .

Barely thinking, Tessa staggered back, treading on the feet of her enemy. She heard the dull sound of swearing. And another sound. The sound of a car rumbling forward.

Yes. Get back . . .

She could feel the hardness of the metal car on the side of her leg.

No screams. No cries. The car was empty. But . . .

Remember . . .

With the last of her strength, the last of her thought, she flung herself sideways, letting her weight drag her down, down, till she was hanging on the edge of the car, and her enemy was toppling with her.

"Shit!"

The voice was hard, rasping with anger. The iron fingers pressed harder. . .

The edge of the car was biting into the soft flesh of her arm.

Hold on.

She could do no more. Dimly she heard the shouts of the riders stranded in the dark bowels of the ghost train maze. The metal underneath her arm and shoulder was shuddering. The scarlet in her eyes was pierced with pinpoints of light, bright light. Beautiful . . .

"What's going on? Hey! Gawdalmighty . . . What in the bloody hell—? Hey! Let 'er go! Hey!"

A voice from the past, far away. A voice from another time, when she wasn't dreaming, when she wasn't dying . . .

There was a dull thud. A gasping sound.

And then the fingers on her throat were loosening, She could breathe. She gulped at the air.

Pain.

Her throat—a pain like a knife—her chest—aching. The breath—hurt. She was choking . . . tears were stinging in her eyes.

Someone was patting her back. "You're all right, love. You're all right."

You're all right, love.

Jacko.

Tessa choked, her shoulders heaving. "Where . . . ?"

"It's okay, love. I got 'im. Gawdalmighty . . . I come in to see why the bloody thing's stopped an' I find you . . . Gawdalmighty."

Jacko, coming into focus. His face, creased into a thousand wrinkles. The spanner hanging loose in his monkey paw hand.

Tessa staggered to her feet. Released from the pressure of her weight, the car jerked forward. From deep inside the ride there were cheers and catcalls from the unseen customers whose own cars had finally moved on.

"Bloody hell!" Jacko rubbed his mouth with his sleeve.

"Torch," Tessa croaked.

The light wavered and bobbed in Jacko's shaking hand as he retrieved the flashlight and brought it to her. She aimed it at the moving, groaning body on the floor.

"He's coming round," said Jacko. "Better clout 'im again, eh?"

"No," whispered Tessa. "No." She shone the torch around, saw her gun lying by the rails, and picked it up.

The whites of Jacko's eyes showed in the darkness as she aimed it at the skeleton man. "I'll be all right," she rasped. "Turn on the lights. Stop the train. Get—help."

Jacko nodded, and ducked out through the exit doors.

The figure on the floor was crawling now.

"Stay where you are," croaked Tessa. "I've got a gun and I'll use it. It's aimed right at you. I'll shoot you straight through the leg. It'll hurt. It'll really hurt."

The crawling stopped.

"Get down. Lie facedown on the floor. Do it!" Every word hurt. But she knew it was vital that she seem strong, in control.

"Tessa!" It was Steve's voice, shouting above the amplified cries and groans.

"Here!" Tessa yelled, tears springing into her eyes as the cry tore at her throat. "Here! Exit!"

And he was running towards her, out of the blackness. He had just reached her when the lights went on. They blinked at one another, dazzled.

"Cramer—okay?" she whispered.

"Breathing," he said. "Ambulance on the way. I'll have to get back to him." He looked down at the silent, black-clad body on the floor. Painted bones and back zipper mercilessly illuminated, the skeleton-man was no longer a figure of horror. Rather he was tawdry, laughable, almost pathetic.

"You got him."

"Jacko did. Hit him." Tessa gestured at the skeleton-suited dummy hanging from the rafters. "There's the second costume. He'd organized himself a stand-in. I think he ran in here because he had some idea he could get the dummy down and back where it belonged, then take its place here before we caught him. But I sprung him, so he went for me. He's not too bright. He could have gotten away."

Steve shook his head. "This is bloody incredible," he said. "So it's—"

She nodded tiredly, rubbing her throat.

"Oh, yeah. He spoke to me. It's Marty Mayhew, all right."

They took off the balaclava and between them they hauled Marty back to his room, where Lindsay Cramer was still on the floor, lying in the dark. Lindsay's neat hair was ruffled, his tie was askew, his throat was bruised and swollen, he was breathing harshly, unevenly. But he was alive. As they entered, he moaned in fear, staring at Marty, scrabbling on the floor with his beautifully manicured hands, trying to sit up.

"It's all right," said Tessa. "He can't hurt you. We're here."

How strange life is . . . Lindsay Cramer lives—so many others died.

"Best if we stay here till the ambulance arrives," Steve muttered in her ear. "You all right?"

"Fine. Why do you ask?"

He glanced at her and saw she was making an attempt at humor. Her teeth showed white in the dimness as she smiled.

She flicked the torchlight around the little room—the sparse, well-organized little room she'd so admired when she first saw it. Something white was sticking out from under the pillow on the bed. A plastic supermarket bag. Tessa went over to the bed, crouched, and shone the torch into the bag, being careful not to touch. An opened packet of steak knives. A birthday card.

"Do you want to tell us about these, Marty?" Steve drawled.

Marty Mayhew said nothing. He sat propped against the wall, his eyes half-closed, his face an expressionless mask. Tessa had seen that look so many times before, on other faces, in other places.

Admit nothing, say nothing.

"He said to come over," rasped Lindsay, holding his throat. He gazed at Marty in fascinated horror. "He agreed—we should talk. But—it was a trap. He was in here, waiting. He tried to kill me. He was the killer—all along. I left my mother—"

Marty Mayhew spoke at last. "Not *your* mother, you pathetic creep," he snarled. "*Our* mother. *Ours!*"

There was a sobbing sigh in the darkness.

My sigh? Or Lindsay's? Or was it both of us?

"You're Mrs. Cramer's son, from before she was married," said Tessa. "That's it, isn't it, Marty? She had you, and she had you adopted out, and she didn't tell anyone."

"My bastard of a father left her flat. She had to do it. Give me up. She was scared. She didn't have any money. Thought I'd have a better life if she gave me up. They all told her I would. At the hospital. That's what she said." Marty bared his teeth. "Better life! That's a joke. Ten sets of so-called parents in fourteen years, that's what I had. Pigs and pervs and bastards, all of them."

Lindsay stared at him in fascinated horror, white skin gleaming, sweating in the dark. "How could . . . ?" he began.

"Shut up, you freak!" spat Marty. "This has got nothing to do with you. You know nothing! Nothing about my bitch of a life. You've had it all. Everything I should've had."

He turned to Tessa. Tears hung on the ends of his thick black eyelashes. His mouth trembled. "She found me," he said. "She tracked me down. She wrote to me. Oh, God." He closed his eyes, leaning his head back against the wall. "I couldn't believe it. She said—her husband was dead, and she wanted—she wanted to see me. She'd had another child. But she'd never forgotten me. Her first child. She said that, in her letter. Her lost baby, who hadn't even had a name . . ." Tears rolled down his cheeks.

Her baby.

Marty opened his eyes. "We were going to meet on my birthday—at Fairview. I suggested that. Thought it was the sort of place she'd like. But she never turned up. I thought I'd blown it. Pushed her too fast. She was nervous, she said." He sneered at Lindsay. "But it wasn't that. You found out about it, didn't you? You got round her. You persuaded her not to come. Not to write to me any more. Didn't you? You prick!"

"No!" mumbled Lindsay. "No, I didn't stop her. I didn't even know about you till—"

"Bullshit!" Marty's eyes were still wet, but now his face was distorted with anger. He looked at Tessa, eyes blazing. "She was scared to tell him about me. Didn't want to upset him. The way she talked about him, you'd've thought he was really something. She thought he was so wonderful. So special. She thought the sun shone out of his ass."

His beautiful face twisted into a sneer. "Can you believe that? Look at him! Nearly fainted when I finally met him this afternoon. So this was the wonderful Lindsay Cramer! Some weedy, constipated, snobby, baldy little prick in a suit!"

Lindsay made a strangled sound.

Tessa turned to him. "You went to Fairview to see Marty in your mother's place, didn't you? That's why you were there on the same day he was. It couldn't possibly have been a coincidence."

He stared at her, swallowed, and nodded. "I found the letters," he croaked. "His letters. I was looking for Mum's medical insurance papers. After she went to hospital."

Tessa saw Marty Mayhew's head jerk upward. "Why's she in hospital?" he asked roughly. "What's up with her?"

He turned his head as the sound of sirens floated through the window. Sirens, coming closer. Down the promenade. Ambulance. Police cars.

Thank God.

Lindsay didn't seem to hear the sirens. He didn't look at Marty. He went on talking to Tessa, as if there had been no interruption. "I found the letters. It was—a shock. Mum had—she'd had him before she married Dad. She'd been writing to him for a couple of weeks. Every day. They'd set up this meeting, at Fairview. I was—curious. I wanted to see—what he was like. So I went."

"Why didn't you tell us that was the reason you were there?"

He ran trembling fingers through his thinning hair. "I didn't think—it had anything to do with anything. It was private. I never thought for a minute he was—dangerous."

Marty gave a snorting, disgusted laugh. Lindsay's eyes widened slightly, but still he didn't look away from Tessa's face.

"I went. But when I got there—I couldn't face it. I saw him, but I didn't—didn't go near him. He wasn't—what I was expecting, from the letters. I just walked around for a while, and then I left."

"Then, today, you met him."

Lindsay swallowed, and nodded. "He knew who I was. I could see it in his face. But he didn't say anything. I thought I might have been imagining it, but later on he said he'd never met his parents, and he looked straight at me. He was telling me who he was. I decided I'd just ignore it. I didn't want . . ."

His voice trailed off. He seemed to be fighting for control. Then he cleared his throat, and went on. "I'm not a snob," he said with feeble defiance. "But it was—it took a bit of getting used to. I couldn't imagine being related to—someone like that."

Marty sneered.

Lindsay bit his lip. "Then, at the hospital, I started to feel guilty about it. I thought, whatever I think—she should see him. Whatever he is. I mean, whatever he's like. So I rang him. But—"

"Look, will you bloody tell me?" Marty broke in. "What's she doing in hospital? How long's she been in there?"

"Months."

Feet sounded on the concrete path. "In here!" Steve called sharply through the door.

"*Months. Is that* why she wasn't at Fairview?" Marty yelled. "Answer me, you bastard! Is that why she hasn't been answering my letters? I've been writing every bloody day. Nearly going off my head. Is she sick or something?"

"She's dying," Lindsay muttered.

Marty gaped at him, battling to take it in. Shock, disbelief, anger, bewilderment, and grief chased each other across his face.

There were people at the door. Paramedics. Police. Marty looked around, showing the bloodshot whites of his eyes.

Nowhere to run.

He looked directly at Tessa.

"Under the cupboard," he said, in an almost unrecognizable voice. "Under the floorboards. Her letters."

Tessa nodded.

One of the paramedics was crouched beside Marty now, shining a light into his eyes, checking the wound on his head. The other was attending to Lindsay Cramer.

"You get the letters, you read them," babbled Marty, brushing the paramedic away impatiently, dodging around him so that he could still see Tessa. "You'll see. It's all written down there. She's left me half her dough. She said. She's fixed it with her lawyer. If she dies . . ."

The paramedic got up and murmured to Steve. Steve nodded

and gestured to two uniformed police who came in and started hauling Marty to his feet.

"She said she'd look after me." Marty struggled feebly against the strong arms that held him. "She said she'd make it up to me. She said Val and I could get a house, a car—everything. Read the letters! They say, 'Dear Baby,' because that's what I sign myself. 'Marty' doesn't mean anything to her. She likes to call me 'Baby.' "

His eyes were wide; black holes in a haunted face. "That's okay with me. I told her. I didn't want to blow it, did I? Had to keep her sweet. But I kept all the envelopes, just in case. You can see they're mine. You listening?"

Tessa nodded.

He licked his lips. "Look, I'm sorry about before. I didn't want to hurt you, but I had to, didn't I? I didn't have any choice, did I? You fix it, will you? You make sure I get the dough."

I tried to kill you. Sorry about that . . . didn't have any choice.

Lindsay moaned softly and put his head in his hands.

"Look at him!" yelled Marty. "He's a bloody nobody. Why should he get the money? Why should he get any of it? Why should I share my money with him? He's had everything, all his bloody life. I've had nothing! Nothing!"

"Time to go, Marty," said Steve.

The man screamed, as if only now was he realizing the full extent of his trouble. The dashed hopes. The failed plans. The ruin of everything. "I've got a right!" he shouted, as he was manhandled from the room. "She's my mother! She owes me. She owes me."

It took a long time for the screams to die away.

Tessa shone the torch at the gaping cupboard.

"We'll leave the letters for Fisk. He's out in the courtyard," Steve murmured.

With Bonnie Gay. All that's left of Bonnie Gay.

Tessa nodded, moved the torch around. The beam caught the empty light socket, the hangman's noose, hanging from a rafter above the phone and moving gently in the warm, salt-smelling breeze that drifted into the partly open window. On the floor was a small pink button.

Just when had Bonnie come blundering in here, she wondered. At the wrong moment, anyway.

Poor, silly Bonnie.

Lindsay struggled to his feet, leaning heavily on the paramedic. He was a bedraggled, unprepossessing figure. "I've got to get back to the hospital," he croaked, his hand on his throat. "My mother—it could be too late."

"His mother's dying," murmured Tessa in answer to the paramedic's inquiring look. She turned to Lindsay. "And that was the deadline, wasn't it?" she said softly.

He stared at her, uncomprehending. "I—I have to get back," he stammered. "I shouldn't have left her. I wasn't going to stay away—so long."

"Just long enough. Right?" said Tessa, in that same, soft voice. "To finally do what you've been trying to do all along— kill your rival for all that lovely money. This afternoon you finally found out exactly who that rival was, didn't you? So you set up a meeting and came here to kill him. Ironic, isn't it, that he had the same idea? The one thing you didn't take into account."

Lindsay moved, but Steve moved faster, blocking the doorway. "Lindsay Cramer," he said pleasantly, "I'm arresting you for the murders of Peter Grogan, Tracey Fernandez, Lloyd Greely, Jasmine Ho, Bonita Gay . . ."

Twenty-three

Found out, waiting until reinforcements arrived so that he could be taken to Homicide to be charged, Lindsay Cramer was petulant and garrulous. He ignored the warning. He had no interest in remaining silent. He wanted to explain that his logical, efficient plan should have worked.

"I found the letters. Practically illiterate, grossly sentimental, typed, and signed 'Baby'—nauseating. It was—as I said—an appalling shock. My mother was planning to give this creature half her money. Half of my father's money. According to one letter, she'd actually changed her will already, without breathing a word to me. It was grossly unfair, and typical of my mother, completely illogical. I had to do something about it. Well, of course I did."

"But Marty hadn't used his real name on the letters, so you didn't know who he was, did you?" asked Tessa gently. "You lied to us about that before. You didn't even know if Baby was male or female. All you knew was an approximate age."

Lindsay frowned. "The will was with our solicitor. For obvious reasons I couldn't approach him . . ." He paused and looked at her, severely inquiring, like a schoolteacher waiting to see if a rather dull student had gotten the point.

"Because you'd already decided that Baby had to go," Tessa responded obediently. "To protect yourself from becoming a suspect, you had to maintain the fiction that you had no idea there was another child. Right?"

A sharp nod. She'd passed the test. "And obviously once my mother died, and the will became public knowledge, the opportunity would be lost for similar reasons. So it was necessary to attack the problem differently. I went to Fairview on the day my mother and this Baby person were supposed to meet. But there were several people of the right age there. I couldn't risk approaching them, could I?"

His brow corrugated as he leaned forward. "I secured the list of names from the Fairview visitors' book. It wasn't difficult. Security there is very poor. After that it was just a matter of research and logic. Research, efficiency, and logic. The appalling notes were still arriving at my mother's address every day, getting more and more hysterical. I knew I simply had to continue with the plan until they stopped." Lindsay Cramer, ruffled, bruised, and handcuffed, could have been speaking to the managing director of a failing company, so perfect was his lecturing manner.

A matter of research, efficiency, logic . . .

"Unfortunately my mother's condition began deteriorating rather more quickly than had been predicted. I had to speed up the elimination process . . ."

Tessa must have made a sound then, because he looked at her sharply. "I wouldn't want you to think I enjoyed it," he said severely. "It was unpleasant. I'm not without sympathy. But there was no other option. There is a very large amount of money involved, you know."

The elimination process . . . unpleasant . . . no other option . . . He's talking about murder. Mass murder.

He's mad.

He's not. That's the trouble. That's why I feel so sick.

"It wasn't simple, either," Lindsay Cramer was continuing resentfully. "There was a lot of work involved. Research on serial killings. Deciding on the motif—appropriate symbols to leave, and so on. The rhyme was appropriate because of the Gay woman. I was concerned that it was a little obscure, but you picked it up quite quickly. Of course, you had the advantage of seeing the embroidery at Fairview."

"Tell me, what were you going to do for Saturday, Lindsay?" asked Steve. "Stage an attempted murder on yourself?"

"Certainly not. This was never part of the original plan—it would have simply attracted attention to me—and it would have been impossible to accomplish successfully once I was involved with the police." Lindsay Cramer looked rather sour as he said this. He, like Mrs. Sparrow, had been severely discomposed by the discovery that the Fairview visitors' book had been secretly copied. "Nor," he continued, eyeing them severely, "would I consider disposing of a completely blameless person just to fill the gap. Unnecessary risk and effort."

"So you were just going to skip Saturday." Steve was curious. "Did you think we'd just assume you'd been scared off?"

"That, or that the body had simply not yet been discovered. Though of course—" Lindsay nodded seriously "—I did bear in mind that a spare day might be useful."

He held up one finger in a lecturing manner. "One should always have a contingency plan. Should there have been a failure for some unforeseen reason on one of the previous days, Saturday could have been used for another attempt." He smiled at them in a supercilious manner. "Most people regard themselves as working hard for a living, however absurd that may be."

"So you only ever planned for six serial deaths," said Steve, glancing at Tessa.

"Of course," said Lindsay patiently. "There are only six steak knives in a set, you know."

There are only six steak knives in a set.

He sighed. "I don't know if you realize exactly how much was involved in all this," he said, raising a hand to probe his reddened neck. "Securing the phones. Securing access to the various premises. Establishing the correct timing. It was a massive enterprise. I had to work on it almost full-time. My own work suffered, unfortunately."

"That's a shame," murmured Steve. "You organized it all down to the last detail, didn't you? Thought of everything. You left birthday cards in the houses of all the people you killed, so that when forensic picked up traces of you, we'd think you'd just entered to leave the card. We wouldn't realize you were looking for something—your mother's letters. You didn't find them though, did you, when you searched Marty's room on Monday night? Not so efficient after all, were you?"

"Why would I think the stupid fool would keep them under the floorboards?" snapped Lindsay. "At the time, I thought that, if he was the one, he'd thrown them away. And afterwards, of course, I thought he wasn't the one, because those idiotic letters kept coming. . . ."

His voice trailed off. He looked, for the first time since he'd started talking, uncomfortable. He'd been reminded of his one real inefficiency. "There was no name printed in the paper," he said bitterly. "How was I to know I'd made an error?" He shook his head. "I felt sick when I realized it today," he said. "All that work! Four days of completely wasted effort."

Four days of completely wasted effort. Peter Grogan, Tracey Fernandez, Lloyd Greely, Jasmine Ho . . .

"I would like to examine this room, if you don't mind." Lance Fisk was at the door, splendid in an impeccable dinner suit. Dragged away from a first night or something, thought Tessa.

They moved outside, onto the covered veranda. Over by the fence, Bonnie Gay's body, sealed in plastic, was being strapped to a stretcher.

Lindsay shook his head crossly. "Tonight should have ended it," he said. "I had finally found out exactly who the Baby person was."

"It was when Rosemary got sick, wasn't it?" asked Tessa. "When people were talking about their parents? Heredity?"

"Yes. The two women knew who their parents were. Mayhew didn't. And what's more, he looked at me when he said what he did. I knew he was the one. I revised the plan. You have to be flexible—react quickly. And I did. It should have worked perfectly." Lindsay frowned at Tessa resentfully.

"You rang Marty and left the hospital after our five o'clock call," she prompted.

"Certainly. There was plenty of time. I should have been able to do the job and get out of here before your six o'clock call, and get back to the hospital without being missed. The hospital staff would think I was away having dinner—if they even noticed I was gone, which I doubted. They're rushed off their feet. Very overtired. Shocking work practices. If that stupid girl hadn't butted in the whole thing would have worked perfectly."

His eyes followed the stretcher coldly as it was carried away, behind the brick outhouse, onto the concrete path.

Tessa swallowed. "Tell us about Bonnie Gay," she said. She was surprised at how level her voice sounded.

He shrugged petulantly. "She came in while I was in his room, preparing. Just knocked and came in. Can you believe it? She seems to have thought that Mayhew was interested in having some sort of affair with her. She was flirting with him all afternoon." He pursed his lips. "A yahoo like that. She must have been desperate. She was all perfumed, covered in makeup. Of course she was very ordinary-looking. But that doesn't excuse having the morals of an alley cat."

For a moment Tessa couldn't speak. Steve glanced at her.

"So Bonnie came in," he said. "And—"

Another sharp nod. "Well, naturally I had to dispose of her. I didn't want to. It was the last thing I wanted. So when it was done, I rather panicked." Lindsay frowned. "It was unexpected. I decided I had better take the body outside. Conceal it. So I did that. And then I left. But of course I hadn't even gotten to the end of the passageway there before I realized that nothing had really changed. There was no reason to run. It was only 5:25. Mayhew wasn't due to come out of the ghost train to meet me till 5:30. I still had time to get back into the room. Everything was set up. So I went back. But in the meantime . . ." He broke off, looking outraged.

"He'd come out of the ghost train early, and when you went into the room, he was waiting for you."

"That's right." Lindsay's eyes bulged, and he touched his neck gingerly. "He—attacked me. It was such a shock. It was terrifying. I couldn't breathe. He had a knife . . ."

"Must have been a bit of a shock," drawled Steve. "Lucky we came in when we did, huh? He could have killed you."

Lindsay nodded, apparently completely unconscious of any irony in the situation. "It never occurred to me he'd try anything like that," he said.

Steve shrugged. "The human element," he said dryly. "As you said yourself, you've always got to take it into account."

"Unpleasant fellow. I prefer the brutish brother," Lance Fisk commented as they rejoined him after handing Lindsay over to his escorts. Fisk was prowling the small room, opening cupboards and peering inside.

"Nothing so far," he said. "Are you positive—?"

"Try the bed," Tessa suggested.

Fisk peered into the supermarket bag and looked down his nose. "Wrong knives," he said. "Wrong sort of card."

"That's poor old Marty's stuff," drawled Steve. "He had a great idea, Marty had. Nearly upset our applecart, all right. He was going to do a copycat murder. Knock off the competition for Mum's affections, and money, and blame it all on the serial killer. But he'd invited the killer in."

Fisk raised his eyebrows. "They were planning to kill each other? How extremely—operatic."

"I meant *under* the bed," Tessa murmured. "Suitcase."

Lance tweaked at his trousers, squatted, and pulled the suitcase from under the bed. Fastidiously, he opened it. Nestled among the sweaters was a box containing one steak knife, some birthday cards, and a rubber koala stamp.

"That's more like it," he said approvingly. He turned around and looked up at the noose hanging above the phone. "I see a suicide was in the offing," he commented.

"Oh, yes," said Steve somberly. "Lindsay Cramer's not a time and motion expert for nothing. He was going to kill two birds with one stone. He got here early, killed the light, rigged up the noose, and planted the evidence. It was all very efficient, even for a revised plan. Marty was going to suicide, and all the evidence that he was the serial killer was going to be here. An efficient end to the whole case. Right on deadline. Bonnie Gay was a hiccup, but he thought he'd fixed that. The one thing he didn't count on was that Marty was as bad as he was."

"They underestimated one another, in fact," said Lance airily, standing up and poking at the noose with a gloved hand.

"Not an uncommon phenomenon among people who have only recently met. You'd both agree with that, I presume?"

Point taken, Fisk.

Jacko waylaid them as they left. "They wouldn't let me in," he complained. "Wouldn't let me into me own place. Or see Marty or nothing. Wouldn't listen to me. But listen, I been thinking. Marty can't have done all them murders. He . . ."

"He didn't, Jacko." Tessa smiled at him briefly. She was tired. So tired. She gestured to Lindsay Cramer who, lips pursed disapprovingly, was being escorted to the gates. "That's the accused."

"*Him?* He don't look like he could bloody fight his way out of a paper bag." Jacko was stunned.

"He's Marty's brother—half-brother."

Jacko's eyes narrowed. "Go on," he jeered. "He can't be. They're like chalk and cheese."

Tessa sighed. "They don't look alike," she said. "But they had the same mother."

She suddenly felt inexpressibly sad, thinking of the woman lying dying now, alone. The woman who'd kept a secret for nearly thirty years, and had tried to find a way of telling it, but never had. At least she'd never know what devastation and misery that secret had caused. She'd never know how totally she'd misjudged her sons.

"They couldn't be more different," said Steve. "But they're brothers, all right. Both killers when they saw something in it for them."

They said goodbye to Jacko, and walked on. The lights of Funworld were once again blacked out. Once again it was empty.

"You know, Dr. Hermin told us why they'd both kill," said Tessa. "Profit, anger, jealousy, or when threatened. He was right."

Steve shrugged. He was feeling rather sore with Dolf Hermin.

"He was right about something else, too," said Tessa. "Lindsay Cramer thought he was being so cold and logical and efficient. But when he had to choose a motif for his fake serial killings, he chose the very thing that was most on his mind. Babies, mothers, children. The thing that was going to lead us right to him."

Steve looked at her. "Lead you, you mean. If it hadn't been for you—"

"If it hadn't been for me—if I hadn't organized that reenactment—Bonnie Gay would never have taken a fancy to Marty Mayhew. She'd still be alive." Tessa looked down at her hands. She knew she'd never forgive herself for that.

"If your aunt had balls, she'd be your uncle."

"What?"

"Old bush saying, Tess. You can try your best, but you've got to take some things as they fall. There'll always be things you can't change. You've got to accept that, or you'll go crazy."

She sighed.

"If it hadn't been for you working out about the rhyme, Rosemary Mackintosh would be dead," Steve said quietly. "Have you thought of that?"

Have you thought of that?

No. Does it help?

It should. It does. It helps, but . . .

"You worked the whole thing out just in time. You made me come here. If we hadn't gotten here when we did, Cramer would be dead as well," Steve went on.

I wish he was.

Say it.

Tessa lifted her chin. "I wish he was dead," she said aloud, staring straight ahead. "I wish he'd died in fear, and pain, and . . ." Her throat seemed to swell, choking off her voice.

Why should the mad, bad ones live? While others . . .

Steve was watching her. "We might never have known the truth of it then. Cramer would never have been tried, convicted—"

"Would that matter?" Her voice was trembling.

You know it would. It's why you do this. Why Steve does it. Why . . .

"Your dad thought it mattered," Steve said carefully. "He died because he thought it mattered."

Yes.

The scene of crime tape was again strung across the Funworld gates. In silence they ducked under it and walked towards their car. People stared, licking ice creams, eating hot-dogs. Music was playing in the cafes farther along the promenade.

On the beach, the tide was rising. You could hear the waves, dully roaring, slapping against the sand. As they'd done fifteen years ago, when a little girl and her father had a day out together. As they'd always done. Always would. No matter what happened. No matter who was there to see, or to hear.

Steve opened the car. "I'll drive," he said, and got in before she could argue.

Tessa didn't want to argue. Her left arm was stiff, throbbing. She went around to the passenger side of the car and looked back at the fun park. One last look. The illuminated ghost train gleamed through the dark. Against its light, small figures moved.

Ghosts.

"I'm never coming back here," she said. "Never again."

Steve watched as she slid into the passenger seat, leaned back, and closed her eyes. She looked very fragile, very alone. Defenseless. Very beautiful. He wanted to touch her. To say . . .

Her eyes opened. She turned her head to look at him.

"You right?" she murmured.

He hesitated, then half laughed. "Sure," he said, and started the car.

He thought he understood.

A Conversation with Jennifer Rowe

Q. *Jennifer, you've had a very eclectic writing and editing career. For starters, let's talk about the days before you became a crime novelist. You've had some of the most coveted jobs in Australian publishing. In the 1980s you were the publisher at the esteemed house of Angus and Robertson. Then you became the editor of* The Australian Women's Weekly. *Tell us about those years.*

Until I went to *The Australian Women's Weekly*, I worked in book publishing all my life, and found it very fulfilling. I had started with Angus and Robertson as an assistant editor, and fourteen years later, having moved through the ranks in a classic pattern, I was publisher. While working for this company, I had my four children, including boy twins. I had also started writing books in my spare time. Life was very, very busy, but I loved the company, I loved working with books and authors, and I loved the people I worked with. Then, when my boy twins were just one year old, I was offered editorship of *The Weekly*, which is an Australian icon, a general interest women's magazine which, despite its name, is a monthly! *The Weekly* has a huge circulation in Australian terms. I took the job. I did this because I felt I should try something new (midlife crisis, maybe?). Looking back, I suppose it was an opportunity I couldn't resist. I suppose I should have had more doubts about my ability to do the job, but I went into it, when I think about it, in a spirit of recklessness. I'm sure all the journalists on the magazine had many doubts and worries about what this strange woman from another industry would do to their magazine, but in fact, fortunately, it all turned out very well. I found that because Angus and Robertson was a company that published a very wide range of books—everything from poetry to the mass market—I could handle the demands of a general interest magazine without great stress. Again I found myself working with terrific people, and facing new challenges—just what I needed at the time!

Q. At the same time, under the pseudonym Emily Rodda, you were writing stories for children (and you won the Children's Book of the Year award five times) and had begun writing mysteries for adults. As a wife and mother of four, how did you manage this busy schedule?

I think after the twins were born it wasn't so much a matter of management as of survival. I have never been a perfectionist as a housekeeper—far from it!—so that helped. I had a lot of domestic help—a cleaner came once a week, and of course I had child care. My mother helped too—she was marvelous. For a period, she even did my shopping. She said she enjoyed it—but I'm so grateful to her.

On a personal level, I'm lucky in that I do have a lot of physical stamina, and I'm good at compartmentalizing. I had three areas of my life—work, family, and writing—and I was continually refreshed by moving among them.

Life is more settled now. I loved working at *The Weekly*, but after five years I was ready for another change—the big one—into full-time writing. I had quite a few books in print by then, and they were doing well enough for me to afford to write full-time. In a way it feels very indulgent being a full-time author—it's terrific to make a living at something I love so much.

Q. When did you decide to turn to a life of (fictional) crime?

In my early twenties I had become a big fan of the classic "clue-puzzle" murder-mystery writers like Agatha Christie, Ngaio Marsh, and Dorothy Sayers. I found that I shared this love with a lot of my women friends. It was our favorite form of leisure reading. It was fascinating to me that it seemed to be typically women who enjoyed this genre and wrote in this area.

When I was still at Angus and Roberston, in the mid-eighties, I thought I might write a Ph.D. thesis on this theme. Then I thought, why not try to write a classic murder mystery instead? I'll learn just as much about the genre that way. And so I wrote my first mystery, *Grim Pickings,* which starred a private detective called Verity Birdwood. To my (genuine) surprise and pleasure this book was accepted by Allen and Unwin Australia and subsequently published not only in Australia but in the U.S., the U.K., and in translation in Japan and Europe. So after that, it seemed natural to write more.

Q. Suspect, the debut of the Tessa Vance series, is a significant departure for you. You've entered an edgier, grittier, psychologically darker arena. Was this another conscious career switch?

I love classical whodunits, and I hope I'll always go on writing them. At times, however, it's a frustrating genre. It has restrictions. The private detective can't get onto crime scenes easily, and there is always a certain artificiality involved in getting them into the murder in the first place. After meeting a couple of real homicide detectives and being impressed by their commitment and intelligence, I found the idea of creating a working detective very appealing. It gave me the opportunity to take a different perspective and to explore the grittier side of life to which professionals are exposed every day. This wasn't so much a conscious decision as a broadening of interest. Both gentle and "gritty" sides of life are true and real. You meet one, you meet the other—and you write about them.

Q. We know that the Tessa Vance books are linked to a twenty-two-episode TV series entitled Murder Call. *Here in America we haven't seen* Murder Call *yet. How direct was your involvement with the TV show—and what is your critical assessment of it?*

I created Tessa Vance, and *Murder Call*, in response to a request from a very successful Australian TV producer named

Hal McElroy, who was a fan of the Verity Birdwood books. Hal felt that there was room on TV for a series of one-hour whodunits, but he felt the series had to feature a professional homicide detective to make it seem "real" to the networks. So I created the series and its characters with Hal's help, and then I wrote all the storylines for the first series.

Murder Call features a homicide team—Tessa Vance's partner, Steve Hayden, their boss, Inspector Malcolm Thorne, the pathologist Imogen "Tootsie" Soames, the forensic expert Lance Fisk, and the photographer Dee Suzeraine. But Tessa Vance is the focus, the main character. Although the mysteries are classic whodunits, the episodes are faster and tougher than one might expect from a normal murder series. In other words, I tried to blend two genres. I think this is reflected in *Suspect*, which is based on the storyline I wrote for a double episode.

As for my critical assessment . . . as the creator of the series, and having written all the storylines for the first series (there's a second series being produced at the moment, and I've written as many storylines as I could for that, too), it's hard for me to put myself outside the show and see it in perspective—of course, I can always see things that I think could be better. But the first series rated brilliantly in Australia and the critics liked it, so I suppose I should believe what everyone tells me and decide it's a success.

Q. You mentioned your heroine in an earlier cycle of novels—TV researcher Verity "Birdie" Birdwood. As their creator, would you say that Birdie and Tessa are equally fun to write? What are the special joys (and difficulties) in writing about each?

Tessa can do things that Birdie can't do—and vice versa. They come at the problem from different directions, and following different rules. Tessa has to deal with police politics, has to work strictly within the law, and according to procedure. She deals almost invariably with complete strangers who know she's a homicide detective. Birdie can be incognito and, of course, very often works with people she knows. They are different characters but equally fun to work with.

Q. For that matter, what are the special challenges in writing mystery series—as opposed to stand-alone novels?

The challenge in writing series novels is to develop the regular characters and to come up with new ideas while staying true to the flavor of the series and to the characters themselves. I don't find this a frustrating challenge; in fact, it's interesting to be writing regularly about the same characters—the opportunity to explore their histories and plan their futures is irresistible. The big adventure in establishing a character in a series is that you can also establish a reading audience who looks forward to new books about this character. This, pragmatically, is important to a full-time writer with four children to support.

But I must say that some of the most satisfying children's books I've written have been single novels, and I would like to write an adult stand-alone novel in the future. The trouble is, once I've created and written about a character, I feel that they really exist—I really miss them after I stop writing! It's a bit like losing touch with an old friend. I had to stop writing Birdie books for a couple of years in order to concentrate on Tessa and found that even though I was enjoying myself, I missed Birdie a lot. I wrote a few short stories about her to keep in practice—to keep in touch, I guess!

Q. We know that you have completed the sequel to Suspect. . . . *Without divulging any top secrets, what can you tell us about your future plans for Tessa Vance?*

In the next book, I've taken Tessa out of her normal environment, into a semirural area, the Blue Mountains west of Sydney, where she feels a bit out of her depth. As she and Steve Hayden, her partner, work on the case they are thrown together (as outsiders generally are!). This gave me the opportunity to develop both Tessa's character and the relationship between her and Steve. As I live in the Blue Mountains myself, I enjoyed writing this book very much. I hope others enjoy reading it, too.